# A POCKETFUL OF POISONS

# A POCKETFUL OF POISONS

A Collection of Deadly Short Stories

BRIAN PRICE

This edition produced in Great Britain in 2025

by Hobeck Books Limited, 24 Brookside Business Park, Stone, Staffordshire ST15 0RZ

www.hobeck.net

'Payback' first published in *The Dark Side of Christmas* (Hobeck Books, 2021)

'Murder on the Hop' first published in *Cooking the Books* (Hobeck Books, 2022)

'A Scent of an Ending' first published in *Music of the Night,* a Crime Writers' Association anthology (Flame Tree Press, 2022).

Earlier versions of some stories were uploaded to the Crime Writers' Association website during 2020.

ISBN 978-1-913-817-81-5 (pbk)

ISBN 978-1-913-817-80-8 (ebook)

Cover design by Jayne Mapp Design

Printed and bound in Great Britain

# Contents

# Contents

## Are you a thriller seeker?

*To everyone who wants to write but hasn't yet started. Go for it!*

# Introduction

Many people are fascinated by poisons, and I first became interested when I read the James Bond book *You Only Live Twice*, as a teenager. Ian Fleming had collected together details of a wide range of poisonous plants that were grown in Blofeld's Japanese garden for the use of would-be suicides. I read all this with close attention, surprised and intrigued by the lethality of some members of the plant kingdom.

As an adult, and a chemist/biologist, my interest in toxicology moved away from compounds used for murder to the effects of chemical pollutants, such as lead and pesticides, on the environment and the creatures, including humans, which it supported. But when I wrote my guide to science for authors, *Crime Writing: How to Write the Science*, and began to advise other writers on the subject, the criminal use of chemicals came once more to the fore. When I began to write fiction, it was inevitable that I should write stories involving poisons.

This collection of short stories includes tales of the ruthless, the tragic, the vengeful, the desperate and the terminally inept.

A wide range of substances is covered, most of them not too difficult to obtain. I have added notes at the end of each story to put them into context.

Earlier versions of some of these stories have appeared before, either in conventional print/ebooks or in the annual anthology produced by Writers In Stone, the writing group in Weston-super-Mare to which I belong. Details appear on the copyright page.

When considering poisons it is always worth bearing in mind the doctrine of Paracelsus, the 16th-century scholar who wrote:

*All things are poison and nothing is without poison. Solely the dose determines that a thing is poison...*

...a principle of which at least two of the protagonists in these stories are unaware.

There are many popular books about poisons, some excellent and some not so good. A particularly interesting one is *A is for Arsenic: The Poisons of Agatha Christie* by Kathryn Harkup. Dr Harkup discusses all the poisons used by Dame Agatha in fascinating detail. Toxicologist Dr Hilary Hamnett's *Poisonous Tales: A Forensic Examination of Poisons in Fiction* is a superb account of toxic substances in fiction from Chaucer and Shakespeare onwards. It provides much useful detail of how many poisons work and how they are detected by modern methods. It abounds with case studies. There are, of course, chapters on poisons in my crime science guide.

As many writers do, I have telescoped somewhat the time taken for police investigations, post mortems and toxicology tests. The speed of action of one or two poisons has been accelerated slightly, but I hope purists will not be too offended.

I hope you enjoy this collection and will sign up to my newsletter, via my website www.brianpriceauthor.co.uk

# The Scent of an Ending

IT STARTED WITH A TICKLE. A faint irritation in his chest. Then his eyes began to water and he started to cough. He had no idea he was dying.

'Bloody Julia,' muttered Keith Watts. 'Giving me her sodding cold. And it isn't as if she was standing anywhere near me.'

Feeling the need for something loud, Keith eased a rare, signed, copy of the Pink Floyd's 'The Piper at the Gates of Dawn' from its place on the shelf, removed the disc from the sleeve with cotton gloves and placed it reverentially on the turntable. He sat back to listen, immersing himself in the psychedelic swirls and crazy lyrics of his favourite band.

By the end of 'Interstellar Overdrive' Keith was beginning to feel quite unwell. His breathing was painful and his chest was tight, but swallowing a couple of paracetamol tablets made no difference. Realising he was seriously ill and needed help, he tried to open the door but the key wouldn't fit in the lock. Something had jammed it. Shouting or banging on the door would be pointless as Emily and Julia wouldn't hear him – his den was soundproofed extremely well. He could reach the windows, if he stood on a chair, but they were too small to climb through and no-one would hear him if he opened them and shouted for help.

Perhaps he could Skype or WhatsApp Emily? He staggered over to his laptop and switched it on. 'No Internet Connection' flashed up when he tried to log in. Panicking, he stumbled to the door and tried once again to get the key in the lock. No joy. By now he could hardly breathe. He vomited, coughed up bloody mucus and collapsed on the floor. Ten minutes later, he took his last agonising breath.

---

Keith Watts's death had been reported by his wife, Emily, at 10.40 that morning. He hadn't appeared for breakfast and, getting no reply by hammering on the locked door of his den, Emily had stood on a ladder, peered through the window and shouted to her sister, who was holding the ladder.

'Get an ambulance. He's on the floor, not moving.'

With Emily's permission, the paramedics had forced their way in. Keith was lying near the door, a small pool of vomit by his, obviously dead, body. A repetitive 'Hiss, click, hiss, click,' was emanating from the enormous speakers at the back of the room as an LP rotated on the turntable, the music long since finished. A paramedic switched it off, checked for signs of life and called the doctor.

---

The faint smell of new mown hay tickled Dr Singh's nostrils, reminding him of summer holidays in the country. Odd for

December, he thought, but he dismissed it from his mind and focussed on the corpse in front of him. After examining Keith's body, he closed his briefcase, straightened up and addressed a weeping Emily sympathetically.

'This is very strange. It doesn't look like a heart attack, stroke, or seizure. I really can't say why he died. There will have to be a be a post mortem, I'm afraid, and we'll know more then. I'm very sorry.'

Emily's sobs echoed down the hall as the doctor arranged for Keith's body to be moved to the mortuary.

---

'What is it, Nick? Tell me you've got a tricky murder or an armed robbery for me.'

Detective Inspector Matilda Barrett, tired of reading budget projections and yet another force mission statement, welcomed the interruption when Detective Sergeant Nick Lane poked his head round the door.

'There's a message from the pathologist. Could someone go down to the mortuary and look at a suspicious death?'

'Gladly – I need a break from this bloody computer. I joined to catch criminals, not sit in an office all day.'

Stepping into the shoes she had kicked off under her desk, she straightened her jacket, smoothed her skirt and strode down the corridor.

---

'Good afternoon, doctor,' she said as they shook hands. 'I gather you're worried about a recent death?'

'Yes, I am. A Mr Keith Watts. Came in yesterday. I've not

seen anything like this before. I first thought it may have been an asthma attack, precipitating heart failure. When I opened up his respiratory tract, however, I saw extensive damage to its lining and fluid in the lungs. I was puzzled so I rang up a friend of mine, a lung specialist. He said it sounded like poisoning with phosgene – a First World War gas. When I mentioned Dr Singh's comment about the smell of hay in the room, he was convinced.'

'What does phosgene do?'

'In a lay person's terms, it wrecks the lungs. It smells a bit like cut hay but Mr Watts wouldn't have noticed it. His GP notes mention that he suffered from anosmia – he had no sense of smell.'

'Phosgene sounds horrible.'

'It is. Anyone handling it needs specialist training to avoid killing themselves.'

'So he couldn't have come across the stuff by accident?'

'No, certainly not. I can't give you an estimate of time of death, I'm afraid – we don't know how warm the room was throughout the night. From what Dr Singh said, he was probably dead for at least six hours before he was found. Anyway, I'll email you my report tomorrow.'

'Thank you, doctor. I'll look forward to it.'

Barrett phoned Superintendent Arnold as she walked to the hospital car park.

'We have a suspicious death, sir. Keith Watts. I'll notify the coroner and put a team together.'

---

Two hours later, SOCOs were busy in Keith's den. A red-eyed Emily showed Barrett into the untidy kitchen, a scrunched-up tissue dangling from the sleeve of her cardigan and her hair in a mess. Declining coffee, Barrett offered her condolences and began gently.

'I'm afraid I have bad news, Mrs Watts. It looks like Keith was poisoned. We need to search the premises, if that's all right with you, but we'll do our best to avoid making a mess.'

Emily paled and collapsed into a chair.

'Oh my God. Poisoned? I don't believe it.'

'I know it's difficult for you, but can you tell me how you found Keith?'

'He didn't come down for breakfast. He usually needs his caffeine fix before ten so I went looking for him. He wasn't in his bed – we have separate rooms – but I thought he could be in his den. He sometimes falls asleep there.'

'Were you worried? Did you think something had happened?'

'No, not really. I just went looking. I banged on the door of his den but he didn't answer, so I looked through the window. I knew something was wrong as soon as I saw him. An ambulance came quickly and I got the paramedics to break open the door.'

Emily sobbed.

'It was horrible. He was lying by the door, his face all twisted and his eyes streaming. He'd been sick. I'll never forget how he looked as long as I live.'

'It must have been dreadful for you. I'm sorry to add to your grief but can you tell me more about Keith's habits?'

'Keith collects, I mean collected, old records. They were his life and he was never happier than when playing them in his den. It was his private space, away from the rest of the house, and only he had the key. He would stay there all day sometimes and hated being disturbed, so I didn't knock on the door when I went to bed.'

'What time was this?'

'About 10.30, I think. The central heating had stopped working during the afternoon, and we couldn't get an engineer to come until today, so I wanted to be somewhere warm. Keith had a portable gas heater and was comfortable in the den.'

'Who else was in the house?'

'Only my sister, Julia. She came to stay that morning.'

'Has anything in his den been touched?'

'Not since the doctor left. I couldn't bear to go in there again.'

Emily fiddled with a bracelet as she spoke.

'Can you help me by running through everything that happened during that day?'

'I'll try but I'm not sure I can remember everything. It's been such a shock. Julia was helping me in the workshop during the morning. I restore furniture for a living. We went off to the garden centre for lunch, I suppose about twelve. We bought some plants and got back around three. Keith was in his den with two fellow record collectors, Simon Napier and Jimmy Chandler.'

'Did Keith know the others well?'

'Fairly. They were friends but also rivals, each trying to outdo the others by acquiring the most obscure rarities. Keith was very good at that.'

'What time did they leave?'

'Napier around five, I think. Chandler about forty minutes later.'

'And then?'

'Keith stayed with his records until dinner, around seven. Afterwards he tried to restart the central heating, but couldn't, and then went back to his den. I never saw him alive again.'

Her voice caught in her throat.

'Can you think of anyone who would have wanted to harm him?'

'God, no. He didn't have any enemies. There was friendly rivalry, as I said, but no hatred. Thinking on it, I did hear an argument in the kitchen, later in the afternoon.'

'What was it about?'

'Oh, I couldn't catch it all but it seemed to be something about low numbers.'

'Low numbers? Numbers of what?'

'I've no idea. Something to do with records, I expect.'

'Did you hear any noises in the night?'

'No, nothing. But Keith's den was soundproofed so he could listen to his music, as loud as he wanted, without disturbing the rest of the house. Also, so I wouldn't disturb him.'

'Did you have a key to the den?'

'Definitely not. Keith wouldn't let anyone else in the room alone. He kept both copies in his pocket.'

'I see. One last thing. Have you seen anyone suspicious around the house at all?'

'No, Inspector. No one. But our security lights aren't working so I can't be sure there was no-one out there.'

'Thank you, Mrs Watts. That's all for now. I'll need the addresses of the two collectors before we go. I'll arrange for a family liaison officer to support you and we'll need your finger-prints and a DNA sample for elimination purposes. Here's my card. Please get in touch if you can think of anything that might help us.'

In the lounge, a brisk Julia had little to offer DS Lane. Smartly dressed, her business clothes contrasting with Lane's casual jacket and chinos, she was clearly irritated about being interviewed. Her elegant appearance was marred somewhat by a red, runny nose which she continually wiped with a tissue.

'I'm staying for a couple of days while they replace the boiler in my flat. Ironic, isn't it – I leave a freezing flat for a house with no heating. And I've got a cold. Anyway, I didn't see much of Keith. Apart from helping Julia in the morning and going out for lunch with her, I was working on a case. I'm a barrister. You can check my internet use if you need proof.'

'I hope that won't be necessary. Did you see anyone else around the house?'

Julia sneered slightly.

'Only those collectors. Nerds like him with their boxes of records and one-track minds.'

'I take it that you weren't fond of Keith. You don't seem distressed at his passing.'

'No. If you must know, I disliked him.'

'Why?'

'He was a creep. We all went on holiday once and he was forever ogling me and 'accidentally' brushing against me. I stopped wearing my bikini when he was around. I'm sure he would have made advances if Emily hadn't been there.'

'But he never actually tried it on?'

'I didn't give him the chance. I avoided him whenever I could.'

'I see. Anything else you can tell me?'

''Fraid not. Can I go now? I do have work to do.'

'Yes, thank you. We'll need your fingerprints and DNA and may need to talk to you again, though,' Lane called, as Julia left the room abruptly.

Keith's den was the epitome of tidiness and organisation. Records were arranged alphabetically on shelves around three walls. An expensive audio system took pride of place against the fourth wall and everything in the room was spotless. The only things out of place were the record sleeve, which belonged to the album still on the turntable, and a white double album which lay on the desk, with three pairs of cotton gloves next to it.

'That Beatles White Album,' said Lane, 'is worth a fortune. Hence the gloves.'

'What's so special about it?' queried Barrett.

'I collect vinyl. Each of these albums was individually numbered and very low numbers go for massive prices. This is number 27 – it's probably worth three grand if it's in good nick. I bet he's got a few more treasures on those shelves.'

Barrett whistled.

'Amazing. I didn't realise you were such an anorak. You can drool over the rest later. Right now, we have to work out how Watts was poisoned, in a locked room to which no-one else had access.'

Between them they went over every inch of the room, checking for holes through which the gas could have been injected. They found none. There were no suspicious cylinders, canisters or bottles in the room. The small, high-up windows were all locked securely, although a trapped green leaf suggested that one had been opened and closed recently. The only oddity was a large, roughly rectangular, mark on the varnished floorboards beneath the gas heater.

As they were leaving, Barrett stopped to talk to a heating engineer, who was just getting into his van. She then caught up with Lane at the car.

'I don't understand why he didn't call for help when he started to feel ill,' said Lane, as they drove back to the station.

'Perhaps he couldn't. Maybe someone stopped him from opening the door,' Barrett speculated.

'Yeah. That's a thought. Did the SOCOs find anything?'

'Nothing obvious. We're still waiting for reports. We'll send his laptop and phone to IT forensics. There are some paper financial records, but a quick glance suggests nothing unusual. I'll talk to the record collectors this evening and get their finger-prints. In the meantime, find out what you can about phosgene. Get someone to look into the family background. I'll send DC Gilmore to check the outside of the house for signs of intruders. Team briefing tomorrow at 8am.'

When Barrett, accompanied by a detective constable, visited Simon Napier he was rubbing down a stripped-back door frame, his muscular chest stretching a faded Grateful Dead t-shirt. He showed her to a study lined with shelves of records and sprawled into an armchair, inviting Barrett to sit in its twin and leaving the DC standing.

'Can you tell me your exact movements at Keith Watts's house, sir?' she asked, after showing her warrant card.

'Sure. I arrived about two, the same as Jimmy. We talked records over a few beers and discussed our latest finds. I left about five, got home around half-past. I was shocked when I read about Keith's death on my newsfeed this morning. He seemed fine when I left him.'

'Did you go anywhere else in the house?'

'Well, I went for a pee at some point. Otherwise, no.'

'Where was Mr Chandler while you were doing this?'

'In the kitchen with Keith, getting beer.'

'Were you alone at any time?'

'Only in the toilet.'

'I understand there was an argument.'

'Jimmy said that Keith had paid too much for a low number Beatles White Album. Keith was furious and argued that it was a fair price and that low number examples would only increase in value. I didn't get involved. They calmed down eventually.'

'Can you think of anyone who might want to harm Keith?'

'No, not really. He was a bit odd. No-one really liked him that much but he knew his stuff. I don't think anyone actually hated him.'

'Odd? How do you mean?'

'He was just so paranoid about his records. He seemed to think people would want to tamper with them. No-one was allowed in his den alone. He went spare when a key was missing a few weeks ago, although it turned up again shortly afterwards.'

'I see. Well, thank you sir. I'll be in touch if I have any more questions.'

---

Pale of complexion and nervous of manner, Jimmy Chandler wasn't just a record collector. The table in his hobby room was littered with model cars, some freshly painted and some taken back to the metal for repainting. More were displayed in cabinets on the one wall not occupied by records. Chandler stammered slightly but his answers were similar to Napier's. He confirmed that there'd been a disagreement – 'Nothing serious' – and said he waited in the hall while

Keith saw Napier off. He, too, had used the toilet and was adamant that he hadn't been anywhere else in the house. Jimmy agreed that Keith had been odd. He also described him as being rather obsessive in his search for bargains, which he would crow about to others.

---

The chatter in the incident room subsided as Barrett started the briefing.

'Keith Watts, avid record collector, died in his vinyl sanctuary between about 8pm on Tuesday and 4am on Wednesday. His portable heater was switched on but the gas bottle was empty. He died from phosgene poisoning but the chemical couldn't have been injected into the room. He was found by his wife, Emily, on the floor near the locked door, with one key in his pocket and the other close to his hand. The windows were locked and there were no signs of anyone trying to open them from the outside. The ground was hard, so there were no shoe prints. If Keith had called for help, no-one would have heard him as the den is soundproofed.

'The couple had no children and there are no offences on record, apart from a speeding ticket each. Keith wasn't well-liked but no-one seemed to hate him, although there is rivalry amongst record collectors. He had no obvious reason to commit suicide. That's our starting point. What have we learned since?'

DS Lane spoke first.

'Keith's collection is worth a couple of hundred grand. It's full of highly collectable rarities.'

'Inheriting that lot could be a motive for murder,' said Barrett, 'although his wife isn't short of money. She restores antique furniture and has an excellent reputation. All the big museums and auction houses use her. They have separate bedrooms so there could be some marital issues there, which we haven't discovered yet. Other collectors might like to see Keith's treasures come onto the market but, surely, they wouldn't kill for them? Anything else?'

'DC Wyman found these among the LPs, next to the Jefferson Airplane.'

Lane held up a large envelope and tipped out its contents. Two dozen photos of a woman, in various states of undress, fell onto the desk. Some were shot through a bedroom window and others were taken on a beach, where she was changing into swimwear.

'That's Julia,' said Barrett.

'She told Nick that Keith had been pestering her. Maybe it went further than that. He could have been blackmailing her. Putting these on the internet wouldn't exactly help her legal career. A motive for murder, perhaps?'

'So we have four potential suspects for now,' said Lane. 'What about means and opportunity?'

'We need to work on those. What did you find out about phosgene?'

'You can't buy the stuff but it's made when some solvents are burned.'

'Which solvents?'

'One used to strip paint, mainly. Something called dichloromethane. It was banned a few years ago but is still permitted in the US for a few purposes.'

'But how could someone burn it and get the phosgene into the room?'

'Well, they couldn't,' replied Lane. 'There was no point of entry to the room. We looked everywhere. If a window had been opened and the gas pumped in, Keith would have noticed. Anyway, they were all locked from the inside.'

Barrett frowned and thought for a minute. Then she smiled.

'Got it! It was the heater! The killer must have poured paint stripper onto a shallow vessel of some sort, perhaps a plate or dish, and slid it underneath. Some spilled, which accounts for the mark on the floor. As the stuff evaporated, the gas flame did the rest.'

'Lucky for the killer that Watts used the heater.'

'Not luck. Planning. I talked to the boiler repair guy and the timer was disconnected. It's unlikely to have happened by accident.'

'Did the SOCOs find anything?'

'Not much. A few scratches around the lock on the inside of the door. No unidentified fingermarks – just Keith's, Emily's and the two collectors'.'

'Why didn't Keith phone or email for help when he started to feel ill?'

'Good question,' replied Barrett. 'Get on to his internet service provider and see if it was working. And check his phone records.'

Barrett summarised her conversations with the record collectors and continued.

'Of the four, only Julia has a particularly strong motive – and that assumes Keith was blackmailing, or had assaulted, her. All had access to the boiler, it's in a cupboard next to the toilet. All four could have possessed dichloromethane. There must be old stocks around and you can buy it as a pure laboratory chemical on the internet. Napier is doing some house renovating, possibly using old paint stripper. Chandler could use the stuff on his model cars. Emily probably used it for removing varnish from furniture and Julia helps her from time to time, so she would have known about it, too.'

'But would they know how to turn it into phosgene?'

'That we don't know. Might be worth looking at their internet searches, if we can get a warrant to look at their computers. We'd need stronger evidence first, though.'

She continued.

'A key disappeared some weeks ago. Emily or Julia would have had plenty of opportunities to copy it and one of the collectors could have taken it on a previous visit and replaced it later. A bit risky but feasible.'

'How did the killer get the stuff under the heater?'

'Julia or Emily could have put it there around dinner time. The collectors both brought those large LP carriers which would easily hold a plate and a can of paint stripper or a bottle of the chemical. Chandler could have nipped in while Watts was seeing Napier off. Napier could have done the same while the others were arguing in the kitchen. The heater wasn't switched on until after they left and Keith wouldn't have noticed the smell of the stripper or the phosgene because of his anosmia.'

---

When Barrett returned to the Watts house the following day, Julia had gone home and there was no answer when Barrett rang the bell. She walked round the side of the house and found Emily in her workshop, no longer red eyed, French polishing a fine old writing desk. The workshop smelt pleasantly of wood dust, polish and wax. Tools were arranged neatly on hooks on the wall and shelves carried jars holding screws and nails. Brass fittings lay on a plate on Emily's workbench and a row of glass bottles held mysterious liquids.

Emily looked up from her work, visibly irritated.

'Can I help you, Inspector?'

'A few more questions, if I may.'

'OK, but I need to keep polishing this piece. Concentrating on work helps me cope.'

Barrett wondered if that was an excuse to avoid eye contact.

'Could anyone have copied Keith's key?'

Emily started. 'No, certainly not. He had two copies which he never let out of his sight.'

'I see. Do you use dichloromethane in your work?'

'I wish I could, but those strippers have been banned for years. For some woods they were the best you could get.'

'So what's in the bottles?'

'Various polishes and stains I've mixed up – my own recipes. Take a look if you like.'

Barrett declined.

'You said Julia helps you.'

'Yes. She's quite useful and she says it makes a nice change from the stress of the courts.'

'I see. How did you get on with Keith?'

'OK. We basically led separate lives. He was obsessed with his records and had little time for me. I have my restoration work. Still, we rubbed along and remained good friends.'

'Did he support you financially?'

'He didn't need to. The mortgage is paid off and I earn enough from this. He was an accountant but was made redundant when his firm downsized. He got a decent payout and made some profitable investments.'

'How about Julia?'

'What do you mean?'

She coloured and her hands gripped the desk tightly.

'I gather she didn't like him and thought he fancied her.'

'She avoided him. She's younger and prettier than me so I suppose he did look at her, that's all.'

'Was he blackmailing her with those embarrassing photos?'

Emily blinked.

'Photos? I don't know what you mean Inspector. I haven't seen any embarrassing photos. Look, I don't want to be rude, but I must finish this desk. Is there anything else?'

'No, you carry on. I'll see myself out.'

Barrett walked slowly back to her car, something niggling at the edge of her mind, something she'd seen. But what was it? She returned to the station for lunch, all the while worrying at her memory.

---

Talking to Lane in the canteen, Barrett ranked the suspects in reverse order.

'Least likely are Napier and Chandler – weak motives and not the easiest of opportunities, although either could have done it. Forget about them. Emily seemed to be indifferent to her husband, rather than hating him, although she did seem distressed when we first met her. She was nervous during our conversation today, especially when I asked about dichloromethane. But if Julia was being blackmailed, she had the strongest motive, so we'll have a serious chat with her. She could well know how to tamper with the boiler. Her own was being replaced, which is why she stayed with Emily. We'll pick her up at her home address this evening. Did you find out anything about Keith's phone and internet use?'

'Yes. The router was switched off for several hours during

the night, so he couldn't email, WhatsApp or Skype out. There's no mobile reception or land line in his den either.'

Barrett stared thoughtfully at her empty plate and recalled her interview with Emily. She stood up suddenly.

'It's not Julia. It's Emily. Bring her in and caution her. I'll get a couple of DCs to search the workshop and any other outbuildings for old paint strippers. I need to collect something.'

---

Barrett repeated the caution, switched on the recording equipment, identified those present and started the interview with a defiant Emily. A smartly-suited solicitor sat next to Emily, making indecipherable notes.

'Thank you for coming in, Emily. We'd like you to clarify a couple of points for us.'

'I didn't have much choice and I don't know why I'm here. I've got better things to do than answer yet more questions. And my solicitor is costing me money.'

'We have reason to believe you were involved in Keith's death.'

'Absolute rubbish.'

'Then let me outline the case against you, Emily. Keith was killed with phosgene, produced from a plateful of dichloromethane which you placed under his heater. For the benefit of the recording, I am showing Mrs Watts a rectangular sandwich plate, which I retrieved from her workshop. The base matches a mark found under the heater in Mr Watts's den. Although the plate has been cleaned, there are some small brown marks on the bottom where the glaze is missing. We believe that tests will show that the stain is from varnish on the floor.

'You copied the key to Keith's den some while ago. Last Tuesday evening you tampered with the boiler to make sure he would use the heater. You slipped into his room, probably while he was finishing his dinner, and turned it into a gas chamber. We know that Keith couldn't get help – you switched the router off and he couldn't phone. He couldn't get out because you had jammed your key in the lock.'

'Pure speculation, Inspector,' interjected Emily's solicitor.

Barrett ignored him.

'In the morning, holding your breath, you retrieved the plate and opened a window to allow the gas to escape. Before staging the discovery, you shut the window again, trapping a leaf which you didn't see. Despite your efforts, a few traces of gas remained, which Dr Singh noticed.

We found an old can of dichloromethane paint stripper hidden under the floor of a garden shed, with your fingerprints on it. I've no doubt that your internet searches will show us how you found out about phosgene. We also found a key to Keith's den, hidden in an empty soup tin and left in your recycling box.'

As the evidence against her accumulated, Emily's despair grew. Her defiance evaporated and she crumpled in her chair, crying quietly. Barrett gave her a few moments to compose herself.

'So, why did you do it?' Barrett asked, her tone now sympathetic.

'It was for Julia,' Emily sniffed.

Ignoring her solicitor's warning look she continued.

'I found the photos on the printer a couple of months ago. The filthy pervert didn't know I was at home and hadn't retrieved them. When I challenged him, he blustered but I knew he was planning to blackmail her into sleeping with him. I saw how he lusted after her.

'I'd saved up some old paint stripper for my work and a warning on the can led me to find out about phosgene. I realised how I could kill him. Stupidly, I hoped it would look like a heart attack or something else natural. I copied the key a few weeks ago, planning to use it when I had the chance. I thought he was going to make his move while Julia was staying, so I had to act then. Julia knew nothing about it, I swear.'

Emily sobbed as Barrett said she would be charged with Keith's murder and handed her over to the custody sergeant.

'A devious murderer and a nasty man, Nick,' sighed Barrett. 'But at least she confessed. Our evidence is pretty circumstantial.'

'Mixed feelings, boss?'

'No, not really. He may have been a creep but Keith Watts didn't deserve to die, certainly not like a gassed soldier, trapped in a First World War trench. No-one deserves that.'

'True enough. Pub time, then. Your round or mine?'

---

*This plot device was prompted by the warnings on a can of paint stripper and a report, in the British Journal of Industrial Medicine, of phosgene poisoning caused by the use of dichloromethane in a poorly-ventilated room heated by a naked flame.*

*Have fun spotting the sixties music references!*

# Dead Man's Fingers

CAROLINE AND GRAHAM FORDHAM had no idea it would be their last anniversary. They had shared the cooking, dined well, and relaxed together, an unusual occurrence of late.

It wasn't until the early hours of the morning that it began to go seriously wrong. Both started to tremble, sweat and vomit but, while Caroline was depositing her dinner in the toilet bowl, Graham suffered a seizure and passed out. Stumbling to the telephone, Caroline called for an ambulance, only to be told that it would be an hour before one could reach their remote part of Cornwall, as all units were dealing with a multiple crash on the A30. Caroline tried frantically to make her husband comfortable, wiping his face with a cool, wet flannel and checking his heartbeat, all the while trying to control her own nausea. After what seemed like forever, blue lights on the drive signalled the arrival of an ambulance.

In A&E, Graham alternated bouts of vomiting with further seizures. Caroline continued throwing up although, by now, her stomach was empty and painful. Baffled by the couple's condition, the medical staff could only transfer them to intensive care and make them comfortable with sedatives, anti-emetics and fluids.

---

The following morning, a weak and confused Caroline looked blearily at the consultant stood at her bedside.

'I'm very sorry', said the doctor, 'but your husband didn't make it through the night. We don't know what caused your illness, but we're running tests on you, and there will be a post mortem on Graham.'

Caroline, fell back on her pillows, aghast.

'Have you any idea at all what it might be? I'm a GP, so don't spare me. Tell me your suspicions.'

'I'm afraid I haven't any. It could be an infection – a particularly nasty Norovirus, perhaps – or something you both ate, containing microorganisms or a toxin. We won't know until the test results are back. You need to conserve your strength and try to get better. It would help us, though, if you could try to remember everything the two of you ate last night.'

Caroline thought back, her head still muzzy from the sedative.

'Ummm... soup – mushroom, I think. Lamb with roast potatoes, carrots, parsnips and broccoli for the main course and tiramisu for dessert. We drank a bottle of wine and Graham had a brandy.'

'Did you both eat the same?'

'More or less. Graham ate most of the parsnips and I had most of the broccoli. He doesn't – I mean didn't – go much on brassicas and I'm not particularly fond of root vegetables.'

'And you were both feeling perfectly well before the meal?'

'Yes, yes – fine.'

'OK. I'll leave you to rest,' said the consultant, frowning. 'Please tell one of the nurses if anything else occurs to you.'

Caroline slumped back, her head spinning. Nightmare thoughts about Graham's death and how she would cope without him swirled through her mind, until she lapsed into sleep again.

---

'It's very odd,' mused Dr Chandra, the pathologist, on Monday afternoon. 'There's no obvious indication of infection, although I'm waiting for the results of some cultures to come back from the lab. It could be some kind of chemical poisoning, but I've no idea what.'

'Are you saying it looks suspicious?' asked Pete Watkins, the coroner's officer.

'Maybe. I'm not sure. But it's worth taking a look at any food residues in their home, especially the soup.'

'I'll ask the police to drop round when Dr Fordham's discharged.'

---

Dr Chandra ushered Adrian Mitchell, Lecturer in Botany at the university, out of the pathology laboratory, thanking him profusely for his help. Ten minutes later, he was on the phone, speaking to Detective Sergeant Sue Leakey.

'It looks like the Fordhams were poisoned by a dangerous plant.'

'What sort of plant?'

'There was a small root in the food remains collected from their home. A botanist has identified it as Hemlock Water

Dropwort, probably the most toxic native British plant. The roots contain most of the poison and look like small parsnips, hence the nickname Dead Man's Fingers. Some teenagers in Scotland nearly died some years ago, when they put it in a curry by mistake. Dr Fordham was extremely lucky to have survived.'

'Nasty. OK, thanks, doctor. We'll get on to it straightaway.'

---

Red eyed and still weak from her ordeal, Caroline led DS Leakey into the kitchen.

'Doctor,' she began, 'It looks like you and your husband were poisoned with Hemlock Water Dropwort, a deadly plant which looks like parsnips. I need to know when and where you got your vegetables.'

'Skinners Farm delivers our organic veg box every Thursday. It's left on the doorstep until someone comes home.'

'Do you have their phone number? I need to contact them urgently.'

Stepping out of the room, Leakey called the farm office. Two minutes later she returned, a grim look on her face.

'There were no parsnips in the box, Dr Fordham. Someone must have added the poisonous roots after it was delivered.'

What little colour there was left in Caroline's face drained away completely.

'You mean someone deliberately tried to kill us?'

'Unless it was a particularly dangerous practical joke, I'm afraid so, yes,' replied the DS. You're extremely lucky not to have died. We're launching an investigation into the incident so we will have a number of questions for you. I have to get back to the station for a briefing but someone will be along later to take a formal statement. I'll arrange for a family liaison officer to support you.'

'There's no need, thank you,' Caroline said, distractedly. 'I'll go and stay with my sister for a while. She's in the next village.'

'OK. I think that's a good idea. Please let us know the address. I'm really sorry about what's happened. Do be careful and don't hesitate to call us if you see anything suspicious.

'Yes. Thank you. I will.'

Caroline closed the door when DS Leakey left and put the chain in place. She grabbed a few essentials, shoved them in a bag, and waited nervously for the next officer to arrive.

***

'Attention please,' shouted DI Blake, rapping on the desk at the front of the incident room. Faces turned towards him as the hubbub subsided.

'We have two poisonings at Wheal View, one of them fatal. Roots of a deadly plant, Hemlock Water Dropwort, were slipped into an organic veg box and eaten by Graham and Caroline Fordham. He died but she survived. He was a property developer, she's a GP.

'So. Jobs. We need to find out who could have put the roots in the box, sometime on Thursday afternoon, and who wanted to cause the Fordhams harm. I want a couple of DCs to knock on doors to see if anyone was hanging around that afternoon. Someone needs to ask the driver who delivered the veg if he saw anyone lurking. DC Porton – have a chat with the doctor and collect Graham Fordham's tech. We also need a couple of people to ask around the local shops and pubs to see if anyone knew of any tensions involving the couple. The couple's finances need looking at, and someone should. talk to the botanist that the pathologist consulted. Find out where this plant grows. Sue – can you divvy up the tasks, please? We'll meet up this afternoon at five.'

Actions identified, Blake wrote up the policy book and went to brief the DCI.

'An obvious question, Dr Fordham,' began DC Shirley Porton, opening her notebook, 'but can you think of anyone who would want to harm you or your husband?'

'Not enough to want to kill us,' Caroline answered, doubtfully. 'I've had a few disagreements with patients about diagnoses or treatments – Google has a lot to answer for – but nothing really serious. One patient was angry because I wouldn't prescribe the drug she wanted. Another resented my advice that he should drink less and became quite abusive.'

'How about Graham?'

'He was popular locally – a patron of several charities, golf club secretary and a parish councillor. His property developments brought jobs and income to the area.'

'Any conflicts there?'

'Well, there are always people who want to block progress. There was a rather nasty dispute with a farmer about land, though I don't know the details.'

'How about the two of you? Any problems?'

Caroline shifted slightly in her seat.

'No more than most busy couples, I suppose. We should have spent more time together,' she sniffed, 'But with my practice and Graham's business it was difficult. The meal was an anniversary celebration and the first time we'd spent quality time together in months.'

'Thank you doctor,' said Shirley, closing her notebook. 'Please get in touch if anything else occurs to you. I'd like to take Graham's computer and phone, please. I'll give you a receipt.'

'Of course. I'll fetch them for you.'

Caroline stood thoughtfully at the door as the DC drove away, then grabbed her bag, locked up and drove to her sister's.

---

Five o'clock saw the detectives drifting into the incident room, with few signs of triumph on their faces. Sue Leakey reported first.

'Nothing from door-to-door, guv. The houses are far apart and people keep themselves to themselves. No-one saw anyone suspicious or an out-of-place vehicle. A neighbour out walking thought she heard the Fordhams rowing a few weeks ago but couldn't be sure. The van driver saw nothing out of the ordinary.'

'Right. Shirley?'

'The couple seemed to be OK, apart from the stresses of two busy jobs. Caroline couldn't think of any enemies for either of them, apart from a few disgruntled patients and a farmer Graham upset over a land deal. Nothing looking like a motive for murder. IT Forensics are looking at Graham's tech and will get back to us tomorrow.'

'What about their finances?'

'Seem to be fine, guv,' replied DC Lisa Wesley. 'Graham's business account is healthy, and he had plenty of work on. Caroline gave us access to their personal accounts, and they're OK, too. They don't have a mortgage and they pay off their cards in full every month.'

'Nothing odd at all?'

'There is something. Until recently Graham took £500 in cash from the business every month, but most of his transactions are plastic or by internet banking. That's a lot to spend as petty cash.'

'Was he paying people off the books?'

'Possibly, but HMRC have no suspicions.'

'How about the shops and so on?'

'They seem pretty popular in the area' reported DC Alan Stopes. 'No-one in the shops or cafés said anything bad about them.'

'Nothing from me either,' said DC Gary Craven. 'I'll go back to the local in my own time tonight and chat to a few people over a pint.'

Blake's praise for Gary's devotion to duty raised a laugh.

'How about this plant? Mike, you were talking to the botanist?'

DC Mike Trowbridge consulted his notes.

'Dr Mitchell said it normally grows in marshy areas, but a storm in 2018 exposed it on beaches at Lelant and Pentewan. It made the papers and online news. One bite of the roots can kill, but cooking destroys some of the poison.'

Blake summed up.

'Not much for a day's work then. No suspects, no sightings and no motives. Anyone who reads the news could find the murder weapon. Tomorrow, I want the farmer interviewed. Talk to the receptionist at Caroline's practice, Shirley. Find out how Caroline's thought of at work. Try to have a word with the partners. Check the wills, please, Lisa. Dave, see if anyone has CCTV covering the lanes and take a look at traffic cameras, if any.'

'There's no private CCTV guv – I looked. There's an ANPR camera on the dual carriageway.'

'OK – check it out. Meet up at five tomorrow.'

---

Gary sat in the corner of the pub, blending in with rugby shirt and jeans, although a few shadier drinkers spotted him for a copper. He eavesdropped on an argument between a couple of local farmers.

'Just shows that organic stuff's rubbish. Nonsense like that's putting growers like me out of business.'

'Bollocks. My lad works for Skinner and his veg is good.'

'Huh. Someone should have done something about Fordham, long ago, mind. Mary Bennett never got over Dan's death and it was Fordham's fault.'

'Oh, come on, Steve, just 'cos he died after Fordham bought his land doesn't mean they're connected.'

'We all know it was suicide. Coroner was being kind when he recorded an accidental overdose. He lived for that farm and hated having to sell it – at a crap price, too.'

'Leave it. And it's your round.'

Gary asked the barman who the two were. With their details in his notebook, and a note to talk to Mary Bennett, he drank up and left.

---

Shirley called at the surgery at one o'clock. Melanie Wright, a slightly plump, well-dressed woman in her thirties, started when Shirley approached the reception desk and showed her warrant card.

'Oh,' she said. 'Yes. Err. I'll be with you in a minute. I'll close the doors. We can talk in the staff room. No-one's using it at the moment, and the doctors won't be there for another half hour.'

'Busy?' asked Shirley, smiling sympathetically.

'Well. You know. Too many patients and not enough doctors. Austerity and all that. Come through.'

The staff room was quiet, apart from a coffee machine gurgling in the corner. The walls were covered with posters about drug recalls, professional organisations, fees for services and medical news, including a faded press cutting about the local Hemlock Water Dropwort discoveries. Photos of the staff enjoying a Christmas party were displayed next to posters on acceptable alcohol intake and the dangers of smoking.

'Melanie,' began Shirley, 'Can you tell me about Dr Fordham. Is she popular? How does she get on with colleagues? That sort of thing.'

Melanie thought for a few moments.

'She gets on all right with the other doctors. The patients seem to be OK with her. She has a no-nonsense approach that puts a few people's backs up, but no-one's formally complained.'

'What about non-medical staff such as yourself?'

'She's all right, as long as we do our jobs properly. She's been a bit cold with me lately, but I've no idea why. She's good friends with the practice nurse.'

'How about her home life. Were you aware of any problems?'

Melanie fidgeted and her eyes flickered around the room. She leaned forward and whispered.

'Rumour is, she was having an affair with Dr Redgrave, the senior partner.'

'Did her husband know?'

'I don't think he had any idea. I don't blame her, though. He was a swine and Dr Redgrave's lovely.'

'You didn't like him?'

'Well, he... Oh, never mind.'

Before Melanie could say any more, the practice nurse came in, heading for the coffee machine with an air of desperation.

'Thank you, Melanie,' said Shirley. 'Here's my card. Please get in touch if you think of anything else.'

---

The incident room stilled as Blake got up to speak.

'What have we got then?'

Gary spoke first.

'Dan Bennett, the farmer Fordham upset, is dead. Officially, an accidental overdose, but locals think it was suicide because he hated selling his land to Fordham. I've spoken to his wife and she believes this, too.'

'Motive for murder?'

'Possibly. She seemed very bitter towards Fordham but also rather frail. I can't see her sneaking along the lanes with poison parsnips in her pocket.'

'Anything else?'

'Steve Carton, a local grower, hates the organic farming crowd which he sees as competition. Don't see him as a murderer though – all bluster.'

'Right. The wills, Lisa?'

'Both their wills are in favour of each other with a few small bequests to medical charities. There are no children.'

'Shirley?'

'We may have a suspect, guv. The receptionist said Caroline was sleeping with another doctor. There's a cutting on the staff room wall about Hemlock Water Dropwort. If she wanted to kill Graham to get him out of the way, she could have arranged to take a non-fatal dose while making sure Graham got a lethal one.'

'Good work. I think we'd better interview Dr Fordham under caution. Bring her in.'

---

A bewildered Caroline sat facing DI Blake and DS Leakey, her solicitor by her side. With Caroline cautioned, and those present identified for the recording, Leakey started the interview.

'Dr Fordham, we have evidence which suggests you had a motive for killing Graham. Furthermore, we suspect that you knew about Hemlock Water Dropwort and ate just enough to make yourself ill, while making sure Graham got a lethal dose. Would you like to comment?'

Caroline responded furiously.

'What evidence?'

'We believe that you're having an affair with Dr Redgrave. Were you planning to leave Graham? Did you want his money?'

Stunned, she almost laughed.

'That is absolute nonsense. The idea of me sleeping with Stephen is laughable. I see a lot of him it's true. He's my mentor. But as to sex, it would be extremely unlikely. He's gay and is marrying a lifeguard from Newquay. He's keeping it quiet until after the wedding. I'm the only one in the practice he's told. As to money, I have plenty of my own.

'Your suggestion that I deliberately took a small dose of the plant is ridiculous,' Caroline continued. 'I looked it up in the medical literature. You can't mess around with the doses and predict what's enough to make you ill without killing you. It's too bloody toxic. It was pure luck that I didn't die as well.'

'If that's all, Inspector,' interjected the solicitor, 'we're finished here. Come along doctor.'

---

Leakey and Porton exchanged rueful glances.

'A nice idea, Shirley. Pity it didn't work.'

'But Melanie was sure she was playing away, sarge.'

'Yeah, well. Workplace gossip.'

'Or jealousy, perhaps.'

'What do you mean?'

'Melanie didn't seem to like him, when I spoke to her, but I saw the Christmas party photos on the staff room wall. There's a shot of Melanie dancing closely with Graham. Maybe she fancied him. Perhaps she wanted them both dead, because she couldn't have him.'

'Sounds a bit improbable. We can't arrest her because she might have fancied Graham. We need something we call evidence.'

Stung by the DS's sarcasm, Shirley muttered 'Yes, sarge' and left the room.

'What is it?' she snapped, as Bob Moore, the IT technician, leaned over her desk.

'Phone records and images from Graham Fordham's laptop. Thought you wanted them. No need to bite my head off.'

'No, sorry. I'm just a bit pissed off. Anything interesting?'

'A couple of things. There's loads of calls to and from an unlisted mobile number. We'll get the location tomorrow. Also, there's this.'

Bob played a video on Graham's laptop. It showed a woman performing a striptease in what looked like the Fordhams' bedroom. Her face wasn't visible but she was clearly not Caroline. Her short, but well-rounded, body contrasted with the doctor's tall, slim frame.

'So, Graham was up to something,' Shirley muttered. 'Thanks, Bob.'

'Guv?' she called, as Blake entered the room. 'Caroline does have a motive. Graham was the one playing away, not her.'

Blake studied the video.

'OK – that shortens the odds a bit, but we need to identify the other woman.'

'Well, she has a mole on her shoulder. And that's a scar where she had her appendix out – my sister has one just the same.'

'Not helpful unless we have someone in mind.'

'It could be Melanie Wright. She's about the same shape as the woman in the video.'

'Well, we can't bring her in and ask her to take her top off, can we? But you could be on to something. We'll leave Caroline for the moment and have another word with Melanie Wright tomorrow.'

---

'The unlisted phone was mainly used in the vicinity of Tregorran Farm, a dozen miles from the Fordham's place,' Bob announced at the morning briefing.

Shirley frowned. Tregorran Farm rang a bell but she couldn't remember why. She pushed it from her mind as Dave waved a printout.

'Traffic provided a list of ANPR hits for the times between the veg box delivery and Caroline's return home. I'll go through them this morning.'

'OK' said Blake. 'We're talking to Melanie Wright this afternoon and, depending on what she has to say, we'll pull Caroline in again this evening. Thanks guys.'

---

Melanie Wright came into the station, smartly dressed in a cream chiffon blouse, tailored jacket, matching skirt and designer shoes. Shirley saw what she was wearing and had an idea. She slipped into the interview room while Melanie was being signed in and turned the heating up to maximum.

'I like your outfit' she said, as they walked down the corridor. 'I wish my salary stretched to such nice things.'

Melanie preened.

'Oh, they're not that expensive when you get them online.'

*That's a thousand quid's worth of designer gear*, thought Shirley, as she guided Melanie into the interview room. *She won't get those on a receptionist's pay.*

Deliberately, Blake kept Melanie waiting for half an hour. Apologising for the delay, he reassured her that she was there voluntarily and asked if she needed a solicitor. She declined. He recited the caution and started the video recorder.

'You look very hot, Melanie. Let me help you out of your jacket,' said Shirley.

As the jacket slid off, both detectives looked at the pale chiffon blouse clinging damply to Melanie's shoulders. Shirley nodded to Blake who began the interview.

'What you said about Caroline's affair, Melanie. It's rubbish, isn't it?' Melanie blanched.

'No, no – it's true.'

'But it isn't. Dr Redgrave is Caroline's mentor. And, for your information, he's gay.'

Melanie looked stunned.

Changing tack, Blake asked, 'when did you have your appendix out, Melanie?'

'Er, when I was fourteen, I think. Why?'

Blake continued. 'You live near Tregorran Farm, don't you?'

'Yes. I've already given you my address.'

'Well, here's a few facts for you. Until recently, Graham had frequent conversations with someone on a mobile in the vicinity of Tregorran Farm. We found a video on his laptop of a woman stripping in the Fordhams' bedroom. You can't see her face but she has a mole on her shoulder like yours and an appendectomy scar. She's also your shape.'

Melanie blushed and shuffled in her seat.

'We also know that Graham was withdrawing £500 a month in cash and we think he was giving it to you. That's how you could afford designer clothes. He was the one having an affair, and it was with you.'

'So? It's not against the law. Caroline must have found out and killed him.'

Shirley took over the interrogation.

'I spoke to Caroline this morning. She knew about the affair but, amazingly, she forgave him. The dinner was an attempt at reconciliation. She had no motive.'

Melanie shrugged.

'You, on the other hand, did. Graham dumped you and stopped your clothing allowance a couple of months ago. So, goodbye to your lover and to your designer wardrobe. You tried to kill the Fordhams with the deadly plant in a twisted revenge attack.'

'Nonsense. I don't know anything about poisons and I've never been to the house.'

'There's a cutting about the plant on the staff room wall, so you knew about its properties. You were spotted by an ANPR camera on the road between town and the area of Wheal View on Thursday. You knew about the veg box and rushed to the house before anyone could take it in. You added the poisonous roots and then drove home.'

Melanie's temper snapped and she snarled at the detectives.

'So what? They bloody deserved it. The bastard used and dumped me, and that smug bitch knew. She looked at me as if I was a piece of shit. But I gave him a better time than she ever did – and look how I was treated.'

Shirley stood up and addressed the suspect.

'Melanie Wright, I am arresting you on suspicion of murdering Graham Fordham and of the attempted murder of Caroline Fordham.'

She repeated the caution and advised Melanie to call her solicitor, eliciting nothing but a look of fury in return.

---

'The root of all evil?' grinned Sue Leakey, when Melanie had been taken to the cells and the team reconvened in the incident room.

'Ouch,' said Blake, 'That's dreadful. For that, you're getting the beers in.'

---

*The exposure of Hemlock Water Dropwort roots after a storm in Cornwall did happen, although no-one (reportedly) died from consuming them. The incident with the Scottish teenagers also really happened.*

# The Dose Makes the Poison

CARRIE COULD STAND it no longer. Darren had gone back to using and was out of it most of the time. He'd been stealing money from her purse, she was sure, and now he was screwing Tracey. That was the last straw. She didn't want him in her life any more but she couldn't just leave. She'd tried to before, and it took all her skills as a trainee beautician to cover up the damage to her face afterwards. She didn't have the money to set up a new life in a different town; her job and her friends were here. She couldn't bear the thought of moving and she knew he'd always be able to find her.

She thought back to how he was in the early days of their relationship. He was funny, charming and generous, never shouting at her and always supportive. He'd encouraged her to go to college and she was the first one to do so in her family. They had even talked about having a family. Then he lost his job and turned to drugs, metamorphosing into a sullen, violent sponger. Meanwhile she had found a career she really wanted and had studied hard at college, getting a placement in one of the town's best beauty salons.

All the advice columns, online and in the magazines, advised people in abusive relationships to leave, to go to a refuge or to get restraining orders. But that assumed there was somewhere to go and she hadn't been able to find a refuge locally. Anyway, Darren knew where she worked. She could report his drug use, but all he would get for possession of a small amount of heroin would be a fine. And he would make her pay.

Sleepless nights saw her brain whirling, desperate to find a way out of the trap. If only he would take an overdose. She could then get on with her life. It would be worth living again. The trouble was, Darren was always careful with gear, never taking more than he needed each time. He didn't keep large amounts in the flat either, just in case he was busted. Any idea of somehow giving him too much, perhaps when he was zoned out, was impractical. *If only there was another drug he could take with the heroin*, she fantasised. *Something that would make the gear more deadly.*

---

'Hey! You'd better be careful with that. It's expensive.'

Carrie started as she nearly dropped the tray of Onabeaut anti-wrinkle vials.

'Sorry, Jane. I'm not quite with it today.'

'Come on, Carrie. We pay you to be with it.' Jane's tone softened. 'Is there something the matter? Can I help?'

'No, no. It's OK. I didn't get much sleep last night.'

'All right for some,' chipped in Lisa, Carrie's fellow trainee. 'If I had a bloke as hot as your Darren, I wouldn't want much sleep either.'

Carrie forced a grin, unable to tell her colleagues the real reason why she couldn't sleep.

'Why is your mind always in your knickers, Lisa?' she joked.

'That's enough, you two. We have clients to see and a salon to prepare. Save that for your tea break.'

Jane's tone was stern, but she quite enjoyed listening to her trainees' banter when it didn't interfere with work.

'We've got four people coming in this morning: two ladies for facial fillers, one for Onabeaut and a lad wanting a tattoo removed because he's broken up with the girl whose name is on his shoulder. It's going to be busy. Lisa – you can watch me do the fillers and, Carrie, you can shadow Marion as she does the Onabeaut'.

Carrie was happy to watch Marion, as she got on well with her. She welcomed the patient in reception and led her into Marion's treatment room. Despite the soothing music and the muted colours, the woman seemed nervous.

'It's not going to hurt is it? Only I don't like needles.'

'Don't worry, Mrs Cartwright. You won't feel much at all. The needles are very fine and most people hardly notice them. And you did say you were desperate to get rid of those frown lines.'

'Yes, I am. But it says in your brochure that you use a toxin. Isn't that dangerous? I don't want to end up poisoned.'

Marion laughed. 'We only use a tiny amount and it stays in your skin. It's quite safe. I'm fully trained and it's been approved for this since 2006. Don't worry.'

'OK then. I'll give it a go.'

Carrie's mind was only half on what Marion was doing. She watched the beautician administer a series of injections across Mrs Cartwright's forehead but, all the time, she was wondering about the chemical she was using. Was it really poison? What would happen if someone swallowed it or injected it into a vein? She resolved to find out as soon as she could.

The chance to discover more about Onabeaut came at lunchtime. Carrie grabbed her sandwiches and slipped into an internet café, just down the road from the clinic. After buying a coffee and paying for a half-hour session, she chose a computer in a corner where she would not be overlooked. Typing in 'Onabeaut' and 'Poison' she was shocked by what she saw. Botulinum toxin is one of the most toxic substances on the planet, she discovered, and they had bottles of it in the fridge at the clinic! She read on and found out that people can die from food poisoning caused by the microbe that produces botulinum and a few patients have died from overdoses when it's been used in surgery. Used cosmetically, it's perfectly safe as long as the practitioner knows what they're doing. Her mind leapt ahead. Could she use it to get rid of Darren? Could she steal it from the clinic without getting caught? She would have to have a chat with Marion about how it's used. But it was vital that she didn't attract suspicion. Deleting her search history and shutting down the computer, she walked thoughtfully back to work.

Marion was still in the staff room, finishing her lunch. She smiled when Carrie appeared.

'Marion. Can I ask you a favour?'

'Of course, what is it?'

'Well, I've got to do a mini-project for my college course and I was thinking about Onabeaut. It seems so interesting that a few tiny injections can make someone look so much younger. Can you tell me more about it.'

'Sure. I don't really understand the chemistry and that, but I'm sure you can look it up on the manufacturer's website. I'll give you some of their leaflets. What I do know is that it relaxes muscles and, after a day or so, the frown lines smooth themselves out.'

'Magic! Is it difficult to do?'

'You have to be careful. It comes as a powder in those little glass vials. I add some saline solution to the powder, shake it up, and it's ready to go. It has to be kept in the fridge and used within a couple of days after I've mixed it, or it goes off. I only use a tiny bit in each injection so one vial goes a long way.'

'Cool. Can I watch you again and maybe try it myself?'

'Sure you can watch, but I can't let you do the injections. I had to go on a special course so I know where to do it and how much to use.'

'OK. Great. Thanks, Marion.'

Jane interrupted the two women's conversation.

'Marion. Your two o'clock's come in bit early. Can you see her? And Carrie, come and watch me do a facial peel.'

Carrie followed Jane into the treatment room, determined to find out more about this fascinating chemical. Could this be the way to rid herself of Darren? She really thought it might.

---

Carrie thought long and hard about how to do it. At first it was just a theoretical exercise, but the more she imagined it the more feasible it seemed. Too much botulinum stops your breathing, she had read. She also knew that users who overdose die because they can't breathe – she'd looked that up as soon as she realised Darren used, in case he needed help. *So, would a dose of botulinum look like a heroin overdose? Especially if the victim already had heroin in his system?*

There was no-one to ask, and she knew it would be stupid to post a question on an internet chat forum. That would leave an obvious trail. She realised she mustn't act in a hurry. Everything had to be planned out and rehearsed, where possible. Not only would she need the Onabeaut, she would need a means of giving it to Darren and an alibi for when it took effect.

The means was easy. She would use Darren's own syringe. When he was really out of it, he wouldn't notice another injection. An alibi was more difficult, but if she could arrange to be seen in public in some way that should cover it.

Getting the Onabeaut was more of a problem. She couldn't just walk out of the clinic with it. Marion kept records and two or three vials going missing would be noticed. Keeping the stuff useable could also be a problem. She couldn't know in advance when Darren would get himself sufficiently stoned for her plan to work and she couldn't keep it for days, even in the fridge. A Friday night was a good bet, but not a certainty. But, after several sleepless nights, she came up with a plan.

---

Thursday afternoon, and the salon was busy. Jane and Marion were fully occupied with clients and Carrie had been given the job of clearing up at the end of the day. Perfect. Putting on vinyl gloves, she rummaged through the waste bins until she found a couple of empty Onabeaut vials. She knew there were two in the fridge with the solution already made up, one which Jane was using and one of Marion's. She used a syringe to transfer most of their contents to the empty vials, replacing the liquid with saline solution, and stuck some surgical tape over the open ends of her vials to stop them leaking. She knew that Onabeaut takes a while to work, and clients wouldn't notice anything was wrong until some days later, by which time the vials would have been long gone. She slipped her prize into a thermos of ice in her bag and carried on with her duties.

Come Friday, Carrie's nerves were as tight as piano strings. She had to work hard to keep focused at work and spent her lunch hour smoking, something she rarely did. She couldn't help feeling that everyone was looking at her and suspecting her intentions. But when Lisa asked her how she was, Carrie turned it to her advantage.

'Just a bit excited, Lise. Darren's taking me out tonight. A surprise. I think he's going to ask me something.'

'You're joking. I thought you were having problems.'

'No, no. Just a tiff a few weeks ago when he looked like he was losing his job. It's all fine, now. We're great. And I'll say yes!'

'Lucky girl. Make sure he buys you champagne not some cheap Prosecco. And I'll want a full report tomorrow.'

'You'll get it, I promise.' *But not the one you're expecting,* Carrie thought.

'Lets go for a curry tonight. I'll pay.'

The numerous takeaway restaurant menus pinned to the kitchen corkboard testified to Darren's liking for Indian food. She hoped she could persuade him to go out, rather than eating in, so CCTV would pick up images of the 'happy couple'.

'What's this all about then?'

'Well, we don't go out much these days but I got some decent tips at work today and Jane was pleased with me, so I want to celebrate.'

'OK. If you're paying, why not?'

The couple ate early and Carrie kept Darren well supplied with lager during the meal. They left the restaurant at eight thirty and, after another couple of drinks in the pub, wandered back to the flat. Carrie made sure that every time they passed a camera she was smiling and holding Darren's arm. He seemed slightly puzzled by her attentions but didn't appear to mind.

Back at the flat, they agreed to stream a movie. Carrie pretended to fall asleep, knowing that Darren would take the opportunity to shoot up. When he did, the combination of the alcohol and the heroin sent him into a deep sleep and Carrie seized the moment.

Slipping on a pair of vinyl gloves she picked up Darren's syringe and needle, removed the vials of Onabeaut from her Thermos and began to inject their contents, slowly, into Darren's arm. She had trouble finding a vein at first but, after several tries, she managed. Darren stirred slightly as the cold liquid entered his bloodstream, and Carrie's heart almost stopped. But he went back to sleep, and Carrie continued. It took her nearly two minutes to empty both vials, and all the time her nerves were almost at breaking point. But she persevered.

Without waiting for the poison to take effect, Carrie rinsed out the syringe and put the empty vials in a plastic bag. She would dispose of them later. The priority was to establish an alibi and that meant getting herself noticed.

---

The bottle of Prosecco exploded spectacularly as Carrie stumbled and knocked it off the shelf with her handbag. Sickly-smelling foam coursed along the floor and fragments of glass were scattered everywhere. The manager of the 7-11 supermarket rushed out from behind the counter and, when he saw Carrie looking upset, his wrath turned to concern.

'I'm so sorry. I must have tripped or something and my bag swung round. I'll pay for the wine, of course. I feel such an idiot, but my ankle has always been weak.'

Manufactured tears appeared on her cheeks and the shop manager, fearful that the store would be blamed for having an uneven floor, was kindness itself.

'Don't you worry about that. It was an accident. Are you hurt? Can I get you some water?'

'No. No thanks. I'll be fine. I just came in for some milk. You must let me pay for the damage. It was all my fault.'

The manager insisted that she didn't have to pay and would only charge her for a pint of milk. Carrie smiled gratefully. She had made sure that the conversation was recorded on the shop's TV cameras and made a point of limping slightly as she left the shop and returned to the flat. Where, she hoped, Darren's body awaited her.

---

Carrie tiptoed into the flat, unsure why she was trying to make no noise. As she had hoped, Darren was lying on the couch where she had left him, his head slumped on his chest. She listened for the sounds of breathing and checked his pulse. Nothing. The Onabeaut had worked. Taking a swig of gin to steady her nerves, she practised what she was going to say and dialled 999.

'Help, please. I need an ambulance. My fiancé. He's not breathing. I think he's overdosed. Hurry, hurry.'

'Stay calm.' The call handler's voice was soothing but

professional. 'Can I have your name and address, please. Can you do CPR?'

Carrie gave the details and said she'd tried CPR. She should have thought of that. The police would want to know why she hadn't attempted to help Darren. As soon as the call finished, she hauled Darren's body off the couch and went through the motions of compressing his chest, so it would show that she'd tried. What if he woke up? The thought terrified her, and she wondered whether she could suffocate him with a cushion if she had to. But it didn't come to that. Darren's corpse remained unresponsive, and she practised sobbing for when the paramedics arrived.

The ambulance turned up a few minutes later. The crew tried everything to revive Darren – oxygen, CPR and injecting a heroin antidote – but to no avail. They commiserated with Carrie as she sat weeping at the kitchen table.

'I'm sorry, Ms Walker. We tried all we could but we were too late,' said a paramedic.

'If only I hadn't gone out for milk. Perhaps I could have saved him,' Carrie wept.

'You don't know that,' he replied. 'We've had several sudden deaths involving heroin this month. Batches have been contaminated with fentanyl, which is much more dangerous. You can't blame yourself.'

At that point a police car pulled up outside and two uniformed officers entered the flat. One of them, a young constable, looked at Darren's body with contempt. The other, a sergeant, looked at Carrie with sympathy in his eyes.

'I'm Sergeant Mike Howell and this is PC Dave White,' he began. 'Can you tell us exactly what happened, Miss Walker? Take your time. I know you're upset. Dave – make yourself useful and get Miss Walker some tea.'

'Thank you', Carrie said, almost whispering. 'We'd been out for a meal and a few drinks. Darren had proposed to me and said we would go and get a ring tomorrow. When we got back, I realised we had no milk, so I popped out to the shop. I made a fool of myself and knocked over some wine. The manager was kind and didn't make me pay for it but I was away for longer than I intended. Darren must have shot up while I was out. I found him like this when I got back. I called an ambulance and tried CPR like they show you on the adverts, but it was no good. The paramedics couldn't revive him either. I'd told him he shouldn't use that stuff and he promised he would give it up. This was the best day of my life and now it's the worst.'

Carrie laid it on a bit thick but she had to convince the officers that she was heartbroken. It seemed to work because the sergeant commiserated with her and asked no more questions.

'I'm afraid Darren will have to go to the mortuary,' he said. 'It's a suspicious drug death, so the coroner may want a post mortem. Also, we'll need a statement from you. Could you come into the station in the next day or two?'

Carrie nodded.

'Thank you. Again, I'm sorry for your loss.'

As the two police officers left, the paramedics carried Darren's body to the ambulance on a stretcher. Once they'd gone, Carrie tipped the cold tea down the sink and poured herself a large gin. A wave of relief swept over her. She'd done it. Now all she had to do was get rid of the empty vials, provide a convincing statement and weather the storm.

Carrie stuffed the empty vials into an old handbag and peered through the window into the street, just in case someone was watching. The pavement was empty so she put on a coat and left the building, leaving her phone at home and heading for the recycling bins at the back of the supermarket. No-one would notice the empty vials amongst all the other glass and, even if they did, they wouldn't recognise them for what they were.

The area at the back of the store was cluttered with rubbish and a dim light shone on the bins. It was hardly an incentive to recycle, she thought, but the lonely spot suited her purpose. She was just about to open her bag when a noise from behind distracted her. A figure on a mountain bike whizzed up to her, grabbing her bag. She pulled back, the handles stretching to their limit. The figure punched her in the face and she stumbled backwards, hitting her head on the glass recycling bin. Dazed, she let go of the bag and slumped to the floor.

Carrie tried to stand up, but couldn't quite manage it. She turned to one side and vomited, the taste of returning gin acrid in her mouth. She stayed that way until a young man, in the uniform of the store, found her and helped her to a bench. Her head was thundering, her face was tender and the hair on the back of her head was matted with blood. Before she knew it, an ambulance turned up, called by the lad who was helping her. It was the same crew that had tried to resuscitate Darren and they seemed surprised to see her again.

'You're having a bad time of it, love,' one of them said. 'What's happened to you here? Been in the wars?'

'Someone hit me and I banged my head. I'm a bit dazed but I wasn't knocked out. I'm all right, really.'

'We'll just take a look at you. To be on the safe side.'

The paramedics examined her, shone a torch in her eyes, inspected the wound on her head and checked her vision.

'You really should come into the hospital for a check-up, you know. Head injuries can be serious.'

Carrie shook her head, wincing at the pain.

'I don't want to. I just want to sleep. I've got some paracetamol at home. I'll be OK.'

'Well, if you're sure. I'll give you this card. If you get any of these symptoms get yourself to a hospital. Call an ambulance if you need to. And can you sign this form to confirm you declined to come with us?'

'Yes, thank you. I'm feeling a bit better so I'll be off home. It's not far.'

Carrie scribbled her signature on the form, thanked the young man from the store and walked slowly away, wishing he hadn't phoned for the ambulance. She really didn't want to come to anyone's attention. Her problem now was not the headache but the empty Onabeaut vials. What if the police arrested the thief before he dumped the bag? Would they get suspicious about Darren's death? Despite the bang on the head, and the alcohol she had consumed, Carrie knew she would get little sleep tonight.

'What's he up to?'

PC Joe Wallace turned on the patrol car headlights and the figure on the mountain bike, dazzled by the beams, covered his eyes with an arm.

'That's Tony Fuller. Petty thief and general scrote. He's out and about late. Let's have a word with him.'

He put the car into gear and drove towards the rider who spun the bike around and disappeared down a narrow alley before the police car could reach him.

'Hold on, Joe,' his colleague said. 'He chucked something as he shot off. I'll get it.'

Joe switched off the ignition and waited for PC Pat Silver to return. A few minutes later the officers were examining a handbag.

'Looks like he nicked this from someone,' said Joe. 'There's no phone or purse, so he must have emptied it out. What've you got there?'

Jack held up an empty glass vial. 'Onabotulum or something.'

'What's that when it's at home?'

'Never heard of it. We'd better pass it on to the drug squad. Probably some new way for kids to get off their faces.'

'Any ID?'

'No, nothing.'

'I think CID will want to take a look, maybe get some prints off the bag. The Super's hot on street crime at the moment, and charging that nuisance Tony Fuller would look good. He's got a lot of previous so he might even go inside this time.'

---

For most of the night Carrie fretted over the vials. Could they be traced to her? She'd left no ID or documents in the bag, and she'd never been charged with an offence, so her fingerprints or DNA wouldn't be on file. She couldn't remember whether she had handled the vials without gloves. She didn't think so, but she couldn't be sure.

By the time morning came, her nerves were jangling and she couldn't face the thought of going into work for the Saturday session. They wouldn't expect her to, she realised, so she phoned Jane and explained that Darren had died. Jane was full of sympathy, although Carrie knew she disapproved of drug users, and told her to take a few days off. At least that would give her face time to heal and saved her concocting a story to explain the injury.

Throughout the day Carrie received sympathetic texts from friends and colleagues at the clinic and college. She took a few phone calls and perfected the bereaved fiancée act; bemoaning the loss of Darren, thanking people for their support, and punctuating the conversations with sobs at appropriate moments. In truth, she did miss him and the enormity of what she had done gradually dawned on her. She was a murderer. There was no going back. And she was now alone.

Carrie was terrified of going to prison and realised that she would have to watch her behaviour carefully for many weeks to come. A careless word or an inappropriate action could attract suspicion, and there were no handy videos on YouTube explaining what to do after you've killed your partner. In the end she decided to keep herself to herself as much as possible, take as much time off work and college as she could get away with and refrain from looking cheerful in public.

Then there was the question of Darren's parents. The police would have told them about his death but should she make contact? She knew they disapproved of her, thinking she could have done more to discourage his drug habit, but surely it would be callous not to commiserate? She feared they would put the phone down on her if she rang, so she settled for writing them a letter, an exercise which took her half the day. She wasn't used to writing personal messages, other than texts or Tweets, and she was anxious not to give the wrong impression. Eventually, she was reasonably satisfied and took a photo of it with her phone, in case they called her to talk about it.

Two days later, Carrie turned up at the police station to make a formal statement. She had rehearsed exhaustively what she planned to say, so she didn't think she'd slip up. Her only worry was that she might sound as though she was reading a script.

Sergeant Howell guided her to an interview room and offered her a hot drink, which she declined.

'I'm going to record this interview, Miss Walker, and I have to caution you as you are a potential witness. Please don't worry, it's just a formality. You're not being accused of anything.'

Carrie's stomach clenched and she wished she'd asked for a coffee. She hadn't expected anything so formal. *Did they know something? Should she have a solicitor?*

'I just need to run through a few things with you,' the sergeant said, after he had recited the caution and identified those present, for the recording.

'You said you'd been out for a meal and Darren had proposed to you. Is that right?'

'Yes. We went to the Bangalore Banquet and he asked me just after we finished the meal. I was thrilled.'

'So everything was all right between you?'

'Yes. Fine. We've had our differences in the past, and the occasional row. But nothing that a kiss and a cuddle didn't heal.'

'What were these rows about? Anything in particular?'

'Minor things, mainly. The only real issue was him using heroin. I tried to get him to stop. When he proposed he said that getting married would be the incentive he needed. I believed him.'

'When was the last time he used it, apart from that night. Do you know?'

'I'm not sure. Maybe a week or two ago. He wasn't an addict. Or at least he said he wasn't. I thought he just used occasionally, but I suppose he could have been doing it secretly.'

'So you were surprised when you found he'd injected himself?'

'Yes. Gutted. I didn't realise he was dead at first, but when I got close I saw he wasn't breathing. Then I tried CPR and called an ambulance. You know what happened after that.'

'Yes, I do,' said Sergeant Howell, gently.

'I don't suppose you know where he got his supplies?'

'Sorry, no. He never told me.'

'OK. Well I'll get your answers transcribed onto a statement form for you to sign. We're not treating Darren's death as suspicious at the moment, but we haven't had the results of the post mortem and toxicology tests yet. Thank you for coming in, Miss Walker.'

As Carrie left the station her head was in a whirl. The idea that they could possibly regard Darren's death as suspicious terrified her. She ran over in her mind all the precautions she had taken and reassured herself that she had left no evidence. The only loose end was her bag with the vials. But surely a thief would simply dump it. Wouldn't he? There was nothing in it of value after all. But still she worried.

---

Dr Durbridge opened the email from the toxicology lab and frowned. *That's odd*, he thought. *It doesn't make sense.* Frowning, he picked up the phone and dialled Mike.

'You know that young man who overdosed a couple of nights ago?'

'You mean Darren Wilson?'

'Yes, that's right. I've had the results back from toxicology and there wasn't that much monoacetylmorphine in his system. And no fentanyl.'

'What does that mean? I thought it was heroin not morphine.'

'It was. Heroin is turned into monoacetylmorphine, and another chemical, in the body. That's what we measure. I'm surprised that someone who used heroin regularly died from such a low dose. I may be sticking my neck out but I think there's something else involved.'

'Any idea what?'

'No. He definitely died from respiratory failure. He wasn't physically assaulted and the only marks on him were where they tried CPR. He had a couple of broken ribs. So I'm thinking there was something in the heroin. Unfortunately, the lab's GC-MS machine broke down part way through the analysis of Darren's samples and they only reported on the heroin break-down product and fentanyl. They're getting it fixed but don't know when it'll be working again. Was there any of the drug on his premises?'

'I think there was a little bit left in a baggie. It'll be in the evidence store if it hasn't gone to the lab already.'

'OK. Can you make sure it's analysed and let me know the results?'

'Will do, doctor. Thank you.'

---

Mike Howell put the young man's death out of his mind and turned his thoughts to Tony Fuller. They'd found his finger marks on the discarded handbag, but he swore he'd found it in the street. A search of his flat had turned up no stolen goods, to everyone's surprise, and no-one had reported the theft of the bag. And then there were those odd glass vials. He'd ask the drug squad about them later. In the meantime, he would have to tell Fuller that they wouldn't be charging him. A pity, he thought. He's overdue a prison sentence.

---

The drug squad office was crowded, the smell of sweat mingling with a pungent odour from a hoard of seized cannabis plants awaiting documentation and transfer to the evidence store.

'Nice work, guys,' said DS Derek Palmer. 'This is clearly intent to supply and even the dimmest magistrate will send it to Crown Court for trial. What have you got there, Chalky?'

PC White showed Palmer a couple of glass vials in a plastic evidence bag.

'Mike Howell wanted to know what they are. Onabeaut, it says on the labels. He thought it might be some new street drug. A patrol chased a local scrote and he dumped the handbag they were in. We've no idea who it belongs to.'

'I've not heard of it. Looks like a trade name and it's clearly an official product. I'll Google it.'

Palmer's hands flew over his keyboard and, a few seconds later, he raised his head.

'It's nothing dodgy. It's a beauty treatment. Like Botox. But why would anyone have it in their handbag?' he mused aloud. 'You can't get off on it, and it's not a DIY treatment. My sister had Botox and it was done by a properly trained beautician. Still, it's nothing to do with us, so let Mike know and we can get back to this amateur botanist who's looking at several years.'

'These vials, sarge. They're some kind of beauty treatment. Nothing to do with us. Odd that anyone should have it outside a clinic or salon, though.'

PC White handed the evidence bag to Mike who sniffed and dumped it on his desk.

'OK, thanks. Just curious.'

Mike was about to drop the vials into a waste bin when something niggled him. Beauty treatment. He'd come across someone involved in that recently. But who was it? He decided to keep the evidence bag for a while, until it came back to him.

An hour later, when reports of another heroin death reached the station, he remembered. That girl who'd lost her fiancé to an overdose. She was studying beauty therapy at college and was on placement in a salon. Looking back over the records he realised that the handbag had been retrieved by a police patrol the same night as the lad had died. *Could the bag be hers? If so, why would she be out with it, having just been bereaved? Curious. Perhaps worth getting CID to take a look.*

---

DC Mel Cotton sipped her coffee and scanned the morning's emails, searching for something interesting. A few burglaries to look at, difficult to investigate thoroughly with their stretched resources, and a series of muggings being handled by the street crime team. Pretty much routine. Then something caught her eye. An email asking whether there could be link between a heroin death and some unusual vials found in a dumped handbag. This piqued her interest and she resolved to talk to Mike Howell when he next came on shift.

---

'It may be nothing,' Mike explained. 'But it seems an odd coincidence that a beauty therapist should lose her partner and her handbag, in separate incidents, on the same night. Assuming that the handbag is hers, of course. And there's those odd vials.'

'It is odd,' Mel agreed. 'Anything else?'

'Well the pathologist, Dr Durbridge, had some reservations about the overdose. He didn't think there was enough there to kill a regular user. Might be worth having a chat with him.'

'I'll do that. Thanks Mike. I'm intrigued.'

An hour later Mel Cotton knocked on DI Emma Thorpe's door and entered when summoned.

'Boss. Darren Wilson. I think his death's suspicious.'

Her excitement was bubbling out of her.

'Hold on Mel. Just who are you talking about?'

'An overdose a few nights ago. Dr Morgan said he didn't have much heroin in his system but he still died of respiratory failure.'

'So? These junkies are pretty unhealthy, aren't they?'

'Apart from a small amount of heroin, and being dead, of course, he seemed quite fit, according to the doctor. I think we need a full home office post mortem. And Dr Durbridge is inclined to agree.'

'Have you any idea how much one of those would cost? And haven't you got enough to do with this spate of burglaries? Surely, they're more important than a drug user who clearly overdosed.'

'But suppose someone killed him? They'd get away with it if we didn't investigate. And might do it again.'

'Look, Mel,' the DI's tone softened, 'If you can find any

other reason to look further I'll consider it. But don't take too long over it. You know how stretched we are. Has he been buried or cremated yet?'

'No. The funeral's the day after tomorrow.'

'Well you can take a few hours today to look around. But if it's going nowhere, get back to the burglaries.'

'Yes guv. Thank you.'

Mel left Emma's office with a tingle of excitement. Catching burglars is important, it's true, but solving a murder? That's much more satisfying!

———

'Dr Durbridge,' began Mel, 'you told Sergeant Howell that you thought there was something else in Darren Wilson's heroin that was responsible for his death. Have you any idea what?'

'I'm afraid not. We know it wasn't fentanyl – that's quite common – but the lab couldn't complete a full analysis. I gather a sample of the drug is being sent to a different lab, and I'll be interested in what they find.'

'Do you know anything about Onabeaut?'

The pathologist paused before replying.

'It's a form of botulinum, used in cosmetic treatments. Why do you ask?'

'Some empty vials have turned up in unusual circumstances, and I wondered if they were relevant.'

'Well botulinum can be very dangerous, in contaminated food, for instance. In large doses it can cause respiratory paralysis – oh, I see where you're going. You think someone gave him this as well as the heroin?'

'Just a thought, doctor. Can you tell if Darren had any in his body?'

'I think it would be a difficult, lengthy and expensive process to get samples analysed, as very tiny amounts of the chemical are involved. A full Home Office PM might reveal something, but I doubt it. The basic clinical PM I carried out certainly didn't.'

'OK. Thank you, doctor.'

Somewhat crestfallen, Mel decided to talk to Carrie Walker, and also check whether the salon was missing any Onabeaut vials.

---

'How are you coping, Carrie?' asked Mel, hoping her solicitous manner would put the woman at ease. DC Sally Erskine smiled encouragingly.

'Not too bad,' Carrie replied. 'It's taking ages to get used to Darren not being here. We were going to be so happy together.'

She stifled a sob.

'Well, I'm really sorry to bother you, but a couple of things have come up. For procedural reasons, I must caution you, but please don't worry, you're not under arrest.'

Carrie nodded, miserably.

'Firstly,' Mel said, producing a transparent evidence bag, 'is this your handbag?'

Carrie started.

'No, no, it's not mine.'

'So we wouldn't find any hairs, fingerprints or DNA that matched yours, if we looked?'

'No. Er...well, I suppose it looks a bit like one of mine I had a few years ago. I gave several old bags to a charity shop last month. Perhaps it's one of those.'

'Perhaps it is, Carrie. OK. Now, what can you tell me about Onabeaut?'

Carrie began to look pale and fiddled with a tissue.

'It's the anti-wrinkle treatment we use at the salon. I'm not trained to use it, but some of the others are.'

'Do you have any idea why two empty vials of Onabeaut would be in a handbag you say you got rid of a month ago?'

'Nnno. No idea. Sorry.'

'OK. Are you aware of any vials going missing at the salon recently.'

'No, I'm sure there've been none,' Carrie replied, confidently. 'It's very expensive and Jane, the manager, keeps a very close eye on the stock. Why would anyone steal it, anyway?'

'Well, I can't tell you officially, but we're exploring the possibility that Onabeaut was used to hasten Darren's death.'

'God, no. That's terrible.' Carrie was barely able to croak out a response, her throat having suddenly dried up. 'I thought it was a heroin overdose.'

'It's not that simple, Carrie. There was another substance involved. Is there anything else you can tell us? Anything at all?'

'I'm sorry. There isn't. It's all such a shock, coming on top of Darren's death. I hope you catch the bastard who did it.'

'All right. We'll leave it for now. I'll write up the notes of this interview. Perhaps you would call into the police station tomorrow to check and sign them?'

'Yes, of course. I'm still not back at work.'

———

*Oh shit! They're on to me,* swore Carrie to herself, reaching for the gin as soon as the detectives left. *Should I make a run for it? But I've got nowhere to go. I wish I'd never heard of Onabeaut.*

*And I wish I'd never heard of Darren bloody Wilson. I'll have to bluff it out. It's all I can do, and I'm not gonna bleeding confess. No-one saw me inject Darren, after all, and I cleaned his syringe after I used it. I didn't leave prints on it and my DNA's all over the flat anyway. They've got nothing, as long as I hold my nerve. A couple of tranquillisers before I go in, and I'll be all right. Won't I?*

'She's guilty, guv, I'm sure of it.' Mel burst into DI Thorpe's office after a cursory knock. 'It's written all over her. She must have injected Darren while he was asleep and then gone out to set up her alibi. Later, she tried to dump the vials, but Tony Fuller nicked her bag before she could get rid of them. And she knew someone had given him the stuff deliberately.'

'OK, Mel. Calm down. Do we have any proof this anti-wrinkle stuff actually killed Darren?'

'No, but that's why we need a full forensic PM and an analysis of Darren's blood for Onabeaut. She's coming in to sign a statement tomorrow and I'd like to arrest her.'

'Mel, all this is incredibly expensive,' said Emma, not unsympathetically.

She thought for a few moments.

'OK. Re-interview her when she comes in and I'll watch on the monitor. Don't arrest her yet. If I think there are grounds, I'll ask the DCI to sanction the expenditure. That's the best I can do.'

'Thanks, guv,' said Mel, grudgingly. 'We'll try to crack her tomorrow.'

'Why am I here?' asked a fearful Carrie. 'I thought I only had to sign a statement.'

'One or two things have come to light, which I hope you can help us with,' said Mel, after cautioning Carrie and asking whether she would like a solicitor present, which Carrie declined.'

'What things?'

'Well, firstly, we've traced the batch numbers of the Onabeaut vials found in your handbag. They were supplied to the salon where you work. Would you like to comment on that?'

Carrie shrugged.

'I'm sorry. I've no idea how they got there.'

'OK. We'll leave that for the moment. Do you know that the chemical in Onabeaut can stop people breathing if they take too much of it?'

All the colour drained from Carrie's face.

'No, I didn't. I mean, you have to be specially trained to use it safely, but I... I didn't know it was that dangerous.'

'Then how would you react to the suggestion that you injected Darren with the contents of those vials knowing that, in combination with the heroin he'd taken, the Onabeaut would stop his breathing?'

Carrie put her head in her hands and started to sob.

'I... I... had to get away from Darren. He abused me, cheated and stole. I was trapped. I...' She could hardly get any words out.

'I strongly advise you to get a solicitor, because, Carrie Walker, I'm arresting you on suspicion of...'

Before she could finish, there was an urgent knock on the door and Emma entered.

'A moment, please, Mel,' she said, grimly.

'Yes, guv', replied Mel, suspending the interview and leaving the room, looking annoyed.

'What is it? I was just about to arrest her.'

'She didn't kill him.'

'You're joking. She was about to confess, I'm sure.'

'I've just had a call from Dr Durbridge. There wouldn't have been enough Onabeaut in two vials to kill him, even with the heroin. It would have taken nearly twenty.'

'So why did he die?'

'Xylazine.'

'What?'

'It a veterinary tranquilliser. It's been used to adulterate heroin in the States for some time and now it's turning up here. The lab found it in the powder in Darren's baggie. We'll probably need that extra PM, but at least it saves us paying for an expensive botulinum test.'

'Shit. OK. Can we get her for attempted murder?'

'I don't know. That's something to ask the CPS. Personally, I doubt it. You'd better let her go.'

When Carrie had been signed out at reception, Mel looked her straight in the eyes.

'I know what you did. You were very lucky something else killed him, and not your efforts. We're still considering a charge of attempted murder. I strongly advise you to stay away from losers like Darren in future. And avoid toxic substances. Always remember this: I will be keeping an eye on you.'

She turned away before Carrie could respond and went in search of coffee.

*One particular type of botulinum toxin is probably the most toxic substance known (and it's perfectly natural). The form used in cosmetic treatments is very much less toxic but problems can still occur if it is used incorrectly. This is why it is not a DIY cure for wrinkles.*

# Killer on the Hop

'A MAN'S BEEN POISONED, professor, and we don't know how. The pathologist, Dr Durbridge, said you might be able to help.'

'I will do my best, Detective Inspector. Tell me about the victim and what happened.' Professor Patterson, Reader in Toxicology at Highchester University, leaned back in his wheelchair and regarded the police officer over the top of his glasses with interest.

'He was Nigel Reese-Johnson, the new owner of the Settleworth Estate,' the DI replied. 'Old money, fallen on hard times. Bad investments on the stock market, and the horses, left him broke and he couldn't manage the upkeep of the house. The National Trust wasn't interested in taking it on – it wasn't that special. He was in the process of laying off staff and selling their cottages to a holiday firm. The family used to be well-liked in the area but, when he inherited the place, a few months ago, he started making enemies and treating his staff badly. The village was up in arms when he announced the holiday cottage plan, aghast at the thought of all the traffic holidaymakers would bring. There was a vigorous local campaign against his proposals. It's fair to say he was seriously disliked, if not hated.'

'Badly enough for someone to want to kill him?' asked the toxicologist.

'Probably not in the village, but who can tell what people will do when they lose their homes and their livelihoods? We've talked to the groundsmen, the gamekeeper, the stable hand and a couple of maintenance workers. They all deny harming him, and have alibis for the night he died.'

'Tell me what happened.'

'Reese-Johnson dined with his wife, quite late, after returning from his solicitor's in London. Sometime during the night, he became delirious and red faced. His wife said he was very hot, appeared to find it difficult to see, and drank copious amounts of water. He refused to call a doctor. She put him to bed but his condition didn't improve, so she called for an ambulance, despite his protestations. It took hours to arrive, and he died of atropine poisoning before they could get him to hospital.'

'Classic symptoms.' said the professor. 'Do go on.'

'That's what the pathologist said, but there was no atropine in the house. The lab found traces in samples from his body, but couldn't explain how they got there.'

'What did the couple have to eat?'

'He had grilled rabbit, roast potatoes and vegetables, followed by trifle. His wife, a vegetarian, had a cheese and nut dish, with the same trimmings, and also trifle. Both had coffee after the meal. He drank brandy, but nothing toxic was found in the decanter. Unfortunately, the residues from preparing the meal, and the waste food, were all disposed of before we searched the place, a day later. Food waste had been collected for recycling early that morning.'

'So, the only thing he ate but his wife didn't was the rabbit. Where did it come from?'

'The estate. There are dozens of them there. The cook swears that no-one tampered with the food while it was being prepared and served, and was most indignant at the suggestion. We talked to his wife at length and we're convinced she had nothing to do with his death. Apparently, they were happy married, and his employees confirmed this. The delay in getting him treatment wasn't her fault. So, what are your thoughts?'

The professor swung his wheelchair round and pulled a book from a low shelf. He opened it at a page of photographs and handed it to the police officer.

'The picture, top left. Ask your officers if any plants like that, with berries like those, are growing in or around a garden on the estate. If they find any, bring the tenant in for questioning. If they don't, get them to search the whole estate. That would make things more difficult to prove. Start the search with the gamekeeper's cottage.'

The DI took the book, looking puzzled.

'I see what you're getting at, but there were no odd plants or berries in the kitchen, and the only green vegetables they ate were peas and runner beans. His wife said there was nothing odd-looking about his rabbit and he ate it with his usual enjoyment. A particular favourite of his, apparently.'

Professor Patterson declined to elaborate on his words, merely smiling and promising an explanation once someone was in custody. 'Humour me,' he said. 'And give me a ring tomorrow.'

The following afternoon, DI Reynolds telephoned the professor.

'You were right. The gamekeeper confessed. We found Deadly Nightshade growing beside the hedge surrounding his garden. How on earth did you know?'

'I assumed he provided the rabbit for the meal. That was where the atropine came from. Rabbits are not affected by the poison and dangerous amounts can accumulate in their flesh. Presumably, he suspected what was coming when the estate passed to Reese-Johnson and, started to feed some captured rabbits on Deadly Nightshade, so he could pay his employer back for sacking him.'

'Exactly. And he showed no remorse.'

'A gamekeeper is used to killing things for a living. Perhaps it's not such a big leap to killing the man who's throwing you out of your home.'

'Well, he won't have to worry about accommodation now,' chuckled Reynolds. 'He'll be in one of His Majesty's guest houses for a long time to come.'

---

*The ability of rabbits to tolerate atropine is a good example of different species reacting in different ways to poisons. A tragic example was thalidomide – it didn't produce the dreadful effects observed after it was given to pregnant women, when it was tested on animals.*

## Taking the Biscuit

THE MISSES LAVINIA MORTIMER and Millicent Frobisher had been mortal enemies for years, ever since Millicent had seduced the young man to whom Lavinia was betrothed. Lavinia denounced Millicent, in front of the whole church congregation, as a woman with the morals of an alley cat who would undoubtedly burn in hell. Millicent fled the church and never returned. From that moment on, the two former best friends never spoke, and avoided meeting in public. When they did encounter one another, the fiery glares which passed between them could have ignited gunpowder.

It came as a great surprise to Millicent when she received a courteous note from Lavinia, suggesting that they should put the past behind them and inviting her to tea the following Thursday. Her initial reaction was to throw the invitation on the fire, but she stayed her hand and thought for a while. *What could she be up to?* she pondered. *Does she really want to forgive me? And do I really wish to forgive her? I'm not at all sure that I do. But what have I got to lose by accepting her invitation, however obscure her motive?*

After a restless night, Millicent was sure of two things: she still hated Lavinia but she would go to tea with her to establish precisely what her enemy had in mind. It was only five years since the events which led to their estrangement, and Lavinia's suggestion that they should finally put matters to rest seemed more than a little optimistic. But she would prepare herself thoroughly for the meeting, and conceal her real feelings until it was appropriate to reveal them. And she made a plan.

Lavinia was delighted to receive Millicent's acceptance, but the smile which crossed her face was twisted rather than a fulsome expression of joy. Before Millicent was due to arrive, she busied herself cleaning the parlour, baking some sweet biscuits and retrieving her Clarice Cliff tea set, with matching teapot, milk jug and sugar bowl, from storage. She hoped that the meeting would settle matters once and for all, and she would do everything necessary to ensure it.

Millicent, too, was industrious. She undertook a number of errands in the High Street, buying herself a new hat, visiting the chemist and purchasing supplies at the grocer's. She would bake some small cakes for the tea, determined to match Lavinia's hospitality with a contribution of her own. She was damned if she would let the woman feel superior.

So it was that, on the Thursday at three pm, Millicent pressed Lavinia's gleaming brass doorbell with a mixture of curiosity and trepidation. Her erstwhile friend opened the door and ushered her into the parlour, her manner cool but not frosty. She thanked Millicent for coming and for the cakes, placing them, along with her sweet biscuits, on a china stand that graced the lace-covered small table in the parlour. She poured the tea, enquired after Millicent's health, and encouraged her to eat, saying that she would like to discuss certain matters shortly.

Conversation ranged over a number of non-personal topics,

such as the heroic flight of Colonel Lindbergh across the Atlantic, and how sad it was about his murdered son, the politics of Mr Oswald Mosely and the likely winner of the cake competition at the forthcoming local fête. Only after cakes and biscuits had been consumed did Lavinia brush the crumbs from her dress and adopt a more serious tone.

'Firstly,' she began, 'I was wrong to have left things as they were in the church.'

Millicent sat up, surprised. Was this really an attempt at reconciliation?

'I should,' snarled Lavinia, her calm tones turning to rage, 'have torn your dress off and kicked you down the street. It was only what you deserved for ruining my life, you evil bitch, and I have always regretted not taking things further. Well, I have now, and you'll find out what I've done when you get home. Matters have been settled at last. Now get out. You won't be seeing me again. I guarantee it.'

Millicent paled and stood up, a look of loathing, tinged with triumph, spreading over her face.

'You must think I'm a complete idiot to trust you. I never believed you wanted to put the past behind you and rekindle our friendship. I know you all too well. Those cakes contained potassium cyanide and you've taken a fatal dose. By the time you get to a hospital it will be too late to treat you and, just to make sure, I'm locking you in this room. I took the key when you showed me in. I don't care if you've paid someone to burgle my house or even set fire to it. I'm rid of you for ever, Lavinia Mortimer, and to hell with you.'

Millicent pushed Lavinia back into her chair, stepped out of the parlour and locked the door. As she picked up her gloves, from the small table in the hall, she realised that she was feeling unwell. Her stomach hurt and she felt sick. Her muscles started twitching slightly. All this she put down to the recent drama, but then she noticed a receipt, dislodged by her movements, falling off the table. With the familiar heading 'James Woolley and Sons., Chemists,' it bore the previous day's date and the words 'Strychnine for moles. 3s 4d'.

Terror gripped her.

She realised.

Lavinia didn't eat the biscuits.

---

*Contrary to what is shown in some TV programmes and novels, cyanide and strychnine don't kill instantly if taken orally (inhaling hydrogen cyanide gas is a different matter). It takes around fifteen minutes for most poisons to reach the intestines and be absorbed. At the time this story was set, it was still possible to buy cyanide and strychnine for pest control as long as you were a reputable person.*

# Payback

## Sally

SALLY NEVER FAILED at anything she set her mind to. But she did this time and it was Pete's fault. If he hadn't come home early from the pub and found her, she would have succeeded at suicide as well. Life wasn't perfect but she had a home, a partner, and was looking forward to starting a family. Until recently, she enjoyed her career, doing a job she was proud of. But a new manager, with the humanity of a chainsaw, had undermined her so much that she felt a failure at everything.

Lying in a hospital bed, a drip in her arm and her stomach sore from the gastric lavage, which washed out the paracetamol before it could wreck her liver, she thought back over the previous six months. The sleepless nights, the exhaustion, the drinking, the rows with her partner – all these she blamed on one person. Kelly Thornbury. The woman who had wrecked her life by making her workplace intolerable.

Nothing she could do was good enough for Kelly. Her workload had increased enormously and her supervision meetings with Kelly consisted of a barrage of criticisms and unreasonable demands. She had to work at home during weekends, just to keep up. Sally was a professional person, capable of making her own judgements and managing her commitments. But, since Kelly had arrived, she had been belittled, undermined and insulted. Kelly's bullying wasn't confined to Sally. Her colleagues had suffered in the same way and several had left their jobs as a result. It was the organisation's culture, of which Kelly was a part, which drove them away.

Sally deeply regretted giving in to her despair and the pain it had caused Pete and her parents. She realised that the prompt actions of the paramedics and doctors had given her a second chance, one she would not waste. The only thing to do was to fight back. And she bloody well would.

The days off while she recovered gave her time to plan. For the first time in months, she was away from work and had time to think. She was determined to pay Kelly back for the misery which she had caused her and her colleagues. Sally wasn't a violent person but she was clever. Maybe there were better ways of getting revenge than through physical confrontation?

Sally spent hours devising ways of humiliating, or otherwise harming, Kelly, from letting down her tyres to poisoning her coffee. The more fanciful and illegal ideas she quickly discounted, as well as those which could throw suspicion on herself. Eventually, she settled on a couple of projects which carried a slight risk but which would be highly satisfying to carry out. She waited until she was about to return to work before starting her campaign. She wanted to see the results of her efforts.

Sally knew where Kelly lived and what her regular movements between the office and home were. She also knew the registration number of Kelly's black Ford Focus. It was easy to hire an identical model for the day, from a firm a couple of dozen miles away. Using painted cardboard and black insulating tape, cut to the appropriate sizes, she made copies of Kelly's number plates. Pulling into a side road not far from the office, and checking that no-one was watching, she fixed the copied plates to the hired car, her hands shaking. They wouldn't fool a police officer but, from a distance, they could pass for genuine. Shortly before Kelly was due to leave the office for home, Sally pulled out of the side road and headed along the route Kelly would take.

As she approached the only functioning speed camera in town her heart went into overdrive and her hands on the wheel became slippery with sweat. Looking around for parked police cars – or possible unmarked ones – she was relieved to see that there were no suspicious vehicles in sight. Just before she reached the camera, she put her foot down, reaching 42 mph as she passed the yellow box, which flashed obligingly.

Sweat pouring from her, and her heart thumping almost loud enough to hear above the engine, she pulled into the next available side road. She removed the false plates and sat in the car, trembling, for ten minutes. Gradually, her terror gave way to a feeling of exultation. Kelly would get a speeding ticket and points on her licence, while she had got away with it. For the first time ever, she felt she had exerted some power over her nemesis and it felt good. So good that she couldn't wait to launch the next phase.

Returning to work, with Kelly's speeding ticket no doubt in the post, Sally underwent an intrusive back-to-work interview. She had to convince Lorna Brake, Kelly's boss and the chief executive of the organisation, that she was fit to return. She didn't dare say why she had overdosed but made up a story about having a blinding headache and accidentally taking too many tablets, because of the confusion it had caused. She knew that, if she blamed Kelly's management style for her suicide attempt, she would be accused of gross misconduct and sacked. Lorna's manner was as sympathetic as a rat trap and all she said was 'Don't make that mistake again.' She countersigned the form on which Sally stated that she felt fit to return and dismissed her without so much as a 'Welcome back.'

Sally's organisation was set up to help vulnerable people in the community, be they homeless, substance abusers, gamblers, victims of domestic violence or in chronic debt. Originally part of the local authority, the organisation had been privatised as a community interest company. Sally, and most of her colleagues, cared deeply about their clients, often putting in hours of unpaid overtime to support them. The managers had different attitudes, however, being driven by targets and statistics rather than the human needs of the people they were supposed to support. They had no training in the fields relevant to the clients yet criticised the way in which those actually doing the work performed. Since privatisation, Lorna had replaced a service ethos with a bullying culture. The four managers followed her lead in squeezing every last drop of productivity out of the staff and anyone complaining was threatened with disciplinary action. Salaries had been cut and working hours extended. Most of the staff were desperate to leave but opportunities for people with their skills, in that part of the East Midlands, were rare.

Many of the organisation's clients had problems with alcohol and were put on various treatment regimes. During a training day, Sally had found out about Antabuse, a drug given to alcoholics which produces an adverse reaction should they drink anything with alcohol in it. She remembered this when she was lying, nauseous, in the hospital bed. Sally discovered that Antabuse can be purchased from overseas sites, via the internet, and she determined to acquire some.

---

Two days after returning to work, Sally had her first supervision meeting. Kelly had always treated Sally with an air of superiority but this time she was downright aggressive, making it clear that Sally would be given no special treatment following her illness. She would be expected to clear her backlog of work without delay. Sally didn't dare to point out the unreasonableness of Kelly's attitude but secretly rejoiced. The ticket's arrived! she thought.

---

Three weeks later, Christmas gatherings were taking place and the Antabuse Sally ordered had arrived. Staff were allowed an extra half hour for lunch to celebrate and most of them went to a local restaurant for a hurried Christmas meal – with no alcohol permitted if they were returning to work. The managers had an evening meal planned and this gave Sally her opportunity. Kelly was an avid coffee drinker, taking it black, sweet and strong. While she was in the toilet, and everyone else was absorbed in completing paperwork before the Christmas break, Sally struck. On the pretext of dropping some expenses sheets on her desk, she stirred two ground-up Antabuse tablets into Kelly's coffee. She wouldn't be around when they took effect, but she could imagine the results at the managers' dinner that evening.

## Kelly

The Swanley Hotel was famous for its food, but was not so expensive that the cost of the managers' meals couldn't be massaged through the company's expenses system. The group took their places at the table, anticipating a fine meal and plenty to drink, all on the company's account. Presiding over her minions, Lorna was every inch the Queen Bee, with her Gucci handbag prominently displayed on the table and an expensive dress straining to contain her chest. Once the waiter had poured champagne, she raised her glass 'To another profitable year,' she toasted. Her colleagues joined in the salute, drained their glasses and settled down to consider the menu.

A few minutes later, Kelly began to feel ill. She broke out in a sweat, started to tremble and lurched to her feet in a frantic attempt to reach the toilets. Unfortunately for her, and for her colleagues, she didn't make it. The full effects of the wine, combined with the Antabuse, kicked in and a torrent of vomit poured from Kelly's mouth, filling Lorna's cleavage and soaking her precious bag. Kelly dashed for the Ladies, trailing vomit behind her, while waiters flapped ineffectually at the pool of sick on the table. Lorna was incandescent and stormed off to confront Kelly, who was hunched over a toilet bowl as her body tried to clear the last of the alcohol from her system.

'You stupid cow,' snarled Lorna, no trace of sympathy in her manner. 'You'll pay for cleaning this dress and replacing my handbag. I'll discuss your behaviour in the office on Monday.'

Reeking with the smell of sick, Lorna stalked out of the restaurant, grabbing a full bottle of wine on the way. Her three remaining colleagues, whose appetites had vanished, also left, promising that the company would cover the restaurant's cleaning costs. Kelly eventually emerged from the toilets, weak and wobbly, and slunk to her car without looking at the staff or the horrified customers. She didn't notice Sally in the corner of the hotel car park, making a call on her mobile.

As Kelly's car pulled out of the car park, somewhat erratically, the blue and red lights of a police car ordering her to stop appeared in her mirror. She knew she wouldn't fail a breath test but the indignity of being stopped and tested, while reeking of vomit, made a ghastly evening even worse. She had never felt so miserable in her life.

## Sally

The next line of attack landed in Sally's lap without her looking for it. She didn't have much of a spam filter on her emails, although she never opened anything suspicious, so it was inevitable that a kindly Nigerian prince would offer to share his wealth with her, in exchange for her bank account details. This gave her an idea. Signing in to her emails at an internet cafe, just in case her own laptop picked up a virus, she opened the email and copied down the address where the details should be sent, filing them carefully away before deleting the message.

Sally's opportunity presented itself after the Christmas break. She needed to talk to Kelly about rearranging a meeting, but Kelly wasn't at her desk. Reaching for a pen and Post-it note, she spotted Kelly's open chequebook. Swiftly, and with her back to the rest of the office, she slipped out her phone and took a snapshot of the open book. At home she printed off the image of the chequebook and immediately deleted it from the phone's memory. Two things interested her, apart from the account number and sort code: Kelly had been in the process of writing a cheque to Lorna for twelve hundred pounds and there was a four-digit number, written faintly inside the chequebook cover, which, Sally surmised, could be Kelly's PIN. Details of the Christmas dinner debacle had filtered down to the rest of the staff and Sally guessed that the cheque was to cover cleaning Lorna's dress and replacing her bag. The size of the sum gave her a warm glow.

Sally held off launching her attack, in case Kelly remembered leaving her chequebook on the desk and suspected someone in the office of copying her account details. So, two months later, she visited an internet cafe in a neighbouring town and logged on to a specially created email account using Kelly's name. She made contact with the 'Nigerian prince', provided Kelly's details and wished him well.

---

While waiting for her opportunity to introduce Kelly to her African friend, Sally had not been idle. Using an image copied from the internet, and text of her own devising, she prepared some rather special business cards which she printed off at home. Taking advantage of the dark evenings, and wearing glasses and a scarf over her distinctive red hair, she stuck the cards up in telephone booths, on community noticeboards, lamp-posts, supermarket customer ads boards and anywhere else she could find.

## Kelly

The results of Sally's business cards were prolonged rather than instant. Numerous naughty punters who dialled Kelly's work mobile number were disappointed to find that 'Kelly the Spank Engine' would not be prepared to 'take them in hand.' Kelly was pestered day and night by would-be 'clients' and was frequently interrupted in meetings. It didn't help when an anonymous tip off to the local paper claimed that a manager in a local community support company was supplementing her salary by providing salacious services. Called up before Lorna, Kelly swore that she was the victim of a practical joke, or a misprinted phone number, and asked for her number to be changed. Lorna agreed, grumbling that it was a nuisance and would cost the company money.

---

Two days after Sally passed on Kelly's bank details, the bombshell landed. Although company policy forbade the use of personal phones during work time, Kelly used her smartphone to check that her salary had cleared into her bank account. When the balance came up on the display she shrieked, dropped the phone and nearly fainted.

'What's the matter with you – and why are you using a personal phone?' snapped Lorna, who had just entered the room.

'I... I... I've been scammed.' Kelly could barely get the words out. 'My account's empty – someone's cleaned it out.'

There were a few murmurs of sympathy around the office and no small amount of disguised satisfaction. Sally proffered a glass of water to Kelly, the concerned expression on her face contrasting with the bubbling glee she felt inside.

'You'd better get on to your bank to find out how it happened. Perhaps they can get the money back,' she said, knowing full well that the funds were gone forever.

Kelly carried on sobbing at her desk until Lorna could stand the noise no longer.

'Take a day's leave and go home,' she instructed Kelly. 'Sort this out and be back in the office tomorrow morning. You need to be at the staff meeting.'

Kelly stumbled out of the office, a look of utter despair on her face. And Sally didn't feel the slightest bit guilty.

---

Kelly slunk into the office with a hangover, as Lorna began the staff meeting with a warning.

'What I am about to say, and the actions which will follow, must remain confidential. Do you all understand?'

She glared around the room, eliciting nods from all present.

'Because of a communication problem at the middle management level' – her eyes briefly flicked towards Kelly – 'we've missed the deadline for completing service user plans for several hundred individuals. We're being audited at the end of the month and our future funding, which means your jobs, depends on these plans having been completed by the deadline. So, from now on, there will be no leave granted, there will be a rota for Saturday working and you will backdate the plans, when you complete them, to a date before the deadline.'

Several people groaned when Lorna mentioned Saturday working and she continued.

'If you look at your contracts in detail you will see that I can require you to work outside normal office hours, if I deem it necessary. And I do.'

'I'm a Christian,' said Katy Maguire, 'and I don't believe in lying.'

'You'll backdate those plans or find another job' retorted Lorna, leaving the room before anyone else could raise objections.

Lorna's accusatory glance was not lost on Kelly. She never told us about the deadline and now she's trying to blame me, in spite of everything I've gone through, she thought.

Kelly had been harbouring a burning resentment of Lorna for some time. She was used to bullying those below her in the hierarchy and didn't appreciate the same treatment from above. She had never dared to challenge Lorna before. But perhaps now was the time to take action? With Lorna gone there could even be a chance for promotion. Despite the recent glitches, her record was better than those of her three colleagues at the same level, so she would be in with a good chance. Yes, getting rid of Lorna would be an excellent idea. She knew that an official complaint to the board of directors would be pointless, and would just get her sacked, but she was determined to find a way to bring her down. And that meant gathering information.

Over three successive Saturdays, staff worked their way through the backlog of service user plans and it wasn't difficult for Kelly to compile a list of those fraudulently backdated. She wasn't IT-savvy enough to hack into parts of the system dealing with Lorna's salary but she did discover, from leafing through a heap of paper expenses claims on the admin clerk's desk, that Lorna was claiming travelling expenses between her home and the office. That may be OK with the company, she thought, but I'm damn sure she's not declaring these to the tax people. Smartphone shots of a selection of these claims joined the list of plans on her flash drive.

Kelly racked her brains to think of other ways in which she

could get a hold over Lorna. She continued to poke around piles of papers, look at unlocked computer screens when no-one was around and listen to unguarded phone calls. Her spying paid off when Lorna's son, Justin, turned up at the office one day, driving a sporty VW Golf. The list price of the car was over £27,000 and she wondered how a student could afford a vehicle that expensive. The answer came to her when she spotted tax and insurance renewal notices in the admin clerk's in-tray. The car was registered to the company and Justin was listed on the insurance as an employee, despite the fact that he had only worked for the company, at an inflated salary, for just four weeks one summer. More evidence went on her flash drive, together with notes explaining its significance.

The next piece of ammunition in Kelly's armoury came about purely by chance. Furious with a staff member who hadn't met his targets, she knocked on Lorna's door and was about to open it when she heard a breathless 'Wait!' from inside. Kelly obeyed and a minute later Dave, the company maintenance hand, left Lorna's office in a hurry, pushing past Kelly without a word. Lorna called Kelly in, her face flushed.

'What do you want?' she snapped, 'What's the idea of inter-rupting our meeting ... about the damp in the male toilet.'

'Sorry, Lorna. It's just that Martin has missed his targets three months running and I want to start disciplinary action against him. He claims it's because their new baby is keeping him awake all night but that's no excuse for skiving.'

'OK. Do what you want. Give him a warning or something. Now get out and send Dave back in.'

Kelly's suspicions as to what she had interrupted were rein-forced as she dropped her eyes from Lorna's and spotted a pair of silk knickers on the floor, in front of Lorna's – unusually clear – desk. She managed to record a subsequent 'maintenance meeting' on her phone by leaving it on the floor outside Lorna's office. Words were barely spoken but panting and heavy breathing predominated. Another item for her flash drive.

It was well known in the office that Lorna enjoyed a comfortable lifestyle. She took holidays in exotic locations, drove a flashy car and, as Kelly knew to her cost, bought expensive clothes and accessories. Her salary was not public knowledge and Kelly had often wondered how she could afford such luxuries. The company accounts, however, were published and, on examining them, Kelly noted a series of payments to design firms, business consultancies and equipment suppliers – a total of £230,000 over three years. It was a matter of minutes to look these outfits up on the Companies House website. Not entirely to Kelly's surprise, the directors of five of the six firms were Lorna and her partner. Kelly downloaded the details onto her flash drive and closed her laptop with quiet satisfaction.

---

The cumulative impact of Sally's efforts had taken its toll. Kelly was jumpy, more aggressive than usual, and prone to making irrational decisions without thinking through the consequences. She was beginning to feel that someone was targeting her. But who? She knew that everyone she supervised, apart from mousy Sally, hated her, but she had them under control. They were too spineless to plot against her. Perhaps she'd ask Sally to keep her ears open, just in case. But could it be Lorna? Kelly knew she was still furious about the incident at the Christmas dinner. Perhaps she hated her personally as well as picking on her professionally.

Kelly was barely sleeping. Her clothes didn't fit properly, because of her overconsumption of wine and chocolate, and were frequently creased and stained. Her mouth often ran away with her and she was heard to refer to the staff she supervised as 'a load of workshy snowflakes'. Unfortunately for her, this outburst happened at a multi-agency meeting, so the damage couldn't be contained within the company. Belatedly realising what she had done, Kelly rushed out of the room. She went home and stayed there for three days without formally requesting leave, unable to face the atmosphere at work. Misconduct, in the eyes of Lorna, for which she would have to pay.

---

When Kelly returned to work, she had come prepared. Lorna summoned Kelly into her office as soon as she entered the building, her face ablaze, and Kelly was delighted to see how upset Lorna was. She smiled to herself.

'Have you any idea what you've done, you crazy bitch?' Lorna shouted. 'You've brought the company into disrepute with your stupid remark and the staff are threatening to make a formal complaint. I've told them that managers are not to be criticised, but they've got the union involved and they won't be so easy to scare off. There's now a question mark over our funding next year and you've put all our jobs at risk. Your performance over the past few months has been erratic, to say the least. You frequently look scruffy and I've smelt alcohol on your breath on occasions. The sex scandal has been an embarrassment, you've taken leave without permission and your behaviour at the Christmas meal was appalling. Do you seriously think you can continue working here?'

'Do you?' replied Kelly, a malicious smile on her face.

Lorna started.

'What the hell do you mean?'

'I mean I have information on you which could get you dismissed, prosecuted for fraud and maybe even charged with tax evasion.'

'Rubbish,' said Lorna, a faint note of uncertainty creeping into her voice.

'I know about the company car you provided for your son – and the inflated salary you paid him. You've been feathering your own nest by sending work to your own companies, I suspect at inflated prices. I have copies of your expenses claims which I'm sure the tax people would be interested in seeing. I also know you've been shagging Dave – on the company time – and I'm sure your partner would be interested in the recording I made. Also, I've listed those plans with the phoney deadlines and that would make interesting reading for someone. It's all on a flash drive and I'm hanging onto it as insurance. Perhaps we can talk about a salary increase when you've calmed down?'

'You blackmailing bitch. Get out of my office,' raved Lorna, unable to think of a suitable response.

Kelly left quietly, leaving Lorna to reflect on her uncertain future with the company and the threat to her family. The other staff in the office were agog. Although they couldn't hear what was said, they formed the distinct impression that Kelly was on the way out. Raised voices in Lorna's office usually meant only one thing. A firing. Surreptitious glee permeated the office for the rest of the day.

## Lorna

For the first time in her career, Lorna felt threatened. She was used to getting her own way, either by bullying or by turning on an oily charm which, along with her blonde hair and short skirts, proved irresistible to a certain type of man. She knew she could avoid trouble with the tax office, by declaring her travel expenses from home to work and paying the tax due. But the business of the car, her companies and Justin's salary would not go away so easily. At best, she would lose her job. At worst, she could face prosecution. If her dalliance with Dave came out it would wreck her family and she had no doubt that Kelly would find a way of publicising it over the internet or in the press.

Firstly, she would consult her solicitor. Then she would devise a way of dealing with the upstart Kelly, who had the temerity to threaten her. She had worked and schemed so hard to get where she was and the idea of losing it all was completely unacceptable. A desperate situation called for desperate measures and Lorna's judgement flew out of the window. Increasingly, she felt as though she was stumbling down a corridor with only one way out. And the walls were closing in.

---

Just before midnight, Lorna parked her car a couple of hundred metres from her target and walked briskly along the street, with a cap and scarf hiding her features and a can of petrol in her hand. A splash of liquid through the letter box, a petrol-soaked rag and a lighter was all it took. Shadowed by the growing flames behind her, the expression of triumph on her face was invisible. Her heart lifted, but something inside her whispered that she had been appallingly stupid.

## Kelly

Kelly shuffled out of the bathroom heading for bed, the combined effects of antidepressants and a half-bottle of wine tangling her feet beneath her. She thought she heard a clattering at the front door but couldn't be bothered to drag herself downstairs to investigate. Anyway, she knew it was locked. A few minutes later, she smelled smoke and lurched towards the bedroom door. She managed to get it open and a thick cloud of hot smoke poured into the room. Coughing and disorientated, she staggered to the window and opened it in a desperate attempt to call for help. Acting like a chimney, the open window only made the fire worse, drawing flames and more smoke up the stairs. But Kelly never felt the flames. Toxic gases from burning carpets and furniture stopped her heart long before flames started licking around her body.

## Sally

When Sally came into work the following morning, she was surprised to find that Kelly wasn't at her desk. She was normally in before anyone else. Instead, someone had taped a sheet of paper across her computer screen bearing the message 'GAL 6:7'. This meant nothing to most people – apart from the person who had put it there.

By lunchtime, Kelly had still not appeared. Lorna had come in late and locked herself in her office, looking unusually haggard. With the two tyrants effectively absent, the atmosphere in the office was lighter than usual. One or two people even made jokes over lunch, in the cramped staff room. A few drank coffee at their desks, something Lorna had banned because she said it looked untidy. This all changed mid-afternoon when a police car pulled up outside and three plain clothes officers got out. After talking briefly with Lorna, one of them came into the open-plan area and asked for everyone's attention.

'Good afternoon, ladies and gentlemen. I'm Detective Sergeant Mike Fellowes and I'm afraid I have some bad news for you. Your colleague, Kelly Thornbury, was involved in a house fire last night. Sadly, she didn't survive. I'm sorry to say that the fire service suspects that the blaze was started deliberately. We are awaiting confirmation from the fire investigator, but we have to treat her death as suspicious.'

When the murmurs of shock and incredulity had subsided, he continued.

'We would like to talk to all of you about Kelly. Ms Brake has made the staff room and the meeting areas upstairs available to us. We'll call you up when we are ready and we'll be as quick as we can. Please don't talk to anyone else about this. Thank you.'

After briefly examining Kelly's desk, and removing the note from her screen, Mike conferred with his colleagues and the interviews began. Mike took Lorna and the other managers initially, while his two detective constables started on the rest of the staff.

---

Sally felt a sinking feeling in her stomach, fearful that her actions against Kelly would come to light. She had been very careful to cover her tracks but realised that at least some of them could be discovered, under the spotlight of a murder investigation. Giving Kelly the Antabuse was tantamount to poisoning her, although it did no permanent damage to her health. Perhaps her purchase could be traced? She was confident that the speeding ticket and Nigerian prince ploys wouldn't be discovered but was she on CCTV somewhere, putting up the business cards? She wouldn't be able to conceal her feelings about her tormentor. She may even be suspected of killing Kelly. Could she be in some way responsible, as a result of her actions? No, that was preposterous. She knew her colleagues would approach the interviews with either nervousness or indifference, unsure as to how much they should say about Kelly and her management style. But unlike Sally, they had no guilty secrets to conceal.

## Police

Interviews completed, the police officers returned to the station to compare notes. Mike kicked off, with an air of puzzlement.

'I'm getting two completely different pictures of the company,' he said. 'According to Lorna Brake they are all a happy family and staff welfare is a primary concern. The other managers said something similar, although not so enthusiastically. But the rest of the staff I spoke to complained of bullying by management, petty rules and impossible workloads. No-one had a good word to say about Kelly, or Lorna for that matter.'

'That's what I found,' reported DC Mellors. 'This was one unhappy ship. Several people had left in recent months, because of management attitudes, and a couple I spoke to were on anti-depressants. I also had accounts of a row between Kelly and Lorna recently. No-one heard what was said, but they got the impression that Kelly was being fired.'

DC Porter nodded her agreement.

'That's odd,' mused Mike. 'Lorna didn't mention that. She said that Kelly was a valued member of the company but she was becoming concerned about her mental health. She advised Kelly to take some sick leave until she felt more able to cope. Did either of you come across anyone who could hate Kelly enough to kill her?'

'Not from what anyone said,' replied DC Porter, 'But Sally

Dawson was clearly hiding something, judging by her body language. She fidgeted a lot during the interview and couldn't conceal her dislike of Kelly.'

'Did anyone explain this note on Kelly's computer? What the hell does Gal 6:7 mean?'

'Katy Maguire admitted putting it there. It's a reference to the Bible. Galatians Chapter 6, verse 7'

'Meaning what?'

'The relevant part of it runs "whatever a man soweth, that shall he also reap".'

'Lou Reed put it better in *Perfect Day*,' muttered DC Mellors, but the others ignored him.

'Did Katy explain why? Could it mean that she knew Kelly was going to die? Did she have something to do with her murder?'

'I don't think so. She was mortified. She thought Kelly was going to be fired and couldn't resist a reference to divine justice. She's a devout Christian. Lorna forced her to lie over some deadline or other, but I don't see her as a killer.'

'Right. I think we need another chat with Sally Dawson and also with Lorna. Both of them are misleading us and I want to know why. I'll speak to them tomorrow.'

## Katy

While the detectives were comparing notes, Katy was clearing Kelly's desk and packing up her personal effects. She noticed that the drawer had been forced open and the filing tray was in disarray. Assuming that the police were responsible, she continued with her task.

There was very little on the top of the desk – company policy forbade clutter – but there were a few items in the drawer. A box of tea bags, a packet of tissues and a personalised coffee mug all went into a cardboard box. When Katy picked up a pair of thin gloves, she noticed a lump inside one of them. Intrigued, she turned the glove inside out and a small silvery object fell on to the desk. It was Kelly's flash drive.

'Give me that,' a voice behind her snarled.

Katy turned round to see Lorna, white-faced and clutching a pair of scissors.

'What?'

'I said give me that.'

'But it was Kelly's'

'No, it's company property. Give it to me or you'll regret it.'

'It not the sort we use. It was Kelly's. Why do you want it?'

Lorna gripped the scissors tightly, her knuckles whitening.

'Never you mind. I need it now or...'

'What are you doing Lorna?' interrupted Sally, who had heard the argument from the main office.

'Just reclaiming company property.'

'No, you're not. It was Kelly's. I heard what Katy said. What's on it that's so important to you?'

'Confidential company information. None of your business.'

'But we never put confidential information on a flash drive unless it's an encrypted Ironkey. You're lying.'

'How dare you. You're sacked, the pair of you.'


## Lorna

Realising that she wouldn't be able to snatch the flash drive, Lorna fled the office, ran to her car and screeched out of the car park. She had to get away and think. For the first time in her adult life, she didn't know what to do and the thought made her sick. She had failed to find the flash drive, after she forced

Kelly's desk drawer and, when she saw Katy holding it, her world collapsed around her.

Sitting in her kitchen, a large glass of gin in front of her, she reviewed her options. That bloody Katy would certainly have passed the flash drive on to the police by now and told them how she had been threatened. The evidence it contained could be damning but was Kelly bluffing? She didn't think so. She knew, from the way Kelly had handled the people she supervised, that she was both efficient and ruthless.

Maybe she could stay and brazen it out. She had no problem with lying to the police. She was skilled at dishonesty. Perhaps a short skirt and low neckline would distract DS Fellowes? No, that was nonsense. He was clearly a professional. If he had his suspicions, she was sure he would investigate.

Lorna was confident she wouldn't be suspected of Kelly's murder. She hadn't woken her family when she slipped out in the night and no-one had seen her when she poured the petrol through the letterbox. She had dumped the petrol can and her gloves in a skip on the way home. Again, her thoughts returned to the evidence Kelly had collected.

There was no denying she could be facing ruin and, possibly, prison. She knew they were bound to catch up with her sooner or later. If she was going to jail she would damn well make the most of her freedom before they arrested her. One last taste of the lifestyle she had enjoyed for the past few years. Paris? Rome? Rio? Wherever she could fly to from the local airport. After a frantic search for flights, she bought a ticket to Corfu, thinking she could lose herself among the Greek Islands for a few weeks.

She packed a few items of clothing, grabbed her passport and cash, and set off, telling her family that she was travelling on business. She realised that it would all be waiting for her when she got back, but at least they wouldn't be after her for murder. She would make her peace with her family later.

## Sally

Mike Fellowes had left his business cards with all the staff in case they thought of anything relevant. After they had calmed down a little, Sally and Katy agreed that they should call him.

'But it's our word against Lorna's,' protested Katy. 'And she's got more authority.'

'Not entirely,' replied Sally. 'I set my phone to record as soon as I heard her shouting. I thought something odd was going on. I didn't get everything but the recording starts with her apparently threatening you.'

They caught Mike in his office, as he finished writing up his notes on the interviews. As soon as they played the recording down the phone, he dispatched a couple of uniformed officers to pick up Lorna for questioning.

'That's very interesting,' he said, 'But it doesn't prove anything. Please don't plug the flash drive in, or tamper with it in any way, or you'll devalue it as evidence. I'm very keen to find out why it was so important. I know it's getting late but can you wait there until one of our forensic IT people collects it? And I'd like to speak to you both tomorrow morning.'

Katy and Sally agreed to wait and arranged to call in to the police station the following day, with some trepidation on Sally's part as she still feared that her campaign of revenge had been discovered.

Mike shook hands with them when they arrived at the station's front desk.

'Katy, could you give DC Porter a statement about what happened, please? I think you met her yesterday. Sally, come with me if you would. I need to take your phone. You'll get it back once we've copied the audio file.'

Sally followed Mike, dreading an interrogation, but the interview was painless with no mention of anything she had done. Once she had signed her statement, Mike spoke to her.

'You and Katy may need to give evidence in court about this. Will that worry you?'

'Court?' said Sally, astonished.

'Yes. Please don't mention this to anyone, until we have issued a press statement, but Lorna has been charged with arson and Kelly's manslaughter. It may even end up as a murder charge. I can't give you any more details I'm afraid, but we'll let you know if you are needed. Oh, before you go, can you clear up something for me?'

Sally's blood froze.

'Of course. If I can. What is it?'

'DC Porter had the strong impression that you were hiding something. It was also clear that you hated Kelly, more than the other people she spoke to. Care to explain?'

Sally wondered what she could hold back. She had to give him something. But how much? She decided to tell part of the truth.

'I did hate Kelly. The way she treated me was awful. In fact, I tried to commit suicide last year because of her. If it wasn't for my partner and the NHS, I wouldn't be here. I didn't say anything to DC Porter, in case she thought I was involved in Kelly's death.'

Mike seemed satisfied. He murmured a few words of

sympathy and showed Sally to the door. She kept her fingers crossed, dreading a Columbo moment, until she joined Katy in the foyer.

## Police

As the two women left the station, Mike gave a verbal report to his boss, Detective Inspector Harris.

'Lorna had left home by the time the PCs arrived to collect her. A neighbour told them that he'd seen her driving off in a hurry, with a suitcase in her car. Her partner said she had to make a business trip, but her briefcase was still in the hall. We put out an alert, and the car was spotted driving into the car park at East Midlands Airport. The airport police picked Lorna up in the departure lounge, on her way to Corfu. Her car boot smelled of petrol, even though it was a diesel vehicle. The tech guys interrogated the satnav and she was in Kelly's street the previous night. This was enough to hold her and, when the IT team looked at the flash drive, they found a load of stuff indicating that Lorna had been defrauding the company, dodging tax and behaving unprofessionally.'

'So, Kelly was blackmailing her?'

'It seems so. We've got motive for murder, means and opportunity, but no confession so far.'

'It's all circumstantial, though.'

'Yes, but once we show her what the flash drive contains, and the satnav data, she'll crack.'

'A nice collar, Mike. Well done!'

Mike grinned as he left the DI's office and then turned his attention to a problem handed to him by the neighbourhood policing team. Someone had been posting a sex worker's business cards around the town and people were complaining. The name on the cards was common enough, but he couldn't help thinking there was something familiar about the phone number.

---

*The toxic effect here is the result of two substances (Antabuse and alcohol) which are (relatively) harmless on their own combining – a process known as synergism. The toxic workplace culture depicted is common in many organisations, especially when a service ethos is replaced by a profit-based one.*

# Lamb for the Slaughter

It was one of those jobs everyone hates doing. Clearing out a deceased relative's belongings. It fell to me because I had the time, and no-one else was available. So, I put on some shabby clothes, packed a selection of cleaning materials and bin bags into a bucket, and drove to Great Aunt Mildred's Victorian semi on the other side of town.

The house itself was in reasonable condition: structurally sound and without obvious signs of a leaking roof, although a mustiness from the unventilated rooms almost overpowered the smell of Cardinal floor polish. It hadn't been decorated for many years. The floral wallpaper in most of the rooms had faded, and the dark brown woodwork showed the scuffs and bashes of decades. The furniture was old-fashioned and solid, but not old enough to be antique and collectable. A charity shop might take it, but a dealer wouldn't be interested. The old sofa and armchairs, lacking the necessary fire safety labels, would have to go to the tip. A few pictures on the wall looked pretty, in a kitschy way, but clearly had no great value. There was some nice china though – a few Clarice Cliff pieces and some Susie

Cooper. They could go to a specialist and the proceeds would be added to the estate, which was to be divided between my husband and his sister.

Mildred had taken her jewellery with her when she went into the care home, barely a month ago, and that was already accounted for. The clothes she had left behind were, sadly, infested with moths and fit only for recycling. In fact, there was very little else of a personal nature left, and I found it hard to form a picture of a woman I had never met. I knew that she was widowed at some point, and, for much of her life, lived with a lady companion who predeceased her. My husband once said 'she was a tough old bird' and, only in her later years, did she employ a cleaner and someone to help with the modest garden.

After a couple of hours exploring the house, and identifying destinations for the various items present, I decided I needed a coffee break and retrieved my Thermos from my bag. I had found an old biscuit tin at the bottom of a wardrobe and thought I would look through it while my drink cooled. It contained a few personal documents – birth certificates, her husband's death certificate – and some letters and Christmas cards, although surprisingly few of the latter. But, at the bottom, was a collection of newspaper cuttings. I glanced through them and nearly spilled my coffee. Aunt Mildred had been tried for murder!

A single yellowed piece of newsprint described how Mildred Gathorn, née Harrison, had been arrested and charged with murdering her husband. Intrigued, I searched through the rest of the papers but couldn't find anything more about the case. There were a few other cuttings dealing with local events, including the visit of the King to the town, but nothing more on Mildred's trial. I resolved to visit the local library the following day, when I needed a break from house cleaning.

The young man at the reference section was most helpful. They hadn't got round to digitising all the local papers, he explained, but they did have them on microfilm. I gave him the date of Mildred's arrest and he provided me with the relevant sections.

For a couple of hours I worked my way through back issues of the local rag. The soporific hum of the microfilm reader's fan, and the stuffy air in the cubicle, almost sent me to sleep. I was just about to go outside for some fresh air when a headline caught my eye: Shocking Poison Trial at Winchester Assizes. That was it!

During the course of an eight-day trial, Mildred was accused of killing her husband, John, in order to inherit his money and elope with a local pharmacist with whom, it was alleged, she was having an affair. The pharmacist had dispensed John Gathorn's heart medicine, and the prosecution alleged that Mildred had persuaded him to supply much stronger tablets than John required, with fatal results.

As the trial continued, duly sensationalised by the popular press, things were looking grim for the defendant. The medical evidence was clearly against her, and the added spice of adultery was bound to sway the jury towards a guilty verdict. Reporters were blatantly suggesting that the judge would be donning the black cap, until the defence case was presented and things changed dramatically.

Mildred's barrister, Raymond Drake KC, described as a mild-looking man with a deceptive appearance but rapier-like cross-examination skills, first drew blood by forcing the police inspector running the case to confirm that the pharmacist had been arrested, a week previously, on suspicion of committing gross indecency with a choirboy. This clearly undermined the prosecution's allegation of an affair. He then called an independent chemist, who analysed John Gathorn's heart tablets, which the police had retrieved. They contained a form of digitalis, and he confirmed that were of the normal strength. Further evidence for the defence came from the examination of the pharmacist's records, which demonstrated that there were no missing digitalis preparations and that every tablet received from the manufacturer had been properly dispensed, in accordance with prescriptions.

Recalling the pathologist to the witness box, Mr Drake elicited the admission that, yes, John Gathorn could have had a heart attack, even with the proper medication, from natural causes. Asked whether an accidental overdose of the tablets could have caused a lethal reaction, the pathologist admitted that it could, although there was some dispute over the exact deadly dose of that particular drug. The pathologist confirmed that a partly dissolved tablet, of normal strength, had been found in the stomach of the deceased, who had recently dined on roast lamb, mint sauce, peas and roast potatoes.

After the jury deliberated for six and a half hours, the foreman returned a not guilty verdict, and my husband's great aunt was acquitted.

---

Well, that was a juicy story, I thought, as I gathered my things together and returned to the empty house. My husband had never mentioned it, but perhaps he never knew. It wasn't as if there was a family scandal to be hushed up – she was innocent.

My last task was to deal with Mildred's books. There were a few old copies of Dickens and other Victorian writers as well as some Edwardian novels. A couple of early Agatha Christies could probably go on ebay. No other first editions or collectable volumes, as far as I could tell. The charity shop for the rest, I thought. Then I caught sight of a familiar name. Mrs Beeton. My gran had been given Mrs Beeton's Everyday Cookery by my grandad when they got married in the thirties. This was obviously an earlier edition, and I leafed through it out of curiosity. I came across the page describing a recipe for mint sauce and, as I did so, a slip of paper fell out. Scribbled across it, in fine pencilled writing, were the words *finely chop an ounce of foxglove leaves and add to the sauce, with extra sugar and mint to disguise the taste. Don't eat more than a quarter-teaspoonful of the sauce yourself.*

I could hardly believe what I was reading. So, my husband's distant relative was a murderer after all, probably aided and abetted by the pharmacist, who would have known about the toxic properties of foxgloves. If he wasn't attracted to my great aunt romantically, perhaps he just wanted a share of the money? Maybe she was blackmailing him over his illegal proclivities? But how had they got away with it? Wouldn't the pathologist have ordered an analysis of the rest of the stomach contents, as well as the partly-dissolved tablet which he must have retrieved during the post-mortem?

Something jogged my memory, and I returned to the collection of newspaper cuttings. One of them had seemed out of place. The headline was brief – *Doctor's assistant dismissed for misconduct.* The short article which followed described how Albert Harrison, an assistant at the hospital mortuary, had been sacked for an alleged incident of drunkenness which had led to the accidental destruction of post-mortem samples. Apparently, he had stumbled against a shelf and knocked the jars and bottles to the floor, where they smashed. The samples were needed for several important trials, but could no longer be analysed.

The trials weren't named, but it was obvious to me that one of them was Great Aunt Mildred's. Why else would she have the cutting? When I saw the miscreant's name, I realised exactly what had happened. For Albert Harrison was Mildred's brother and, by bribery or coercion, he must have been persuaded to destroy John Gathorn's stomach contents. I went back to the library to see if there was anything more in the newspaper about Albert. He was never arrested but died suddenly, two weeks after the trial, apparently of natural causes.

---

I was flabbergasted by the cunning that my husband's great aunt and her fellow conspirators had shown. I hadn't realised what lay beneath the veneer of respectability that covered my husband's distant family. My mind went into overdrive. Was Albert Harrison's death really natural? And why did Mildred's companion die before her. Could the family have once included a serial killer? I realised I would never know. And, as much as I trust my husband, I had a feeling I wouldn't want to eat mint sauce for a while – and certainly not any made to Great Aunt Mildred's special recipe.

---

*You never know what you'll find in Mrs Beeton, but this was a distinctly unusual recipe! Earlier forms of heart medicine based on digitalis were sometimes a little unreliable, and difficult to use without producing unwanted side effects. Modern forms are much safer – digoxin is still extracted from foxgloves.*

# Natural Justice

THE POSTERS SPRANG UP OVERNIGHT, like mushrooms in the morning dew. 'Save Mellors Wood', 'No to the training centre' and, less politely, 'Piss Off Porton'. Every tree, lamp-post and bus shelter in Whitfield Cross was adorned with one of these messages, expressing opposition to Damien Porton's proposals to develop his recently-purchased land. He planned to build a cordon bleu cookery training centre, where he could charge large fees to aspiring Michelin-starred chefs. It wasn't the centre *per se* which enraged the villagers but the fact that it would mean felling Mellors Wood, the jewel of the village.

Carpeted with bluebells in the spring, and home to countless butterflies and other wildlife in summer and autumn, the wood had thrived for centuries. Local people had walked, picnicked and courted in the wood since time immemorial, and the thought of its destruction was like the impending loss of a limb. Unfortunately, the conservation bodies had omitted to designate it as a Site of Special Scientific Interest, so it had no legal protection other than general development controls. Damien Porton could do what he liked with it, provided that he had planning permission, and rumours of his improper influence on the planning committee were rife.

Damien was a celebrity chef, rich on the back of a long-running TV show and a series of expensive cookery books. His Mayfair restaurant catered for celebrities and VIPs from around the world, its eye-watering prices being well out of reach of the normal diner. He had already outraged conservationists by urging people to plunder Epping Forest for its wild mushrooms and he had the same contempt for green issues as he had for food from a roadside burger van. He spent most of his time at his London flat but also owned Constance Hall, a 17th century building, on the outskirts of the village, which he had surrounded with high walls, CCTV and alarms to keep the paparazzi out.

Damien sneered as his Bentley glided past a display of posters attacking his project. 'Bunch of Luddite NIMBYs,' he muttered to himself. He had been pressurised to speak at a public meeting in the village hall the following evening and wasn't looking forward to it. He was confident that he could persuade the 'yokels', as he thought of them, that his project's benefits to the village would outweigh those of a few flowers. But, just in case, he was taking his solicitor and a couple of minders with him.

The opposition was led by Dr Gareth Healey, a 32-year-old ecologist who worked at the nearby Tavister Town Museum. His forty-page document describing the wood's history, biodiversity and importance to conservation was a model of reasoned and fact-based persuasion. The local papers, regional radio and even the *Guardian* had covered the battle, so a considerable media presence was expected at the meeting.

A chilly Autumn mist covered the village the following morning, but tempers became more and more heated as the day drew on. Most of the villagers opposed the project but a few, believing that it would mean work for them, were in favour. The landlord of the Mitre, the pub closest to the wood, supported the project and banned campaigners against the scheme from his bars. His youthful drinkers, in low paid jobs if any, fuelled themselves up with cider and determined to have their say, loudly, at the meeting.

At the other end of the village, the County Arms was the unofficial headquarters of the campaign against the plans. Its patrons were a more sober group, but still became increasingly agitated as the time of the meeting approached.

'We must remain calm and reasonable,' urged Gareth, 'otherwise we'll be dismissed as a rabble. I'm sure Porton will accept public opinion and build his training centre somewhere else.'

'Don't be bloody naive,' snorted Colonel Carmichael, whose estate backed onto the wood. 'He's a profiteering little oik who cares nothing for the village he's invaded. Money and fame are all that motivate him. Trying to reason with him would be like asking the wind not to blow.'

'But we can convince the planning committee to throw it out, I'm sure,' replied Gareth. 'We've got science and the village on our side.'

'Of course,' sneered Jed Butcher, a local farmer. 'Just after they've given me a licence to fly my pigs. They've all got their noses in the trough and the Chairman's as crooked as a corkscrew hazel.'

These arguments had, of course, been rehearsed many times, but Gareth realised that it was vital that they kept calm and behaved themselves. There was no local police constable any more, but two officers and a PCSO had been drafted in from Tavister to keep order at the meeting, should it be necessary.

The village hall was packed half an hour before the meeting was due to start, and the noise was intolerable. The air was full of anticipation, anger and the smells of cider and sweat. Attempts to exclude people without seats, on fire safety grounds, had to be abandoned, such was the strength of local feeling, both for and against Porton's plans.

'Order, please, order, ladies and gentlemen,' shouted Rupert Renfrew, the chair of the local council, from the stage. 'Everyone will get a chance to speak so please settle down.'

The cacophony subsided to a muted grumbling as Damien Porton got to his feet and switched on a projector. A Powerpoint presentation appeared on the wall behind the stage, crinkled and warped where 21st century technology met 18th century plasterwork.

Porton's pitch was as slick as his Savile Row suit. He mentioned, without giving numbers, job opportunities for local people during the construction and operational phases, which brought cheers from a few members of the audience. He assured the village that building and materials deliveries would only take place during the daytime and that the site would be screened to reduce dust and noise. He spoke of the prestige that such an establishment would bring to the village, although few people were interested in that, and promised extra trade for local pubs and the village shop. Intermittent boos greeted his promises and angry looks were exchanged between supporters and opponents of the project.

'And I'm planting just as many trees around Constance Hall as will be lost from the wood,' he declared, triumphantly, hoping to win over the green objectors.

'Yes – leylandii rubbish,' someone shouted, 'Nothing that belongs here,' prompting numerous 'hear, hear' replies.

Porton ignored him. Switching on the synthetic smile that had endeared him to his TV viewers, he concluded with: 'Ladies and gentlemen – I'm bringing something to your village which will take it into the 21st century. Jobs and prestige will follow and we must embrace progress. I hope you will see that this is much more important than a few flowers. Thank you.'

The applause which he had hoped for failed to materialise and the few ragged cheers were drowned out by boos and catcalls such as 'Rubbish,' 'Bollocks,' and 'Philistine'. Porton looked nervously at his minders. It took Renfrew a full five minutes to restore order and summon Gareth Healey to the stage.

Bespectacled and stooping slightly, wearing a work shirt and corduroy trousers, Gareth was the antithesis of Porton's confident suaveness. He spoke from notes rather than a laptop and cleared his throat several times before speaking. Once he began to outline the case against the proposals, the audience fell quiet. Calmly, and growing in confidence as he spoke, he outlined the wood's conservation value, its cultural significance to the village and the place it had in the villagers' hearts. When he stopped, the silence was broken by a couple of jeers which were swiftly drowned out by a tumult of applause. Gareth smiled gently. Porton looked as if he was chewing a tarantula.

Then it was time for the audience to speak. Renfrew tried to allow a balance of opinions to be heard but the few locals who enthused about employment prospects were swamped by those in favour of preserving the wood. Birds, bees, picnics and flagons of cider featured prominently in their accounts, and many a romance had blossomed among the bluebells. At least three of the audience claimed to have been conceived in Mellors wood.

The final contribution was the testimony of an elderly woman who rambled on for several minutes about the glorious mushroom soups she used to make from fungi foraged in Mellors wood and how she would never be able to do this again. Hers was the only voice Porton, a confirmed foodie, paid any attention to, but as the woman spoke a frown crossed Gareth's face.

The meeting broke up shortly after, and the two camps drifted off to their respective pubs, with some mild jostling as opponents pushed through the doors and a brief scuffle outside which required police attention.

'You did damn well, young fellow,' said Colonel Carmichael as Gareth reached gratefully for his pint. 'If there was any justice, the committee would throw it out in an instant.'

'Yes, but there isn't,' replied Gareth. 'We need to set up a fighting fund and get hold of a planning expert. We'll need a decent lawyer, too. They're not cheap, and Porton can afford the best. Local opinion won't stop Porton – and money brings its own momentum.'

Various suggestions for fundraising followed. The vicar offered the church grounds for an Autumn Fair, the landlord of the pub agreed to host quiz nights and the captain of the cricket club thought he could persuade the members of the team to pose for a 'tasteful' nude calendar. Martin Askew, a retired accountant, offered to act as treasurer for the campaign and a committee meeting was arranged for the following week.

'By the way, why was your Aunt Judy waffling on about

soup?' asked the Colonel, as the landlord called last orders. 'She seemed a bit woolly, if you ask me. Not on her usual form.'

'I don't know,' replied Gareth, 'She's normally much sharper than that – and I don't remember her ever making mushroom soup.'

'Oh, well. Age claims us all, I suppose. Good night.'

---

Damien Porton was an early riser and usually jogged around the grounds of Constance Hall before breakfast when he was in Whitfield Cross. Intrigued by the old woman's reference to mushroom soup, he decided to take his run through Mellors Wood and see what he could forage. To his delight he found several species which he recognised – horse mushrooms, chanterelles, penny buns and some just-emerged button mushrooms. Sweeping them into his bag, he jogged onwards, promising himself soup for lunch. A light snack would do, as he had a business meeting over an expensive dinner that evening.

---

The meeting was going well, and he had convinced his potential investors that local opposition to the training centre would be swept aside. 'It's amazing how a few brown envelopes can smooth the planning process,' he said knowingly. The others chuckled. With roast partridge following the mackerel paté, Porton was feeling benign and slightly woozy from the champagne. As they started on the dessert, he began to feel ill. His stomach hurt and he dashed to the gents just before throwing up and succumbing to horrendous diarrhoea.

'I've got to go home,' he moaned to his companions when he

returned to the table some time later. 'I'm really sick. That paté must have been off.'

Porton called a taxi and just made it back to the Hall before he needed to rush to the lavatory again. Exhausted, he eventually crawled into bed, resolving to castigate the restaurant in his monthly Sunday magazine column. He'd often blasted restaurants in print, usually those run by his rivals, and this one would get both barrels.

By the following afternoon his discomfort was beginning to dwindle. He was able to write his column and review the plans for his training centre but was still too feeble to go out for his jog. A day later, however, he began to feel ill again. He was constantly nauseous, his insides ached abominably, his skin began to turn yellow and his gums had started to bleed. Confused and sleepy, he became weaker and weaker and eventually phoned his GP in London, telling him he suspected the mackerel paté.

'Well, I suppose it could be,' said Dr Campion. 'There is a toxic substance called scombrotoxin found in badly-kept mackerel and it can produce some of your symptoms. I really think you need to go to hospital. Get yourself checked out.'

Porton followed the GPs advice and booked himself into the nearest private hospital, requesting an ambulance to get him there. Following a battery of questions, tests, and examinations a worried-looking consultant came into Porton's room the following morning.

'Damien', he said 'I'm afraid you are gravely ill and we don't know why. Your liver is shutting down and your kidneys are seriously damaged. It can't be the mackerel you were worried about. The signs and symptoms just aren't consistent with it. Have you eaten anything else unusual recently?'

'I had some wild mushroom soup,' croaked Damien, 'But it tasted absolutely fine. I know my mushrooms.'

An hour later, the consultant returned with a series of pictures printed off the internet. 'Did any of the mushrooms look like these?' he asked.

Porton's vision was blurring and he was beginning to hallucinate but he managed to look at the pictures. 'Definitely not those,' he said, 'That's Death Cap and that's Fly Agaric. I'm not bloody stupid.'

He continued looking, rejecting the images presented, and nodded when he saw the final image.

'Some of them were like that one – small button mushrooms.'

The consultant paled.

'I'm really sorry, Damien. Those are the early stages of the Destroying Angel. It's deadly and I'm afraid the damage is irreversible. We have looked on the transplant register for a suitable liver for you but we've had no luck. We've even looked abroad. There is nothing more we can do for you except make you comfortable. I'm so, so, sorry.'

Porton barely registered what the doctor was saying as he slipped in and out of consciousness, eventually lapsing into a coma.

———————

A week later the County Arms was buzzing with excitement as the campaign committee held its final meeting. Behind the bar the front page of a tabloid newspaper was pinned up with the headline 'Foraging Foodie's Fatal Fungus.' No-one was actually expressing glee at Damien Porton's demise, but there was much relief that the wood was safe. The remaining campaign funds, after celebratory drinks had been purchased, were given to the local wildlife trust to help them buy the wood from Porton's heirs. It would be protected from development permanently and Whitfield Cross could begin to return to its normal peaceful state.

As the merriment in the bar died down and people drifted off home, Gareth carried the remains of his beer over to his Aunt Judy's table.

'You encouraged Porton to eat those mushrooms, didn't you?'

'Of course not, dear. What makes you think that?' his aunt replied.

'You never made soup from mushrooms in the wood, because everyone knew some of them were poisonous.'

'Oh dear. Perhaps my memory was failing me,' she replied, although her twinkling eyes belied this.

'So you're responsible for his death.'

'Goodness me, no. Everyone knows you should be careful with wild mushrooms. And Porton claimed to be an expert. I like to think of it as nature striking back. Simply a case of natural justice. Goodnight, dear.'

*Not a murder, but who is responsible? Aunt Judy or Damien, for not taking sufficient care when identifying mushrooms?*

## Summertime, and the killin' is easy

'If they hadn't camped on that bit of meadow, I wouldn't have had to kill them. You see, that patch of ground is special to me. I'll explain why, in a minute. I did ask them, politely, not to pitch that horrible orange tent there, but they ignored me. In fact, the man, all tattoos and attitude, threatened to "punch my lights out" if I didn't "do one".'

Hypnotised by the double-barrelled shotgun aimed at her chest, DC Sally Erskine had little choice but to comply with the man's instructions. She sat down and handcuffed her wrist to the arm of the bentwood chair and placed her phone, radio and handcuff key on the table in front of her. How the hell had a routine response to a fire at a campsite escalated to a life-threatening firearms incident? she asked herself. And how the fuck am I going to get out of this alive?

'Technically, he was within his rights to be there,' her captor continued. 'I don't own the land; I just rent a cottage from the farmer, who lets people camp in his fields for a fee. No-one had used that corner before, as it was always overgrown with nettles. This season, the farmer cleared it so as to accommodate more tents, despite my pleas that he should leave it. I said it was because Small Tortoiseshell butterfly caterpillars feed on the nettles and they've become rare in recent years. But that wasn't the real reason.

'I had hoped they would just be there overnight, but it was clear, by the third day, that they were staying for the week. They defiled the tranquillity of that special place, sitting out there all hours with barbaric music playing and cheap disposable barbecues polluting the air. Every time the sun came out, she lay there with her top off and he exposed his flabby beer belly. They just chucked their rubbish into the corner, ignoring the waste bins provided, and he obviously thought it amusing to construct a sort of cairn from empty beer and cider cans, a monument to their boozing.

'They had to go. The farmer wouldn't help; he said they'd paid their money and were entitled to stay. I made a fuss but he took no notice. Perhaps that was a clue for you. So, it was down to me to get rid of them. I'm not a strong man, physically, so I couldn't evict them by force. I needed to find another way.

'Yesterday afternoon I looked, with loathing, at the pile of drink cans and it gave me an idea. When I moved into the cottage, I found a bottle of old Seconal sleeping tablets in the back of a cupboard. I dug them out and examined the label which showed that they had been dispensed in 1966. Would they still work? I wondered. I Googled them and discovered that, combined with alcohol, they could be lethal. And I knew just how I could make them take the tablets.

'I rushed down to the village store. Mrs Tilley was just closing up and wanted to get off home so I had to persuade her to sell me a flagon of local sweet cider. I guess that looked suspicious. Perhaps that's what put you on to me.'

'No, sir, I just...' Sally started to speak.

117

'Don't interrupt. That evening I approached the couple just before nightfall. "Look," I said, "I think we got off on the wrong foot the other day, so I've brought you a sort of peace offering. It's some local cider. Quite strong, but delicious. I hope you enjoy the rest of your stay."'

'The man looked puzzled but grunted a "Ta". She giggled and said something about it putting hairs on her chest, which she pushed towards me, earning her a glare from her partner.

'The cider and the sleeping tablets did the job and, by midnight, they were both sound asleep, their snores no doubt puzzling the fox which scavenged the half-eaten burgers and sausages dropped on the ground. I sat outside the tent, waiting for their breathing to stop but, to my surprise, they kept on snoring. Perhaps the tablets were too old? Maybe they hadn't taken enough? I realised I would have to find another way.

'My eyes lit on a box of disposable barbecues and I recalled a warning sign by the entrance to the campsite. "Do not use barbecues in tents" it proclaimed. So that was how I would finish them off. I pulled one of the barbecues from the box, lit it on the ground outside and, once the flames had died down, manoeuvred it into the tent using a set of tongs. Within minutes, dangerous levels of carbon monoxide would build up in the tent and, soon after, they would die. I closed the tent flap and retreated to my cottage, a sense of gleeful anticipation replacing the nerves which had kept my pulse racing for the past half hour.

'I suppose something flammable fell onto the glowing charcoal as, by the time I got home, the tent was burning. Another camper must have called 999, because a fire engine turned up and put the flames out. When I saw the police tape this morning, I realised that, even if the pathologist recorded death from carbon monoxide poisoning, the Seconal in their systems would give the game away. It wouldn't be long before the police came to question me but I'm surprised you got here so quickly. The farmer and Mrs Tilley, I suppose. I guess I'm not as good at murder as I thought I was.

'Why did I do it? What was so special about that patch of field? Seven years ago, on Midsummer's Eve, I buried Helena there, after I caught her in bed with the farmhand. They fished the farmhand out of the slurry pit the following morning, full of drink and with an unexplained head injury. I was stronger then.

'I forgave Helena, of course, but it was too late after I had killed her. So, I laid her to rest in that corner, and nettles have grown there in profusion every year. Until now.

'My tale is almost complete, Detective Constable. I know you suspect me. I'm not a criminal mastermind and I realise there is evidence of what I've done. So, it's time for me to use this shotgun. Don't worry – I'm not going to shoot you. I'll toss you the handcuff key and, by the time you've freed yourself from the chair, I'll have joined Helena, wherever she is. I apologise, in advance, for the mess. Goodbye.'

---

'Sarge? It's Sally. You'll never believe this. Can you ask the guv'nor to send a team and some SOCOs to the campsite at Miles Cross Farm? Four murders, and a suicide by shotgun. It's horrible. I only came here to take a witness statement about the tent that caught fire. But I've heard the most harrowing story, the suspect has killed himself and I'm sodding well covered in blood.'

---

*Deaths as a result of people using barbecues and cooking appliances in tents and other unventilated spaces are not unusual. Barbiturate sleeping tablets, like Seconal, were largely discontinued many years ago, owing to their ability to depress respiration, sometimes fatally, especially when combined with alcohol.*

# Death After Dinner

'IF I HAVE to listen to another of his speeches about how proud he is to be a self-made man, I'll swing for him,' moaned Rowley Morrison, although 'swinging' for murder had long since been abolished.

'Can't you indulge him this once,' his uncle George replied, as they hung up their coats. 'It's a big day for him, celebrating his engagement.'

'Yes, to a girl half his age,' sniffed Valerie. 'He should be ashamed of himself.'

'Her photo looks nice, though, sis,' Rowley mused. 'I quite fancy her myself. Perhaps someone should warn her that life with Dad won't be quite what she expects.'

'Well go ahead, if you dare. You know how much he appreciates interference in his affairs. I'm going to get myself a drink.'

Valerie headed purposefully towards the decanters in the drawing room.

'Rowley! George! You're here. Splendid! Splendid!' Peter Morrison's voice boomed across the hall as he descended the sweeping wooden staircase to greet his family. 'Where's Val?'

'She's in the drawing room with the Scotch,' said Rowley.

'Ah. Jolly good show. Let's join her,' Peter replied, his immaculate teeth flashing white against his synthetic tan. 'I could do with a snifter myself.'

They had just got their drinks when an attractive blonde woman of about twenty-five entered the room.

'Ah, my dear. There you are.' He turned to his relatives. 'May I present my lovely fiancée, Miss Melanie Myles. This is my son Rowley, my daughter Valerie and my brother George.'

'Pleased to meet you,' Melanie replied. 'I'm so excited to be joining your family. Pete has told me all about you.'

Rowley almost drooled at the sight of Melanie's cleavage, Valerie returned her greeting coolly and George smiled pleasantly. After half an hour's awkward chit-chat, the guests went up to their rooms to change.

'Pretensions to nobility,' muttered Rowley, as they climbed the staircase. 'Making us change for dinner. Listen to the way he speaks. Pretending to be Lord Muck. I'm half expecting a snooty butler to appear. And look at this place. A perfectly decent old manor house done up with execrable taste.'

Valerie grinned.

'Yes. I'm surprised he hasn't bought himself one of those phoney peerages. Lord Morrison of Little Taste.'

Rowley chuckled.

'Now, now,' their uncle interjected. 'Your father is a highly successful man. Forgive him his indulgences.'

'I don't know how you can be so forgiving, Uncle. He practically stole the business from you,' snapped Valerie. 'No wonder Aunt Helen refused to come.'

'Water under the bridge, my dear. Water under the bridge. I'm doing fine. And Helen has a cold.'

'Right. Of course. Glad to hear you're OK, though. But I wouldn't be so sanguine if he'd done that to me.'

---

The dinner itself was a strained affair, at least to begin with. An undercurrent of animosity pervaded the room, never quite spilling over into open conflict. Dark looks were cast in both Peter's and Melanie's directions although neither seemed to notice. It was Valerie who broke the ice.

'And what do you do, Melanie?' she asked.

'I'm the CEO of a computer games company. We entered the market two years ago and the FT described us as one of the most promising start-ups of the year. We're doing rather well.'

Valerie seemed surprised that someone so glamorous could be a successful businesswoman. Rowley's jaw dropped and George smiled to himself.

'I'm very proud of her,' enthused Peter. 'She's not just a pretty face.'

The others nodded, and the conversation flowed a little more easily for a while, until Peter announced he needed an early night. He drained his glass and lurched to his feet, an evening's heavy drinking taking its toll.

'Help me up, darling,' he mumbled, and Melanie draped his arm over her shoulder.

'I'll give you a hand,' said Valerie, taking the other arm.

Between them, the two women manoeuvred him upstairs, with Rowley gazing raptly at Melanie's retreating rear. They returned a few minutes later and Melanie picked up an item from the table, where Peter had been sitting, leaving the room in a hurry.

'I'll go for a walk in the garden before I go to bed,' said Melanie, a few minutes later. 'Help yourself to drinks.'

---

Valerie stood on the terrace, smoking thoughtfully for ten minutes, then joined the others in the drawing room for a nightcap.

'Well, that was a surprise. Not a bimbo after all,' she conceded. 'Pretty well off, as well, I imagine.

'Yes, but I still think she's after his money,' replied Rowley, 'What can she see in him? A pompous entrepreneur with a massive ego and a paunch. Just wait till she finds out what he's really like. No wonder Mama killed herself.'

'Oh do shut up, Rowley. Your mother had health issues before she met your father,' said George, grimly.

'Yes, but the bastard played on her weaknesses and bullied her until she couldn't stand it anymore. Hence the overdose. Pretty Melanie's in for a shock, you wait and see. I still think someone should warn her.'

'There's really no point,' insisted Valerie, 'I've just had a chat with her outside. She knows her own mind and she's not stupid. She's devoted to him, believe it or not.'

The conversation ended abruptly when Melanie put her head round the door and wished them goodnight. Two minutes later, as they were finishing their drinks, they heard her scream.

'Help. Help me please. Hurry.'

They rushed upstairs to find Peter sprawled across the bed in his pyjamas, his face swollen, clearly not breathing. Valerie placed her fingers against her father's neck for a few moments, then stood up.

'I'm very sorry, Melanie,' she said. 'He's dead.'

Half an hour later, Dr Simpson stepped back from Peter's body, a puzzled frown on his face.

'I can't be sure, but it looks like anaphylactic shock. Was he allergic to anything?' he asked a tearful Melanie.

'Yes,' she gulped. 'Nuts. He insisted that tonight's food be prepared in a nut-free kitchen. He was fanatical about it and threatened to sue the caterers if they made a mistake. He inspected the food meticulously when it was delivered.'

'Hmmm. Could there have been nut traces anyway?'

'I doubt it. Peter said Rowley has a nut allergy, too, and he's fine. He would have been affected much sooner if the food had been contaminated. Also, there are no nuts anywhere in the house.'

'Does he have an Epipen in case of an attack?'

'Of course. There it is, on the floor. He must have used it.'

'I'm not happy about this, Miss Myles. Not happy at all. We'd better join the others.'

He ushered Melanie out of the bedroom, locking the door behind him.

'Maybe I read too many crime novels,' the doctor began, when they were all seated in the drawing room, 'but this looks suspicious to me. I'm told he was always extremely careful to avoid eating nuts but it looks as though, somehow, he has ingested some. Which means he was probably given them deliberately. I'm afraid we have to involve the police.'

'What? Why?' asked Rowley.

'Preposterous,' said George.

Valerie looked thoughtful but said nothing.

The responses of his relatives demonstrated little sympathy for Peter or, indeed, for his ex-fiancée. Brandies were poured and the trio waited impatiently for the police to arrive. Melanie remained on her own, slumped at the dining table, staring blankly at the wall and fiddling with the flashy engagement ring on her finger.

'So, what's worrying you, doctor?' asked Detective Inspector Brooke, peering into the bedroom and taking in the corpse on the bed. 'I presume this isn't an accidental death.'

'I don't think so,' Dr Simpson replied. 'Peter Morrison appears to have died from anaphylactic shock. He is strongly allergic to nuts. However, no nuts are permitted anywhere in the house, and it's highly unlikely there were any in his food. To me it suggests that someone, somehow, gave him nuts. So, I've confirmed death and I'll leave it with you. And I recommend that a full Home Office post mortem is carried out.'

Dr Simpson handed Brooke the key to Peter's bedroom and left. The detective glanced briefly around, turned off the radiator, locked the door and went downstairs to the drawing room, where Peter's relatives sat grumbling. Melanie joined them, her eyes red from crying.

'I'm sorry to keep you waiting. I'm Detective Inspector Brooke and, after discussion with Dr Simpson, I'm afraid I'm treating Mr Morrison's death as suspicious. His bedroom is now a crime scene and no-one can go in there. SOCOs will be along tomorrow but, before I go, I would like a few words with each of you. I'll be as quick as I can. Is there somewhere we can talk?'

'Peter's study, I suppose,' said Melanie. 'I'll show you.'

Melanie led Brooke into the room, a designer's idea of a Victorian gentleman's study. It was dominated by a mahogany desk, in front of a velvet-curtained bay window. Two leather club chairs sat either side of the tiled, cast-iron fireplace, that was fitted with a modern gas log fire. Bookcases lined three walls but a close inspection revealed that the books were mainly mock-ups of leather clad volumes, bought by the metre. Brooke perched on the edge of the desk and invited Melanie to sit in one of the chairs. A detective constable, notebook poised, sat in the other.

'I'm very sorry. This is painful for you, I know,' he began, 'But I do need to ask you some questions. The pathologist's report should confirm Dr Simpson's diagnosis, but I'm assuming that Mr Morrison somehow ingested nuts. We will have the food remains checked, but I'm working on the assumption that he was given them deliberately, with malicious intent. Did he eat anything apart from the food at dinner?'

'No, Inspector. Nothing.'

'OK. Is there anyone you know of who would possibly wish him harm? Perhaps someone who wanted to play a joke on him, which had unintended consequences?'

'I suppose you mean someone in the family? Well, I don't really know. Peter has told me a bit about them, but I met them for the first time today. The atmosphere at dinner was strained at first, but I assumed that was because they thought I was a gold digger.' She looked slightly awkward. 'I still think they weren't happy with me marrying Peter, even after I explained I had a successful career and didn't need his money.'

'Tell me more about the dinner.'

'The food was a bit complicated and we gave the caterers strict instructions. No nuts for Peter, low protein for George and me and no gluten or nuts for Rowley. Valerie was the only normal eater among us.'

'Hmm. You'd better give me the contact details for the caterers. I'll need to talk to them.'

Melanie nodded.

'Did everyone stay at the table all evening?'

'Well, it went on for a while – three courses and coffee. I think we all got up to use the loo at one time or another. Peter had a lot to drink and went to bed early. Valerie and I had to help him to the bedroom. I came down to retrieve his Epipen, which he'd left on the table, and then I went for a walk in the garden. I spoke to Valerie, briefly, on the terrace. The others helped themselves to drinks in the drawing room.'

'His Epipen was discharged – had he used it previously at all?'

'Not during the day. In fact, I can't remember when he last needed it. I assume he used it when he began to feel ill. I'm surprised it didn't work.'

'Is there anything else you can tell me?'

'No. No, I don't think so. I'll let you know if I remember anything. I really did love him, you know. His age didn't matter.'

'I'm sure you did. Thank you, Miss Myles. A family liaison officer will be here tomorrow. She'll support you over the next few days. Would you ask Mr Rowley Morrison to come in next, please?'

---

Rowley entered the room, looking tired and smelling of brandy. Brooke motioned him to sit, as he looked nervously around him.

'Bit like being called into the headmaster's study,' he tried to joke. 'Hope I haven't done anything naughty.'

'This is a murder investigation, Mr Morrison, not a game,' reproved Brooke.

'Sorry.' Rowley straightened up in his chair. 'How can I help?'

'By telling me all about your movements yesterday, from the time you arrived to the time Peter Morrison was found.'

'Well, we travelled down together, me, Val, and Uncle George, in George's car. We arrived about five-thirty and Dad greeted us. He introduced Melanie, we had a drink and a bit of a chat and went up to change for dinner after about half an hour. I stayed in my room looking over some papers until dinner at seven. After the meal, Dad went up early, Melanie went for a walk and then to bed. The rest of us were having brandies when she screamed. We rushed up to his room, found him lying there, and Val checked to see if he was alive. Obviously, he wasn't.'

'May I ask how you got on with your father?'

'OK, I suppose. We became somewhat distant after mother died. I hadn't seen him for some while. I have a busy solicitor's practice so I don't get much free time.'

He hesitated.

'To be frank, Inspector, my father was not a nice man. He made my mother's life a misery. She was never very well and, eventually, she killed herself. The family holds him at least partly responsible. Also, his lord of the manor act irritated us – pretending to be better than the rest of the family just because he was a business success.'

'How did you feel about him marrying Melanie?'

'Unenthusiastic. I thought she was after his money. I was surprised when Melanie said how successful she was. I didn't really blame him, though. She's pretty stunning.'

'Can you think of anyone who disliked him.'

'I think he pissed off plenty of people in business, Uncle

George, for one, when he bought him out. I'm not sure his practices were strictly above board.'

'Did you go into your father's room at all?'

'We all did. Horrible décor.'

'OK. I think that's all for now. I'm sure I'll need to talk to you again. We'll need to take DNA samples from all of you, for elimination. Would you send your sister in, please?'

———

Valerie entered the study without knocking and sat down opposite Brooke.

'I hope this won't take long, Inspector. I'm a consultant dermatologist. I have an early morning clinic tomorrow and I need a decent night's sleep.'

'It won't take long, Dr Morrison. Where do you work?'

'The Fortbury. It's a private hospital.'

'So you must be reasonably well off?'

'That's rather impertinent but, yes, I have no money worries.'

'How did you feel about your father remarrying?'

'Largely indifferent, until I saw Melanie's picture and realised how young she was. Then I thought she was probably after his money. But, when she spoke at the dinner, I revised my opinion. I still couldn't see what she saw in him. I suppose she appreciated his entrepreneurial skills.'

Her tone bordered on the sarcastic.

Valerie's account of the events of the previous evening broadly matched Rowley's. She confirmed she had left the table at some point and that no-one had been with her.

'Thank you, Dr Morrison,' said Brooke. 'We'll be in touch. Can you send in your uncle, please?'

George Morrison appeared relaxed. He had donned a black tie but, otherwise, gave little impression that he mourned the loss of his brother.

'Please sit down, Mr Morrison. Can you run through the events of yesterday for me?'

George's account tallied with the others. He admitted leaving the table briefly, to use the toilet. He said he had no particular objection to his brother remarrying. He thought Melanie a little young, but was impressed by her business success.

'How did the others feel?'

'They weren't happy, I'm afraid. Rowley, in particular. They both thought she was money grabbing, although Val changed her mind when Melanie told us about her job at dinner. I think she also spoke to her on the terrace. Rowley lusted after her and couldn't take his eyes off her breasts.'

'Would they suffer if they didn't inherit? Any will made in favour of his children would have become null and void when he married.'

'Val's got a well-paid job in private medicine and has no dependents. I'm sure she's comfortable. I don't know about Rowley. He looks a bit shabby these days, his car is far from new and I've heard rumours about a malpractice investigation.'

'Are you a lawyer too?'

'Heavens, no. Accountant and financial advisor. I'm sure someone's told you that I went into business with Peter, developing property. He was extremely difficult to work with. I agreed to let him buy me out, for what turned out to be a ridiculously small sum.'

'Were you angry?'

'Perhaps for a while. But, when I saw the sort of shady deals and sharp practices he got involved with, I was glad I got out. He was lucky not to have been investigated by the fraud squad. He may have made three times as much as me but he also had five times the stress. I'm more than comfortable doing what I do.'

'Could someone he dealt with have borne a grudge?'

'Maybe. I wouldn't be surprised. You'll have to ask his PA, Selma.'

'Thank you, I will. Do you know anything about your sister-in-law's suicide?'

George grimaced.

'I don't want to speak ill of the dead, but Peter could be unpleasant, especially to women. He was very controlling and several women dumped him before Clara agreed to marry him. I think she suffered from anxiety and depression, and living with Peter tipped her over the edge. It caused something of a split in the family, which hasn't completely healed. Hence part of the difficult atmosphere at dinner.'

'And you left the table during the meal?'

'Yes. Loo break. We all did and no-one was gone for more than five minutes.'

'Thank you, Mr Morrison. That's all for the moment.

It was lunchtime before the SOCOs finished in Peter's bedroom and his body could be removed. With no obvious signs of violence, and the certainty that all those present had been in the room, there was little evidence to collect. All medications and personal care products, from tranquillisers to toothpaste, had been bagged up, just in case they had been tampered with, and tape lifts had been taken of various surfaces to check for nut traces. His Epipen was also collected. The remains of the food served at the dinner were also bagged up for analysis.

DI Brooke examined the crime scene himself, looking for pointers to Peter's death. The bedroom was opulently furnished with a four-poster bed taking centre stage. All manner of extravagant soft furnishings, in clashing colours, combined to produce a suffocating feeling. The bathroom, by contrast, was a model of modernity. Marble surfaces and chrome fittings gleamed and a smoked glass door partitioned off a walk-in shower. Above the Villeroy and Bosch washbasin a shelf held a daunting array of dental care equipment – manual and electric brushes, mirrors, picks, and a long-necked object, about the size of an electric toothbrush, which Brooke didn't recognise. He slipped it into an evidence bag.

---

'What's this?' Brooke asked Melanie, holding up the device he had found in the bathroom.

'It's a water pick. It squirts a jet of water between your teeth to wash out the debris,' she replied, her voice barely audible. 'Peter was obsessed with dental hygiene. He spent a fortune on getting his teeth straightened and whitened. He could be half an hour cleaning them before bedtime.'

She started to sob.

---

Two days later DI Brooke sat in Chief Inspector Drake's office, discussing the case.

'I know how it was done. Someone put peanut powder in his water pick. The lab confirmed this. When he used it, he went into anaphylactic shock. Also, I think someone discharged his Epipen beforehand, so it was useless.'

'OK. Who are the suspects?'

'It has to be those present at the dinner. No-body else could have gained access to his bedroom and the water pick. All four could have inserted the peanut powder when they left the room during dinner and all four could have tampered with his Epipen – Melanie in his room or one of the others while it was on the table.

'I'm discounting Melanie as she would have waited until they were married so she could inherit. I'm not sure George Morrison is as unconcerned about the way Peter bought him out as he claims. Valerie and Rowley would stand to lose their inheritance on Peter's remarriage and this would hurt Rowley particularly – he's in financial and professional trouble. Valerie seems OK, financially, but there are some allegations of incompetence and drinking, on social media.'

'How about the caterers?'

'They delivered the food and left immediately. They didn't go anywhere in the house apart from the kitchen. Melanie served the meal. Anyway, I've had a chat with the pathologist and I know who did it. I expect to make an arrest later today.'

---

'Thank you for coming in Mr Morrison. I'll record this interview, if you don't mind.'

His visitor looked puzzled when Brooke recited the caution and offered him a solicitor, which he declined.

'I'm happy to help, but I don't think I can tell you anything more.'

'Well, you can start by telling me about PKU.'

'What?'

'Phenylketonuria. It's a genetic disease. But, of course, you know that, since you have it.'

Morrison looked cagey.

'So what?'

'Bear with me. I noticed that both you and Miss Myles required a low-protein meal, the type needed by PKU sufferers. I checked with her and she has the same inherited condition. Now, to have it, both parents must have it or be carriers and I was told that your sister-in-law, Clara, was never very well. This got me thinking. I checked Melanie's birth certificate and then the results from the DNA samples we collected. You are her father and you called yourself Morris on the certificate. You had an affair with Clara, presumably some time before she met Peter, and the baby was adopted by Mr and Mrs Myles. The thought of Melanie marrying her uncle was so repugnant that you had to stop the wedding, by any means possible. George Morrison, I'm arresting you on suspicion of murdering Peter Morrison.'

Brooke recited the caution.

Morrison looked aghast, then his shoulders slumped in defeat.

'Yes. It's true. I kept an eye on her as she grew up, discreetly and with the aid of a private investigator. I was so proud of her achievements. When I heard she was to marry Peter I was horrified. I couldn't tell her about her origins. She was so happy with her adoptive family and it would have devastated her. Helen would have found out that I'd cheated on her, too. We had only just got married. Killing him wasn't a difficult decision. I still hated him for shafting me over the business. I knew about his dental obsession so I put peanut powder in his water pick when I left the table, pretending to visit the toilet. I discharged the

Epipen while Rowley wasn't looking and the women were out of the room with Peter, just to make sure. I don't regret a thing.'

As the custody sergeant booked Morrison in, he looked DI Brooke in the eye. 'If it was your daughter, wouldn't you have done the same?' he asked.

Brooke didn't answer.

*Allergens such as peanuts are completely harmless to most people but potentially deadly to individuals allergic to them – an extreme example of the principle that people can react differently to potentially harmful substances.*

# Mind the (Knowledge) Gap

THE INQUIRY CLEARED ME, personally, and I didn't even have to use the Nuremberg defence – that I was only following orders. Emails and records of meetings and conversations, which I had prudently retained, got me off the hook, at least legally, and laid the blame clearly at the doors of company management and certain corrupt officials in other countries. But still...

It wasn't my idea in the first place. It was the kind of thing people speculated about in the bar at conferences. How to develop a new food which could grow anywhere and provide an almost complete meal. *New Scientist* magazine occasionally ran speculative articles on the topic, as well as featuring similar ideas in a cartoon strip, *Grimbledon Down,* which ran in the magazine during the 1970s. But the Director of our lab must have picked the idea up, thought about it over a few drinks, and pitched it to several biotechnology companies. Against all odds, one of them took it forward.

I tried to explain about the knowledge gap. We knew a lot about manipulating genes. After all, we'd been doing it since the last century. But this was different. The idea was to insert drought-resistance genes, from a new, engineered, strain of wheat, into a potato, as well as lentil genes, which would increase the protein content. Adding a few tomato genes could boost the vitamin C levels and maybe a few bean genes would produce folic acid. Some clover could enable it to produce its own fertiliser, by attracting bacteria to the crop's roots which would fix nitrogen from the air.

The result would be a highly nutritious potato crop, that could grow in a wide variety of environments. Coincidentally, it would also be ideal for making crisps, or chips as our backers called them. They had already been trademarked as 'Maga-chips'. Less frivolously, the crop could provide extremely valu-able nutrition for people in a wide range of countries.

What we didn't know was how to combine such a range of genes in the same organism without causing problems. Would they be compatible? Would one lot cancel out the other? Were we simply getting above ourselves with a pick 'n' mix approach to genetics? Knowledgeable as we were about the subject, there were massive areas of ignorance. But we were well-funded, by people who believed that throwing money at a problem would automatically solve it. Clearly, they weren't scientists.

So, we attacked the problem, day and night, working in shifts. As I suspected, trying to shove all these alien genes into the humble potato didn't work. Either the plant didn't grow at all, or it produced weird vegetables which proved inedible. Genetically speaking, it looked like too many cooks were spoiling the spud. The problems kept all the senior scientists on the project awake at nights, as well as a good few of the junior ones. We tried using promoter genes – those which made other genes do their job – from all the plants involved but that made no difference. Then I had an idea. Every organism has loads of junk DNA – stuff which doesn't seem to do anything. Perhaps the answer was there?

I spent weeks mucking around with DNA from all the plants involved, culturing cells in the lab rather than growing the full crops, in order to save time. I did occasionally ask myself whether it was worth it. Perhaps we didn't need to know how to do such bizarre things as this. Eventually, I found something promising and produced the first Superspud. Somehow, I knew it would work. Hubris, indeed.

So, we grew a test crop in a secret, closely guarded, field in Lincolnshire, and ran the usual animal tests. I'd never seen such healthy, well-nourished lab rats as those fed on our creation. We did chemical tests to make sure the desired nutrients were present, and also ruled out many undesirable substances. Green lights, throughout. But there was still a major trial to be done. Could humans eat Superspuds?

I tried to explain to our backers that there could be problems. That we shouldn't rush things. This was a completely new food, after all. But the American company was desperate to get the product to market ahead of their Chinese rivals who, it was rumoured, were working along the same lines.

'Don't worry,' they said. 'We don't have to do the tests in Europe or the US. There's plenty of countries in Africa or Central America where we have influence. They'll welcome a couple of schools and the odd hospital, in return for letting us run a few speedy field trials.'

So, we grew several tonnes of Superspuds, producing seed potatoes for trials in a small Central American country. Initial results showed that they grew quicker than expected, and publicity videos circulated by the company showed bountiful yields. Hundreds of people eagerly came forward to try them.

All was looking well, and the lab Director was rumoured to be preparing her Nobel Prize acceptance speech.

The next videos didn't come from the company, though. They came from activists and, eventually, from mainstream news media. And they paralysed me with horror.

You see, the potato is closely related to the Deadly Nightshade plant. This was of little significance in the chilly fields of Lincolnshire but, in the warmer soils of Central America, a particular gene unexpectedly switched on. The gene that produces the deadly poison, atropine. I will never forget those images of children and adults, stumbling around outside the test canteens, barely able to see, gasping for water, hallucinating and tearing their clothes off as they overheated.

The project was abandoned, the company was prosecuted and our lab was closed down, fortunately without any individuals going to prison. But someone, obviously a disgruntled employee, had graffitied a few words on the boarded-up building, words which I could only agree with. *Knowledge may be power, but when ignorance is bliss, 'tis folly to be wise.*

---

*This is really a piece of science fiction and whether a gene for atropine synthesis could appear in a potato is debatable. It does, however, suggest that manipulating genes willy-nilly could have unforeseen consequences.*

# Peace and Quiet

It wasn't really murder. Just an adjustment. Restoring some calm to David's little corner of the universe. He had been close to the edge for so long. He had to do something.

He loved his parents, he supposed, and wasn't really looking forward to life without them. But he had known, for some time, that he couldn't live with their constant bickering and arguing. That's why he was standing over their cooling corpses, a pillow in his hand, and an expression of sheer relief on his face.

---

David had always been a quiet child – reserved and unemotional. At school he was described as 'no trouble' and got on with his work diligently and reasonably competently, preferring to stay in the school library rather than stand in the noisy playground at break time. He didn't make friends easily, not trusting other children whose brashness and occasional cruelty he found threatening. He wasn't bullied physically but the taunts of 'loser', 'weirdo' and 'no-mates' were just as painful as

141

punches in the gut. He managed to stay on for A-levels and did well, but he was only too glad to leave. He couldn't face the stress of university; all those new people, strange surroundings and demanding tutors.

At home, he felt unthreatened and secure because neither of his parents was loud or volatile, unlike the characters in the soap operas which ran daily on the television. They were polite to each other and any criticisms were mild. He never heard blazing rows – or declarations of adoration for that matter – and he was never the target of verbal or physical attacks. He felt accepted, rather than loved, and the bland atmosphere suited him since the thought of powerful emotions was frightening.

Girls passed him by, literally and figuratively. There was nothing wrong with his appearance but he held no attraction for the opposite sex. In any case, the prospect of talking to a girl, let alone forming a relationship with one, horrified him. Too messy. Too emotional. He had no male friends either – he couldn't talk about football, cars, or beer and had no hobbies or experiences which would interest the others. No-one invited him to parties or the pub and he spent his lunch breaks surfing on his iPhone in the corner of the office rather than chatting with colleagues in the canteen.

Nevertheless, David was more or less content with his lot. After months of scanning the job ads in the papers and calling in at the job centre, he had managed to secure an admin job with the local council. He dealt with applications for bus passes and blue badges for disabled drivers and also licences for buskers and other street activities. It suited David because none of these tasks involved direct contact with people, and he was happy to sit in front of his computer all day. The job paid him enough to live on, although staff cuts and redundancies had imposed unrealistic workloads on him and his colleagues. David just kept his head down and worked harder, without complaint, avoiding stressful conversations with aggrieved colleagues who feared for their jobs and their health.

Things began to change when the work of his department was outsourced to a private company which provided a wide range of services, such as prisons, immigration detention centres and aspects of social care, previously the province of the public sector. While his colleagues joked about working for 'Rentathug', referring to recent assaults in penal institutions run by the company, David couldn't control a mounting sense of unease. This became justified as, despite promises to preserve existing conditions, it was clear that the new employer's management culture was one of challenge, conflict and bullying. He now had to work longer hours for less pay and was often given new tasks to do for which he was neither trained nor prepared.

David lasted five and a half weeks before collapsing under the strain. He simply walked out one morning, avoiding any contact with his colleagues. He was deemed 'voluntarily unemployed' by the DWP and hence ineligible for benefits for some considerable time. He realised he was unlikely to find a new job he could cope with, so he couldn't afford to keep his small rented flat which had been a haven of calm for him. Three years after he had left, he moved back in with his parents.

Things had changed in the meantime. His father had lost his job with Royal Mail and his mother had been made redundant from her post as church secretary at St Matthew's when the parish was combined with St Mark's. They didn't object to his return, but, he sensed, they were less than thrilled to have him there.

He became listless, and anxious, and lacking motivation to do anything that involved leaving his room. His parents persuaded him to see a doctor and an overworked locum GP put him on diazepam, despite the practice's usual reluctance to prescribe it. David took the drug at first, and kept on cashing the prescriptions, although he didn't really enjoy the wooziness it produced and eventually consigned the tablets to the back of a drawer.

The atmosphere at home was no longer the emotional millpond he remembered from childhood. His parents were clearly getting on one another's nerves and also resented not having jobs. At first they tried to keep their disagreements private. Annoyed glances, muttered comments to each other which he was not meant to hear, and the low rumble of complaints when they were in bed and thought he was asleep. His presence seemed like sand in a gearbox and his psychological security was being ground away at an increasing rate.

Whether it was his presence or their enforced proximity that aggravated the situation, he couldn't tell, but, over the succeeding months, the Cold War between his parents escalated into overt hostilities. From breakfast to bedtime his father moaned to his wife about her appearance, her cooking, the ironing, the cleanliness of the house and her failure to get the shopping he wanted. He never considered doing any of these tasks himself – the New Man concept had completely passed him by.

For her part, his mother complained that her husband got under her feet, never gave her time to think and did nothing to improve the deteriorating state of the house. 'Why don't you buy some bloody wallpaper and stick it up, you lazy sod,' she yelled on one occasion, countered by 'You know where you can bleedin' stick it' – sentiments and language which profoundly unsettled David. They started to get at him too. 'Why don't you go out and get a job/some exercise/a girlfriend' were repeated refrains and all they did was force him further into the cocoon-like protection of his room.

David's childhood interest in World War Two aircraft had been rekindled by documentaries on TV and films on the internet. He spent hours watching flickering footage of Spitfires, Hurricanes, Messerschmitts, Lancasters and Dorniers on his computer. He ordered model kits online and his room became festooned with aircraft engaged in dogfights. Whenever his parents looked in on him, they moaned about damage to the wallpaper from his posters and the screws in the ceiling which supported his aircraft. He simply slammed the door on them.

The house's thin walls offered little insulation from the noise of rows. Even in bed his parents would still attack each other loudly over perceived shortcomings, be they cleanliness, attractiveness or sexual ability. They didn't think to moderate the volume when talking about intimate matters, which embarrassed David all the more. All he could do was turn up the volume on his computer in an attempt to drown out the insults. He grew to love the sound of machine-gun fire.

When his parents were not yelling at each other they had the television on too loud. A procession of antiques experts, property gurus, debt enforcers, quiz contestants and wannabe minor celebs paraded through the living room during the day, while soaps and emotional dramas dominated the evening.

The TV's noise had a physical effect on him, but much worse was the emotional tension in the house. As soon as he and his parents were in the same room together, his heart rate went up, he started to sweat, his limbs trembled and a dizziness took over his brain. Every complaint and insult they directed at each other felt like a knitting needle shoved into his ear. As they argued their faces distorted into masks of hatred while a shrieking noise built up in David's head. His father's sneering attitude towards his wife, and his mother's contemptuous glare in return, were like slaps to David's face and, before long, he could no longer tolerate their company. He spent more and more time in his room, coming out only to wash, eat and use the toilet.

Disturbing thoughts began to seep into his brain. They started as whispers but gradually became more insistent, pushing him closer and closer to the edge of sanity.

'What's happened to them?'

'Why don't they shut up?'

'Why are they torturing me like this?'

'Why don't they divorce?'

'They'd be better off apart.'

'They'd be better off without me.'

'I'd be better off without them.'

'They'd be better off dead.'

'There'd be peace and quiet if they were dead.'

'All I want is peace and quiet.'

At first David brushed these thoughts away. He didn't analyse his feelings but he knew that they had been brutally damaged by the constant rows and incessant noise. He considered moving out, but his room was the only place he felt safe and he couldn't bear the idea of leaving it. He couldn't afford to live anywhere else, anyway. But, day after day, the thoughts came screaming into his head, building up the pressure like in an overheated boiler about to explode. Eventually David could see no way to preserve his sanity while his parents lived. He convinced himself that they were so unhappy that they would prefer to die. The voices in his head agreed with him and he became unable to tell the difference between his own thoughts and the whispers.

One evening in September, David resolved to help them on

their way. He was not a violent man, despite the murderous thoughts that crowded into his brain. Knives, blunt instruments and strangulation were out of the question while firearms and lethal poisons were unobtainable. But, then again, he did have the diazepam. That was poisonous wasn't it? He'd read somewhere that anything can be a poison – it's only the dose which differentiates a medicine from a poison.

A few minutes research online showed David that it could be difficult to kill his parents with his medication. The tablets he had accumulated might prove lethal, especially if taken with alcohol, but getting his parents to swallow a fatal dose would be difficult. A smaller dose, however, would render them unconscious, or at least incapable of resistance to another method of killing, should one be necessary.

The problem was how to get them to take the drug. Crushing the tablets and adding them to a drink might work but there could be an unpleasant taste or even a visible residue. His parents drank wine in the evening, but a quick experiment revealed that even the cheap brands his parents drank tasted funny when a few tablets were added. They weren't wine connoisseurs, but they would probably notice. Food was the best option, if he could find something with a strong enough flavour to disguise the presence of the drug.

Browsing through the fridge when his parents had gone to bed, he spotted a chicken curry ready meal for two – perfect! In his room he ground up his remaining tablets between two spoons. With intense concentration he peeled back the film on the plastic tray and stirred the white powder into the curry, mixing thoroughly until the sauce completely disguised it. He then cleaned the edges of the film and glued the package shut with his modelling adhesive. It wouldn't stand up to the closest examination but, as his parents would undoubtedly be arguing while the food was cooked and served, he didn't think they would notice.

The following evening David ordered a takeaway pizza and didn't leave his room to eat – a frequent occurrence in recent weeks. He listened carefully to his parents sniping at each other, the ping of the microwave and the clatter of cutlery on plates. Gradually, the backbiting diminished and things became quiet. David gave it another half hour and tiptoed downstairs.

His parents had made it to the living room and were both unconscious in their recliner chairs in front of the television. He checked for pulses in their necks. They were still alive. Damn! They hadn't taken enough. He had to finish the job, so, steeling himself, he grabbed a pillow from his room. He first suffocated his father, whose arms flapped feebly as he struggled futilely through the drug-induced fog. His mother offered no resistance at all. Muting the television sound, David stepped serenely out of the room, a sublime sense of bliss pervading his entire being. He wasn't pleased to have killed – that was just incidental. He was just so, so glad that the arguments had stopped.

———

Five days later, the police broke down the door after the postie had reported the smell of decay – a smell which, evidently, had not bothered David. They found two rotting corpses apparently watching a silent programme about moving to the country and David in his room with a tranquil smile on his face.

'You wouldn't believe it, Sarge,' reported PC Wadworth. 'The two of them were crawling with maggots and stank to high heaven. The PCSO with me threw up and I'll never get the smell of rotting flesh out of my uniform.'

'What about the son?'

'He was in his room, just sitting there, peacefully. He hadn't responded to our knock and didn't come down when we put the door in. I couldn't move for model planes hanging from the ceiling. It was like the Battle of Britain in miniature in there.

'So you reckon he killed them?'

'No doubt about it. He told me he put drugs in their curry and held a pillow over their faces, just to make sure. I told him I was going to arrest him, and he just smiled.'

'Did he say anything when you cautioned him?'

'Only 'I just needed peace and quiet. Peace and quiet'.'

'He won't get much of that where he's going. Take him to the custody sergeant, put him in a cell and call the duty solicitor.'


David sat on the steel toilet, hidden from the CCTV that covered the rest of his cell. He peeled back the plaster at the top of his thigh and eased out the tiny modelling blade he had hidden there when it dawned on him that he would end up in a noisy prison. Sliding it along the veins in his wrists, his only thought was 'Peace and quiet. At last.'


*Another, tragic, example of a medicine also being a poison. Diazepam is now prescribed much less frequently as it can cause serious addiction issues.*

# The Venomous Bead

ROGER HAD TO DIE, of course. I'd realised, from the way he'd been behaving recently, that he knew something was up. He spent hours obsessively poring over documents and spreadsheets, barely talking to me. It was only a matter of time before he blamed me for the huge hole in our business accounts. That would mean disgrace, prison and the loss of everything I'd worked for. And I couldn't have that, could I?

We started our business, selling chemical cleaning products to local authorities, care homes and commercial companies, when we left university. I was the chemist, he was the business brain, and the firm flourished for several years. Then came 'austerity', forcing councils and companies to cut corners. We suffered because our products, although better and more environmentally-friendly than those of our competitors, were considered too expensive. We refused to compromise on quality, hoping that things would improve and we would be making reasonable profits again.

Meanwhile, I'd acquired a house, a sports car and a glamorous girlfriend, all of which cost a fortune to run. It's the old story. I borrowed money from the company intending to pay it back. As repayment became increasingly unlikely, I started to falsify paperwork and do 'off the books' deals with clients which never appeared in the accounts, although the stock inventory shrank rapidly.

I knew I had little time left. I'd been able to fob Roger off at first – 'Some customers haven't paid,' 'Someone's been pilfering stock,' 'The temp mixed up the invoicing' – but I realised he would soon see through my smokescreen and discover the £80,000 shortfall. I was hardly sleeping at night. Despite the extra alcohol I was drinking, I was losing weight. I was becoming increasingly irritable and I feared that my beloved Jasmine would soon look elsewhere for a partner. I really had no option but to dispose of Roger.

So how could I do it? I was reasonably fit, but attacking Roger physically would be difficult. Blunt instruments and knives were messy and I knew, from true crime documentaries, that it is extraordinarily difficult to get rid of all DNA traces. I wouldn't know how to sabotage a car, and starting a fire could kill his wife as well as Roger. I do have some scruples. Anyway, he might escape. That just left poison. But which one? You couldn't get arsenic or cyanide from a pharmacy, like in Agatha Christie's day, and, although we were a chemical company, buying something toxic, for which we normally have no use, would look suspicious. Then a distant memory came back to me. Abrin. Found in bright red seeds once used to make rosaries. And highly toxic. I'd read about it in Ian Fleming's *You only live twice* and it seemed perfect, as Roger's late mother, a devout Catholic, was always fiddling with the red and black beads on her rosary. I'll bet he kept it after she died. He's quite sentimental about his mother and is a Catholic himself. Five minutes on the internet confirmed the beads' identity and bingo! – I had my murder weapon.

I needed to steal the rosary, but taking just that would have looked suspicious, so I faked an ordinary burglary. Roger kept family memorabilia in a marquetry box on a table in his ground-floor study at the back of the house. I knew that he usually left the French doors to the back garden unlocked until he went to bed, and I could approach them from the lane running behind the house. The job looked simple.

I planned every detail meticulously. On a Friday, fifteen days before the planned murder date, I cycled out, wearing the standard burglar's kit of dark clothes, trainers and, once off the street, a balaclava. Hiding my bike under bushes in the lane, I put on latex gloves and wrapped plastic bags around my feet to blur any shoe prints. I crept up to the house, keeping low and avoiding the garden furniture, whose positions I'd memorised. A noise in the shrubbery made me freeze. I turned. A pair of eyes, bright green, reflected the pale moonlight. It was only Roger's cat, regarding me with a level of disdain that only cats can achieve. When my heartbeat had dropped back a little, I resumed my mission.

Roger and his wife were great ones for routine. I chose a time when I knew he would be watching television and his wife would be visiting her sister – a weekly occurrence. I would have at least an hour to do the job, but I knew I would only need a few minutes.

The French doors opened without a sound, and my feet were almost silent on the carpet. I could hear the noise of a crime drama on the television in the lounge and I relaxed slightly. Roger was unlikely to disturb me. Using only the light from a small torch, I grabbed Roger's laptop and an iPod from the desk, and scooped up the box from the table, checking that the rosary was there. It joined the tech, and a small antique carriage clock, in my rucksack. I crept out, closing the doors with a faint click, and sneaked back to the lane, hardly believing I'd succeeded.

Cycling home I was filled with a mixture of euphoria and terror. Anything that looked like a blue light sent my heartbeat through the roof, and it wasn't until I locked my bike in the garage that I could breathe normally.

I knocked back a large Scotch and examined my haul. There was probably incriminating material on Roger's laptop. I would have liked to have known how much he knew but I didn't have his password and I'm not one of those IT geeks who can run through a few suggestions and crack it on the final try, like in the movies. It would disappear into the river, along with the box and the other stolen items. But I had got what I needed and, in a couple of weeks' time, Roger would die.

---

Roger always ate a late takeaway curry in front of the television while watching the Saturday night football. He would have a vindaloo or a madras – good, strong flavours. His wife would have a korma or a biryani in the kitchen. If I intercepted the delivery guy, I could poison his curry and Roger wouldn't notice the taste. The initial symptoms could be put down to food poisoning, and suspicions would only arise after he died. By then, the curry containers would have been taken away with the rubbish on Monday morning. Removing his laptop had probably hidden some evidence of a motive on my part, and had certainly delayed his investigations, but I would also have to stage a fire at the office to cover my tracks completely.

I prepared the rosary seeds according to instructions I found on the dark web, protecting myself with latex gloves and a dust mask, and sealed the poison in a plastic pot. The protective items, the equipment I used, and the string from the rosary, went in a plastic bag which I dropped in a litter bin a mile from my home. I had the poison, and a plan for delivering it. The alibi came next.

Proving I was somewhere else at the crucial time would be difficult, but I figured that a little leeway would be OK. People jogged in the local park, even late on a September Saturday. I had started doing the same, wearing a distinctive running shirt, as soon as I devised my plan. The park was fifteen minutes walk from Roger's house but I could cycle it in four. It was also covered by CCTV cameras, following a series of muggings. I went over the plan repeatedly and reckoned it would work – provided that no-one saw me doing anything suspicious. I could only hope.

———

Killing time! Shaking with fear, I cycled off with a hoodie over my running shirt, a baseball cap pulled down over my eyes and a pair of plain glasses in my pocket. I left my bike in bushes at the edge of the park, with my 'disguise,' and jogged around for a few minutes, taking care to be picked up by the CCTV cameras. Once out of their range I doubled back, unseen, put on my hoodie and cap and cycled furiously to Roger's house.

Leaving the bike in the lane, I put on the glasses and some latex gloves and hid behind some trees in the front garden until I heard the delivery driver's motorbike. As he approached, I walked along the path as if I was Roger returning home.

'Thanks, mate,' I said, taking the bag of food from him with my cap pulled down and my face shadowed by the light above Roger's door. 'See you next week, OK?'

I put on Roger's London accent, gambling on the fact that the driver was one of many used by the restaurant and wouldn't realise I wasn't him.

Once the driver was clear, I opened Roger's vindaloo and thoroughly mixed in the poison. I closed the tray, put everything back in the bag and left it on the doorstep before ringing the bell and clearing off. Roger would assume that the driver was in a hurry and, since the food was already paid for by credit card, didn't need to wait.

Then it was back to the park as fast as I could cycle, sweat pouring off me and my heart hammering. Wearing my running shirt I set off, timing my appearance at the first camera as if I had been jogging out of range all this time. On the way home, I dropped the gloves, the glasses and the poison pot in a builder's skip.

At home it was clean-up time. I put the cap and hoodie in a plastic bag, to be dumped in a clothing bank in the morning, and showered thoroughly. Then I settled down to catch up with the TV I would have seen before and after my jog. I'd done it! I'd bloody done it! All I had to do was wait for Roger to die, torch the office, attend the funeral and get on with my life.

---

'I'm not sure that curry was quite right,' complained Roger, pouring himself a second whisky. 'It didn't taste the same as usual and I'm feeling a bit odd.'

His wife shrugged.

'Mine was fine. Perhaps they've got a new chef. I'm surprised you can taste anything in a dish that fiery. But you've been a bit peaky recently anyway, haven't you?'

'No. Not really. Just a few odd things at work I need to look into. Nothing for you to worry about.'

He smiled reassuringly.

'I think I'll get an early night. I'm feeling increasingly queasy.'

'OK, Roger,' replied Eloise. 'I'll join you shortly.'

Half an hour later, as she was getting ready for bed, she heard Roger vomiting and calling for help.

'Christ, Roger! What's the matter with you?'

'Sick. The shits,' he mumbled, clutching his stomach in agony.'

'Right. I'm phoning 111.'

Ten minutes later, she got through to the NHS helpline and described Roger's symptoms. She listened intently to the advisor, then turned to her husband.

'You have to go to hospital, they said. I'm calling an ambulance.'

Forty minutes later, an ambulance arrived and she followed it anxiously to A and E.

Two days later, Roger died.

---

'I thought it was supposed to be a dodgy curry, Sarge.'

'It was, constable, but it was dodgy 'cos it was poisoned,' replied Detective Sergeant Dave Shaw, as they waited for the briefing to start.

A dozen DCs and civilian support staff lounged, sat or sprawled around the stuffy incident room, perking up when DI Vernon cleared his throat and started to speak.

'Roger Meredith, aged 37, married with no kids. Home address The Laurels, Woodfield Drive. Co-director of a company that sells cleaning products. Taken ill after eating a curry on Saturday night and admitted to hospital. Died on Tuesday in the Royal Infirmary of poisoning by a substance as yet unknown.'

'At first the hospital suspected food poisoning,' continued Vernon, 'but they did a PM as he hadn't seen a doctor recently. The pathologist was suspicious because his lungs were full of fluid and tests on his vomit revealed no traces of infection. Samples have gone to a specialist lab at the Uuniversity for further analysis. The results will take a while to come back, but we're working on the assumption that he was murdered.'

'Who's in the frame, guv?' asked Shaw.

'No-one immediately obvious,' replied Vernon. 'We need to talk to his wife Eloise, then his business partner, Richard Murdoch, the restaurant owner and the delivery driver. Speak to any relatives and find out if they know of any problems in the family. We also need to contact the environmental health department and all the nearby hospitals to check whether there have been any similar cases. Neighbours will have to be interviewed, but they probably didn't see anything suspicious. Find the empty curry containers. Someone check with Companies House and HMRC to see if there's anything useful about the firm's finances. Divide up the tasks please, Dave. I'll take a Family Liaison Officer and talk to the wife, then I'll see his business partner. We'll meet back here at five o'clock.'

'I know that address, guv,' said DC Trengrove, intercepting

the DI as he was leaving the room. 'They had a burglary there two weeks or so ago – I'll check when and what was taken.'

'Thanks – that's interesting. We'll see if there's a connection.'

———

'I'm very sorry for your loss, Mrs Meredith.'

Eloise barely noticed the time-worn phrase as she showed Vernon and the Family Liaison Officer into the living room. The house was clean and tidy. Apart from a few condolence cards on a mantelpiece, there was little to suggest there had been a death in the family.

'I realise it's painful, but can you run through exactly what happened on Saturday night?' Vernon asked.

'Yes, of course. Our curries were delivered as usual. We always eat late on a Saturday, after a round of golf and drinks at the club house. Roger watched the football and I talked to my Mum on Skype, then surfed the net – football bores me. After the match Roger had his usual whisky and we went to bed. During the night he threw up and, a bit later, the diarrhoea started. He was in so much distress that I phoned 111. They said to get him to hospital and the ambulance arrived 40 minutes later. You know what happened after that.'

'Did you see the delivery driver?'

'No – he'd gone by the time Roger opened the door. He rang the bell and left the food on the doorstep. I guess he was in a hurry.'

'Did Roger have any enemies – at work for instance?'

'I shouldn't think so. His staff seem a happy bunch and Richard, his partner, has been his best friend since school. I suppose he didn't have many friends. He was a bit reserved. He would chat to people at the golf club but he wasn't close to any of them. Richard was the person who knew him best.'

'Had Roger seemed any different recently?'

'Well, he'd been a bit moody. Funnily enough, I asked him about it the night he was poisoned. He just said there was something going on at work which he had to investigate.'

'Did he discuss it with you?'

'No. We had a kind of unofficial rule. No shop talk at home. I didn't like to ask.'

'Tell me about the burglary – what was taken?'

'Just items that Roger kept in his study. A laptop, an iPod, an antique clock. Oh, and a box of family memorabilia.'

'What was in that?'

'Only oddments, really. His grandfather's medals, his father's gold watch, some religious bits and bobs of his mother's, a few photos and some cheap costume jewellery.'

'Were you at home at the time?'

'Roger was, probably watching some crime drama. I was at my sister's. The burglar came in through the unlocked French doors and Roger didn't hear him.'

'Thank you – is there anything else you can tell me?'

'Sorry, no.'

The DI left his card, asking her to get in touch if anything else occurred to her. *Not exactly the grieving widow,* he thought, as he drove back to the station. *Anyone would think she'd lost an unloved hamster, not a husband. We'll need to look more closely at the bereaved Mrs Meredith.*

At Richard Murdoch's home, a mock-Tudor semi in a wealthy part of town, there was no-one in and no car on the drive. Peering through the small widow in the side of the garage, Vernon spotted an expensive bicycle but no car. He drove to the firm's business address, a single-storey building on a small industrial estate that had seen better days. A Mercedes was parked on the forecourt and a notice on the half-glazed door advised that the premises were closed. Vernon knocked anyway. A few moments later, a face appeared.

'Mr Murdoch?'

'Sorry, we're closed.'

'Detective Inspector Vernon, sir,' he said, showing his warrant card. 'I'd like to ask you a few questions about your partner's death?'

'OK. You'd better come in. It's all been very distressing and I don't see how I can help.'

'How did you get on with Mr Meredith?'

'Great. We were best mates. We've known each other for years.'

'Had he seemed any different to you recently?'

'He's been a bit down as sales have fallen off. We're still solvent, but everyone's suffering at the moment'.

'Are there any business rivals who could have wanted to harm him?'

'God, no – we sell cleaning chemicals, not crack.'

'What will happen to the business now?'

'I guess Richard's half will go to Eloise and I'll work with her until she decides what to do with it.'

'OK. Just routine, but can you tell me what you were doing on Saturday night between nine and eleven?'

'Sure,' replied Richard, readily. 'I watched television after dinner and went jogging around ten. The doctor said I should get more exercise as my job's pretty sedentary. I use the local park – it's quiet in the late evening and the CCTV cameras deter muggers. I got home about eleven, had a shower and a beer. Then I watched some more TV and went to bed. I can tell you what I watched if you like.'

'That's OK, sir – I don't think we need that. You live alone, then?'

'Much of the time. My girlfriend, Jasmine Corwell, is a flight attendant with Worldfly and she's away a lot on long-haul trips. We meet up whenever we can.'

'I see. Well, that's all for now but we'll be in touch again.'

As Vernon left he noticed a brightly striped running shirt in the back of what he assumed was Murdoch's car. He noted the registration number and returned to the station.

---

The five o'clock briefing room was buzzing. One by one the detectives reported the results of their enquiries. No similar cases had been reported locally and the restaurant owner was indignant at the suggestion that his food was the culprit – he had served eleven vindaloos that night and no-one had complained. The delivery driver swore that he had handed the food to the customer 'wearing a hoodie, glasses and a cap' on the doorstep before driving off. He had previous for petty theft but seemed truthful. The neighbours saw nothing and the rubbish bins were empty.

'There's one oddity,' DC Wells reported. 'You said that Mrs Meredith was at her sister's during the burglary. I spoke to her and she told me she hasn't seen Eloise in the evening for months. She used to visit every Friday, and they'd have a glass of wine or two, but that stopped. There wasn't a falling out –

Eloise kept making excuses. Apparently, they meet for lunch from time to time instead.'

'Curious' said Vernon. 'I'll talk to Eloise again.'

'How about the business partner, guv?' asked Shaw.

'I'm not ruling him out. He claims to have an alibi for when the curry was delivered and was keen to share it. Perhaps too keen. Can you get someone to check CCTV in the park and around Meredith's house – look for a man in a hoodie and baseball cap plus any suspicious vehicles. Watch for Murdoch's car and, in the park, look for someone in a striped running shirt. Oh, it might be worth talking to his girlfriend in case he's been behaving oddly of late or has had a row with Roger. I'll give you her details. Back here, 1 pm tomorrow, everyone, please.'

---

When Vernon called on Eloise that evening she seemed nervous.

'You misled me about your visit to your sister, Mrs Meredith. She told us that she hasn't seen you on a Friday for quite some time.'

Eloise coloured and fidgeted.

'I suppose I knew you'd find out. It's true. I was planning to leave Roger but I couldn't tell him. He wouldn't have agreed to a divorce – his family's Catholic. I've met someone else and we want to make a new life together. That's what I was doing on the computer when Roger was poisoned – looking for places to escape to. Although he was a bit colourless, and dreadfully boring with his football and his business, I couldn't hate Roger. I would never have done anything to harm him. I didn't want him dead. I just wanted to escape to something more exciting.'

'I'll need your friend's name and address – we'll want to talk to him about his movements on Saturday. And, remember, it's an offence to obstruct the police.'

---

The following day Vernon kicked off the briefing.

'We have a prime suspect – Eloise. She was planning to leave Roger for a man called Peter Groves. She has motive and opportunity but I don't know about the means. Can you speak to Groves, Shaw, and get him to account for his movements? Oh, and get Roger's whisky bottle tested for poison.'

'OK guv.'

There was little else to report. Richard's car had been nowhere near Roger's house and there was no sign of a hooded man. Park CCTV confirmed the presence of a man running in a striped shirt at around the time of the delivery, although he was out of sight of the cameras at the critical moments. Jasmine Corwell was in Hong Kong and would be returning the following day. DC Trengrove left her a Voicemail, asking her to get in touch.

---

Nothing more happened until the next morning, when Vernon had a phone call. He listened intently for ten minutes, scribbling furiously on his notepad, and immediately called the team together.

'I've just had a call from a pharmacologist at the university. She's fascinated by obscure poisons and has analysed the samples. She can't be absolutely sure but she thinks she knows what killed Roger. Abrin.'

'What's that when it's at home?'

163

'It's a plant poison – a bit like ricin.'

Blank looks greeted this comparison.

'You know – Georgi Markov and the KGB killing on Waterloo Bridge. Originally thought to be an umbrella firing a pellet. Anyone?'

Realisation spread across a few faces in the room.

'Where do you get this stuff – not in Boots, surely,' quipped one DC.

Vernon frowned at him.

'It's found in plant seeds called jequirity beans or rosary peas. The plant doesn't grow in Britain but it's common in India, Florida and other hot areas.'

'Why rosary peas?' asked DC Trengrove.

'Because they were often threaded onto wire or cotton to make rosaries.'

'Some religious items were taken in the burglary,' said Trengrove. 'Could one of them have been a rosary?'

'Good thinking – that could be our murder weapon. Ask Eloise if there was one in the stolen box. So the killer, if it is the burglar, must have known that the rosary was there and also that the beans are poisonous. It has to be either the wife, the lover or the partner.'

'But Murdoch has an alibi' interrupted Shaw. 'And why not Eloise's sister? Could Roger have harmed her in some way? She would probably have known about the box and Roger's habits.'

'Murdoch's alibi does look solid, but he has a bike and could have got from the park to Meredith's house and back in plenty of time to reappear when expected on the CCTV. He's a chemist and he may have known about abrin. Also, the company was in trouble – no accounts have been filed at Companies House for two years and HMRC are owed thousands in back taxes and VAT.'

'If he was fiddling the books and Roger found out, that could be a motive,' suggested Shaw.

'OK. Let's get a search warrant for Murdoch's home and office and take a look at his, Eloise's and Groves' finances. Groves was out of the country at the time of the murder, but he and Eloise could have been conspiring. I'll pop round and have a chat with Murdoch tonight and we'll have another go at Eloise tomorrow morning. And, you're right, Dave, we'd better talk to the sister again, just in case she had motive and opportunity. Has Murdoch's girlfriend been in touch?'

'Yes, guv,' replied Trengrove. 'She'll come in for an interview tomorrow. Interestingly, she was out of the country on both the night of the burglary and the night Roger was killed.'

---

A bleary-eyed and nervous-looking Richard opened the door to the DI at nine-thirty.

'Good evening, sir – sorry to trouble you again but can you spare me a few more minutes?'

'If I must. It's rather late and I'm tired.'

Murdoch seemed to have trouble meeting the detective's gaze.

'It's just that there are a few points I need to clear up. Tomorrow will do, if you prefer. I'd be grateful if you'd call in at the police station. Would eleven a.m. be convenient?'

Murdoch licked his lips. 'Twelve would be better.'

'Twelve noon it is, then. Thank you, sir. Good night.'

Something about Murdoch's manner troubled Vernon, so he parked a few yards along the road with his lights off. Moments later, Murdoch dashed to his car carrying a plastic container and took off at speed. Vernon followed at a distance, unsurprised to see Murdoch pulling up outside his office.

Listening at the partly opened door, Vernon heard the sound of liquid sloshing about. A strong solvent smell drifted out. Hurling himself through the door he rugby-tackled Murdoch before he could light the bundle of rags held in his gloved hand.

'Richard Murdoch, I am arresting you for attempted arson,' said Vernon, cautioning him as the handcuffs clicked.

---

At the station next afternoon, Vernon summed up the case against Murdoch.

'Murdoch is up against it, financially. His bank account is deeply in the red and his credit cards are maxed out. The company accounts show a series of large and unexplained withdrawals. If Roger realised what has been going on, Murdoch would have been ruined. So there's motive.

'The forensic guys found traces of red material in his garage. Bits of rosary pea. Even more tellingly, the search team found Murdoch's fitness tracker which showed periods of frenzied activity around the curry delivery time with a stationary period, marked by a fast heartbeat, between them.

'The tracker records are consistent with him cycling from the park to Roger's, waiting anxiously for the driver and cycling back after poisoning the curry. The idiot forgot to take it off when he committed the murder. He'll enjoy wearing that around the prison exercise yard.'

Several officers chuckled.

'Anyway, faced with the evidence against him, Murdoch

confessed and the CPS has authorised a charge of murder as well as arson, so it's off to the pub. First round's on me.'

―――――

*The rosary beads are, of course, not venomous; they are poisonous. In some jurisdictions abrin is classified as a biological weapon. The title is a reference to the history parody by Sellars and Yeatman, '1066 and all that'!*

# Scum

'Mummy, I feel sick and I need the toilet.'

Five-year-old Kieran Worsley clutched at his stomach in obvious distress, as the family's camper van eased its way into the M6 traffic jam heading south.

'Well you should have gone before we left,' said his mother, exasperated, as she passed him an empty plastic sandwich box.

'If you need to be sick, use this. But try and hold on until we reach the services. We'll stop then.'

Her exhortations had no effect and the air was soon filled with the smell of sick as the boy vomited noisily.

'Eeeugh,' squealed his sister, sitting beside him. 'He's pooed as well.'

'Nothing but trouble all holiday, that kid,' muttered his father. 'Losing his trainers, chasing a sheep, falling into the lake before breakfast, and now this.'

He opened the van's front windows to let in some cleaner air.

'He does look rough, Doug,' his wife remonstrated, looking

back at her youngest with growing concern. 'Can we pull off somewhere and clean him up?'

She reached for Kieran's hand.'

'Never mind, sweetie. You must have eaten something bad. You'll feel better soon.'

Kieran's alternating howls and hurls had subsided and he sprawled back in his seat, moaning quietly, his ghostly white face slick with sweat.'

'Sorry Mummy,' he whispered, tears running down his cheeks.

Panicking now, Maura yelled at her husband.

'He's really ill, Doug. This doesn't look like the tummy bugs he used to get. Where are we?'

'A couple of miles north of Lancaster.'

'I'll Google the hospital and put it in the satnav. Now get a bloody move on. Use the hard shoulder if you need to. If the police stop us we'll ask for an escort. Oh God, he's unconscious. Hurry! Hurry!'

---

*Coroner blames pollution for death of child, 5.*

The Technician read the headline in the *Cumbrian Gazette* with mounting fury. The article went on to relate the County Coroner's narrative verdict that Kieran Philips, aged five, had died of kidney failure following the ingestion of water contaminated with a virulent strain of the bacterium *E. coli*, when he fell into Lake Gracklemere. He noted that the source of the pollution was a badly maintained sewage works operated by Ultimate Water Services (UK) plc, the British arm of a multinational water company. At the inquest, the Environment

Agency confirmed that over half the pollution load entering the lake came from the works, and the coroner called upon the Government to take stricter measures against pollution in UK rivers and lakes.

*That is so bloody wrong!* she fumed silently, sitting in the cosy Lake District café. *And the bastards got away with it. The sodding Coroner didn't bring in a verdict which would get them prosecuted. Well, if the law can't do anything, I damn well will!*

---

Cutting short her walking holiday, the Technician drove back south, thinking all the time about how she would tackle the problem. Nothing she could do would bring little Kieran back, she knew, but she could do some damage to the company responsible.

Causing them a financial loss would be a possibility. The trouble was, they would just pass the costs on to water consumers, leaving their salaries and bonuses intact. The directors, though. They could be made to feel pain, and that could be extremely satisfying. As soon as she got home, she would use Tor to research the company and its personnel. Then she would plan a campaign. If things worked out, they wouldn't know what hit them.

---

Two hours anonymous internet searching provided her with all the information on Ultimate Water Services she needed – the names, salaries and bonuses received by the directors and senior executives; the location of its premises; and details of the forthcoming annual general meeting. *That should be enough to be going on with,* she thought. *I can create some mayhem, though I'll need a bit of help.*

She sent an encrypted email to some like-minded hackers based in Leicester and, within the hour, received detailed instructions on what to do. And so the campaign against the water company began.

---

From: ceo@ultwatservuk.com
To: legal@ultwatservuk.com

Derek – are we exposed over that stupid kid who died up North?

Nigel

From: legal@ultwatservuk.com
To: ceo@ultwatservuk.com

No. The family can fuck off. They haven't enough money to sue, and proving it was us would be difficult. I had lunch with the minister and there's no chance of a prosecution.

Derek.

*Information in this email is legally privileged and may not be disclosed to anyone other than the intended recipient. Anyone doing so will be subject to severe penalties.*

From: ceo@ultwatservuk.com
To: legal@ultwatservuk.com

Thanks, Derek. I was worried that some woke law firm might take up their case *pro bono*.

Nigel

From: legal@ultwatservuk.com
To: ceo@ultwatservuk.com

No chance. If they tried, we'd argue that they shouldn't have let the little shit out of their sight. Blame it on the parents.

Derek.

*Information in this email is legally privileged and may not be disclosed to anyone other than the intended recipient. Anyone doing so will be subject to severe penalties.*

---

The leaked, skilfully faked, emails caused a veritable shitstorm. The *Guardian* and the *Mirror* put the story on their front pages, and even *The Times* covered it. Social media was boiling with comments, all attacking Ultimate Water Services. The company argued strenuously that the emails were bogus, but thousands of posters on social media refused to believe them. Ultimate Water Services offered compensation to Kieran's family, which they rejected as 'dirty money', and two law firms, plus three environmental groups, offered to take up the case. Questions were asked in Parliament about the minister's involvement and, following additional revelations in the *Guardian* about her links to the water industry, she resigned her post.

As The Technician reviewed the results of her work, with considerable satisfaction, an encrypted email from her friends in the Midlands dropped into one of her inboxes.

From: anon@anon.net.ukr
To: anon@anon.net.vanu

Loved what you did to the shit magnates. We've had a bit of fun in support. The directors and senior execs have personally donated two grand to each of Greenpeace, Friends of the Earth and Surfers Against Sewage. They don't know it yet, and it will be hard for them to get the money back – it's anonymised.

Keep it up!

Argus.

The Technician laughed and opened a bottle of wine to celebrate.

She had one more thing to do before the grand finale. And it should be fun. From the company website, and various other online sources, she acquired photos of the directors and senior executives running the company. It took half a morning for her to compile them into a short video, with appropriate captioning.

Next, she purchased a small van, for cash, using a false identity. It didn't matter that it would fail its MOT the next week; she would only need to use it once. She fitted out the van with powerful projection equipment, uploaded her video and drove it, cautiously, into central London, parking opposite University College London's Senate House, where a conference of water companies was taking place.

With well-rehearsed moves, she leapt out of the van and slashed the tyres. She shoved a small screwdriver into the ignition and snapped it off. With the vehicle now effectively immobilised, she switched on the projector, shut the door and squeezed superglue into the one lock she hadn't already treated. Pulling her baseball cap down over her face, she quickly blended into the crowds of evening pleasure seekers, changing her outer clothing en route to Tottenham Court Road tube station and the Elizabeth Line. She would be home in time to see the results, and she could hardly wait.

---

The pale façade of Senate House formed a perfect screen for The Technician's projected video. It was a short loop that began with a simple message: 'These people killed little Kieran Worsley.' The photos she had downloaded, with the individuals' names attached, were interspersed with the message, and the sequence concluded with 'Bring them to justice now'. She had considered using a photo of Kieran, from the newspaper, but decided against it as it could bring further pain to the family. Instead, she kept the focus on those she really wanted to hurt.

Within half an hour the video was all over social media as people filmed and uploaded the images with their phones. A few select independent media outlets had been notified shortly before the video appeared, and they duly showed it on their news feeds. None of the mainstream channels broadcast the images, for fear of legal action, but several newspapers reported it, briefly, phrasing their reports carefully to avoid libel suits.

The company issued a furious press release, stating that the claims were libellous and that they were not legally liable for Kieran's death, although they had tremendous sympathy for his parents, Maura and Doug. They would be taking legal action against whichever left-wing group was responsible. Two directors resigned, more out of fear than conscience, and the company's shares on the Stock Exchange slumped. Privately, the directors agreed that a shadow hung over the forthcoming AGM but they resolved to press on, regardless. At home, The Technician smiled contentedly at a job well done.

---

She'd never liked the 'creeping about in the dark' bit. It made her feel vulnerable and, even though she and her equipment were well-camouflaged, she constantly feared discovery. But at three o'clock in the morning, when the only creatures moving on the caravan site were rats, mice and the occasional fox, the risks were minimal. She found a caravan near the edge of the site which looked as though it was fully occupied and crawled along the ground beside it. With a bit of fiddling with a screwdriver, she managed to extract the cassette which held the toilet waste and, breathing only through her mouth, dumped the contents into a large, lidded plastic tub. She did the same alongside another caravan and filled a second tub, wrapping both vessels in sturdy plastic bags. Driving cautiously home, avoiding any bumps in the road which could cause her malodorous haul to leak, she wondered if she would ever get the smell of shit out of her hair.

Ten days later, the Ultimate Water Services AGM was due to be held at the company's headquarters just outside Birmingham. The Technician had no trouble in identifying the catering company providing the buffet lunch for the Board and, with the aid of some forged references and a skilful spot of acting, got a job on the team. She also scoped out the building, a large single-storied structure with easy access to the roof for a reasonably competent climber. Which she was.

She still had other preparations to make. Two bottles of strong limescale remover, a couple of burner phones, two small battery-powered electric motors, two corked bottles, some electronic components and a large pack of baking soda, joined the buckets of sewage in her garage which, in the summer heat, was becoming almost unusable.

There was one more item to acquire. In sturdy waders, a hard hat and a hi-vis jacket stencilled with the name and logo of the Environment Agency, she looked every inch the pollution inspector. Wearing gloves and a face mask, she carefully scooped up stretches of the blue-green algal scum at the edge of the lake, one featured on social media as the most polluted in the area. Another plastic tub for her garage, but one with considerably less offensive contents.

After two hours of work at the kitchen table, the day before the AGM, the devices were ready. Sealing them in plastic bags, having checked that all the batteries were functional, she slipped them into the tubs of ordure and strapped tape over the lids to ensure nothing leaked in transit. She knew security at the company headquarters was lax and she had no problem reaching the roof without being picked up by CCTV. She placed her tubs underneath the intake duct for the air conditioning, removed the tape from the lids, and made her way home.

The Technician reported for work at the catering company early on the Saturday morning, with coloured contact lenses, a wig and a series of removable tattoos disguising her identity. Scum from the lake, filtered and concentrated, filled an opaque water bottle that she carried with her throughout the morning. Every time a suitable dish appeared, and she was unobserved, she stirred in some of the liquid. The sweet chilli dip was an obvious choice, as was the pasta salad, already flecked with basil. A bowl of coronation chicken, a dish of spiced hummus and a large pot of what she took to be caviar also received doses. For good measure, she sprinkled some on a tray of smoked salmon. *It's a shame I can't get it into the champagne,* she thought. *But this should do.*

Stepping out from the dining room, once the food was all laid out and the AGM was well underway, she dialled two numbers on her mobile phone. On the roof of the main building, inside the Technician's tubs, two phones lit up and some electronics clicked. Two motors whirred into life, winding nylon thread, attached to corks, around spindles. The acidic descaler poured out of the now opened bottles and fell onto the baking soda. The resulting tsunami of carbon dioxide blew the lids off the tubs, sending a fountain of sewage into the air conditioning intakes. The Technician walked slowly away, rather wishing that she could be in the room when the horrendous stink came pouring through the air vents. But perhaps not.

It started with a faint whiff of something unpleasant, just as the Chairman was announcing the increases in salaries and payments to board members proposed for the following year. Rapidly, the odour built up and within a few minutes people were feeling sick and rushing for the door, heaving. Above this pandaemonium the Chairman could be heard closing the meeting, saying that any additional voting would be carried out online.

The directors hastened across a paved area to the dining room, gratefully inhaling clean air. Pre-lunch drinks helped to clear their sinuses and restore their appetites – none of them wanted to pass up a decent lunch, and there was a gala dinner at a hotel to look forward to that evening, as well.

'So what the bloody hell was that about?' asked the Chairman, spreading caviar on a thin piece of toast.

'Sabotage, George. Some bloody ecoterrorist put shit in the aircon,' replied the CEO, dipping a battered prawn into chilli sauce. 'We've called the police and they said they'd send someone round. We can't clean everything up until they've been and examined the scene, which will be hours yet.'

'Has anyone claimed responsibility?'

'Not so far. But when they do, we'll sue their arses off, don't you worry.'

'I'd like to hang the bastards. Probably a pathetic protest against pollution or something.' He paused. 'You don't think it's anything to do with that kid who died, do you?'

'No. I've had a private investigator take a look at the parents. They're too wet to do anything like this. Nothing to worry about.'

'Good man. Now, do have some of this caviar.'

The notice in the foyer of the Crown Hotel was brief: 'UWSUK dinner cancelled owing to illness.' The illness in question related not to the hotel staff, but to the directors and senior officers of the company. They had succumbed to violent vomiting and diarrhoea, following the buffet lunch consumed earlier, as toxins from the blue-green algae wreaked havoc with their digestive systems. Two board members and the CEO were hospitalised, and the local Environmental Health department urged everyone affected to contact 111 for advice, or speak to their GP.

The newspapers had a field day the following Monday, with headlines such as *Sewage company in the sh\*t*, *Water bosses down in the dumps*, and *Black SaTURDay for water meeting*. Broadsheet papers covered the incident in more sober tones, apart from the *Mail*, which claimed that left-wing terrorists were responsible. Only the *Guardian* suggested that the odour attack and the outbreak of food poisoning were linked.

The police were unable to find any forensic evidence on the devices on the roof to identify the perpetrator. There were no fingermarks, and any DNA traces were swamped by the material in the sewage. The identity of the member of the catering staff who disappeared part way through the event, and never sent in a claim for payment of wages, remained a mystery. CCTV yielded nothing of use.

Investigations into the company's practices, by the media and official agencies, showed that it had failed, for many years, to maintain its sewage treatment plants and water mains, despite paying out large dividends to foreign shareholders. Its share value fell further and, nine months after the death of

Kieran, it was taken into public ownership. No prosecutions of individuals ensued.

*Not a bad job,* mused The Technician, in the aftermath of the AGM. *It's a pity I couldn't get some of them jailed. But at least they got a taste of their own sewage.*

*The blue-green algal scum which forms in lakes polluted with fertiliser and other sources of nutrients contains toxic chemicals which have caused death to livestock and domestic pets. Humans have been made ill as well, notably a group of soldiers kayaking on Rutland Water. E.coli is a bacterium found in human and animal faeces and some strains can be extremely dangerous.*

# The Case of the Poisoned Apple

*I wrote this when the challenge posed to my writing group was to rewrite an old story in a new way. I trust Holmes purists will not be too offended!*

READERS of these chronicles will be aware that the cases solved by my friend, Mr Sherlock Holmes, have frequently been peculiar, macabre, and, in some instances, terrifying in nature. In all such instances, Holmes' matchless powers of deduction proved superior to the schemes of the malefactors and n'e'er-do-wells he encountered. Disregarding the tale of the giant rat of Sumatra, which still may not be told, perhaps the most unusual case was one in which we found ourselves involved purely by happenstance.

It began thus. Holmes, as an avid beekeeper, was intrigued by reports of a new strain of bees whose production of honey far surpassed that of our native insects. These prolific creatures were said to inhabit an obscure corner of a European forest.

Having no cases of importance at the time, Holmes invited me to join him in an entomological foray to Transylvania. My medical practice was also quiet, so I agreed eagerly. The next morning we departed from fog-swathed Baker Street by hansom, heading for Victoria Station and the boat train.

Two weeks later, we were working our way through undergrowth that obstructed a, clearly little-used, path through the dense forest. A mellow buzzing of bees competed with delicate birdsong for our attention and we followed its trail. Holmes's teeth were clamped tightly over his unlit pipe, and his face bore an uncharacteristically excited expression. We pushed our way into a clearing and stopped in amazement. There, on a rough wooden plinth, stood a glass coffin. A young woman lay within, apparently deceased, but with none of the signs of mortal decay which normally accompany that dreadful state.

We approached, my colleague frowning. Perhaps, I thought, the young woman was still alive and my medical training would prove of service in treating whatever ailment afflicted her. Holmes eased off the coffin lid and I examined her, as closely as the proprieties permitted. She was as cold as the grave. Yet, was there a faint pulse of some kind beneath the ivory skin of her slender neck? Holmes, too, examined her and her glass tomb but, as was often the case, declined to share his ruminations with me.

Our cogitations were interrupted by a crashing in the undergrowth. A young man in peculiar clothing burst forth and charged towards us, brandishing a sword.

'Put up your weapon, sir, I cried,' pulling my old Army revolver from my pocket and aiming it squarely at his chest. 'Who are you and what do you know of this young lady's condition?'

'I am Prince Rupert of Hentzau,' he replied, lowering his

blade. 'I am on a sacred quest to find a maiden in this forest who has been bewitched. It is known that a kiss from a prince will restore her to life, and she shall be her saviour's bride. I am that prince, sir, and you are standing between me and my intended fiancée. Step aside or I shall run you through.' He raised his sword again. 'And what, pray, is the device that you are brandishing?'

'This, sir, is a Webley revolver and, if you do not lay down your sword forthwith, I shall shoot you through the heart.'

'Gentlemen,' called Holmes. 'There is no need for such bellicosity. I have examined the young lady and it is evident to me that she is under the influence of some kind of poison. See, here, in her mouth A fragment of fruit of a most unusual colour. It is not impossible, albeit a little improbable, given my current knowledge of pharmacology, that this is responsible for her unfortunate state of suspended animation. There is no need, your highness, for you to impose an unlooked-for impropriety on the young lady. I shall extract the material and examine it in detail when I return to London. It will be of signal interest to observe the effects of its removal on her condition.

Holmes bent over the coffin and, using a pair of tweezers extracted from his knapsack, gently withdrew an almost iridescent morsel of what was clearly an apple from between her ruby lips and placed it in a small glass jar. Within moments she began to stir and whispered in a confused manner.

'Old woman. Apple. Funny taste. So tired.'

'Do not distress yourself, my dear young lady,' said Holmes, soothingly. 'You have been poisoned and I have removed the noxious agent. The substance concerned is beyond my experience, but I will certainly identify it when I have the opportunity to carry out a full chemical analysis back in London.'

The young woman looked at him, incomprehension flooding her delightful countenance.

'For now,' continued Holmes, 'this young gentleman craves an audience with you. It may be that I am speaking out of turn, but I understand that his intentions towards you are of a romantic nature. My colleague, Dr Watson, and I will retire to an appropriate distance but, should you feel uncomfortable in the gentleman's presence, you have only to call and we will come to your aid without delay.

Holmes and I withdrew along the path, out of earshot of the two young people but maintaining a clear view of them. It was obvious to both of us that the young prince was enamoured of the former occupant of the glass coffin, but it was unclear to us whether his feelings would be reciprocated. After a little time had passed, matters appeared to have been resolved and the couple approached us.

'I thank you, gentlemen, for your attentions,' said the young woman, addressing us. 'Prince Rupert has kindly invited me to accompany him to a state ball some two weeks hence. I am minded to accept but, before I do so, I must return to my parents and seek their approval. His highness has offered to drive me home in his carriage, which awaits a short distance away. His sister is travelling with him and will act as chaperone. I must bid you farewell and wish you a safe return to whichever country is your homeland.'

As we returned to our lodgings in the nearby village, I turned to my companion.

'What exactly happened there, Holmes?' I asked.

'I cannot say with certainty,' he replied. 'Grim deeds have certainly been afoot. I shall look forward to applying a scientific approach to the problem when we return to our lodgings. But for now, Watson, we have bees to investigate.'

# The Sound of Death

PETER MERRISON LAY SPRAWLED on his study floor, with a flushed face and traces of froth at his lips, clearly dead.

Detective Inspector Carton, sweating in his forensic suit and annoyed at being called out to a suspicious death on his day off, briefly examined the body. He stood up and viewed the scene as two CSIs busied themselves with cameras and sampling gear. He looked around Peter's book-lined study, taking in a desk cluttered with bits of paper, a tablet, a speaker and a laptop. A printer sat on a separate table, next to a cardboard box containing books and a bottle of Scotch. A spilt glass of whisky lay on the floor, next to a tea tray bearing an empty cup and a half-eaten biscuit. *Is this a typical writer's room*, he wondered?

He took a last look around the room, just as the pathologist entered.

Downstairs, Peter's relatives and colleagues had assembled in the lounge, under the watchful eye of DS Shona Muir. Gina Merrison, Peter's widow, sat motionless and mute in the corner, brushing away attempts to comfort her and sipping slowly from a glass of brandy. Derek Ford, Peter's agent, perched on the sofa, a glass in one hand and his other arm round the shoulders of Alison Fearne, Peter's PA, who was sobbing sporadically. Conway Graves, a crime writer, sat looking disappointedly at the half-served dinner visible though the doorway of the dining room, while Gavin Merrison, Peter's son, sat ostentatiously reading Proust as if nothing had happened. Caroline Felton, Peter's editor, stood next to the French windows, muttering angrily into her phone. They all looked up as DI Carton entered the room.

'I'm sorry to keep you,' he began, 'But DS Muir and I would like to talk to you all. You're not under caution, we just need to establish a few facts about Mr Merrison's death. Is there a room we can use?'

'You might as well use the kitchen,' replied Gina, listlessly. 'No-one feels much like eating, but I'll make some tea first, if that's OK.'

'Yes, thank you, Mrs Merrison. Perhaps we could chat while you're preparing the drinks?'

'Of course.'

---

Before Carton could start the interviews, the pathologist put his head round the door.

'A word, please, Detective Inspector,' he murmured.

Carton led him into an empty room.

'I can't be sure until I've carried out the post mortem,' he said, 'but there are signs of cyanide poisoning. Mr Merrison's pink complexion and the froth on his lips are suggestive, but not definitive. I'm one of the many people who can't smell cyanide, and I wouldn't want to try, anyway, so I can't say he smells of bitter almonds. I suggest you get any food and drink in the room analysed.'

'Thank you, doctor. I'll tell the CSIs to bag up everything relevant.'

Carton returned to the lounge where the others were waiting.

'I'm sorry to tell you,' he said, 'that we are treating Mr Merrison's death as murder. It is possible he was poisoned. I'm afraid everything from the bottom of the stairs upwards is a crime scene, so you will all have to stay downstairs until the CSIs have finished.'

Carton's announcement provoked a variety of reactions, from scornful looks of disbelief to apparent fear.

---

'Can you tell us what happened, Mrs Merrison,' asked the DI, raising his voice to be heard over the clatter of crockery and the sound of water boiling. 'I believe Peter's door was locked when you found him?'

Gina switched off the kettle and turned to face him.

'Peter's latest novel has just topped the bestseller list and we were having a dinner to celebrate. He'd been working in his study all afternoon but had promised to come down at six-thirty for drinks and dinner. When he hadn't appeared by seven, Alison went up with Derek to chivvy him along. His door was locked so Alison came down and asked me for the spare key – they'd heard strange noises and were worried. When we opened the door, we found him dead. The key was on the floor beside him.'

'I'm sorry. This must be painful for you, Mrs Merrison. When did you last see your husband alive?'

'Just after lunch. About two. I took him up a tray of tea and biscuits at half past three but I just put them on the floor and tapped on the door.'

'Did you speak to him at all after that?'

'No. We rarely speak when he's working.'

'Thank you. I'll let you get on with the drinks. Can you send Alison Fearne in when you serve them, please?'

---

Alison entered the room, red-eyed and twisting a damp tissue in her hands.

'Ms Fearne. Can you give me your account of this evening's events, please?' asked Carton.

'Yes, Inspector. Gina was annoyed at Peter's non-appearance, so I went to call him. Derek came with me. As we approached his door, we heard some strange noises – a choking sound and a sort of thump.' Her eyes widened. 'Oh, God, he must have died while we were outside. That's horrible.'

She started crying and Carton gave her a few moments to recover.

'We banged on the study door but Peter didn't answer. When Gina got the door open, we could see why. Peter was lying on the floor, not far from the door. I rushed towards him and felt for a pulse. There was none. Gina called an ambulance and after the paramedic confirmed he was dead he said we should call the police.'

'When did you last have any contact with Peter?'

'About two. I just missed lunch. He sent me a text at five-fifty, asking me to rearrange a meeting, but that's it.'

'Thank you, Ms Fearne. I won't be much longer. What can you tell me about the cardboard box in his study?'

'It was from his publishers. Author copies of his next book and a bottle of whisky. They always send him one when he has a new book coming out.'

'I see. Can you think of anyone who would want to kill him? Did he get hate mail?'

'No, I can't. I never saw any hate mail. He was very popular.'

'OK. Thank you. Can you ask Mr Ford to come in please?'

Derek's account of the events, curtly delivered, tallied with Alison's. He agreed to accompany Alison to Peter's study as he wanted a quick word with him before dinner. He said he knew of no-one with a lethal grudge against his client and couldn't understand why anyone would want to poison him.

Caroline Felton was next.

'Ms Felton, you are Peter Merrison's editor at Randall and Smythe?'

Caroline nodded.

'Did anyone hate him enough to kill him, do you think?'

'Not that badly. I was less than pleased with him because he'd got a new agent and was moving to a different publisher, once his current contract had expired. He had a falling out with Conway a couple of years ago. Conway claimed that Peter had stolen a plot idea and threatened to sue, but it didn't go anywhere. I think Peter invited him to try and patch up the differences. They had been good friends before that incident.'

'Did you see Peter at all after he went to his study?'

'No. I went for a drive after lunch. I had a meeting with him in the morning, though.'

'He had a box of books on his desk. Did they come from you?'

'Not from me personally, but the firm sent him a box of proof copies, and a bottle of his favourite whisky to congratulate him.'

'When was that?'

'You'll have to ask at the office.'

'All right. Thank you. Could you send Peter's son in now please?'

Gavin Merrison slouched into the room exuding irritation.

'I'm sorry for the loss of your father,' began DI Carton.

Gavin shrugged and drawled a reply.

'You'll find out soon enough that we didn't get on. I'm a literary novelist and he wrote popular trash. I suppose I regret he's gone, but he's no loss to the world of literature. We've hardly spoken in years.'

Carton suppressed his shock and asked, 'So why did you come to the dinner party?'

'It was a free meal and loads of drink. I get on well with my mother. At least she reads proper books.'

'Did you see your father today?'

'Briefly. He walked past me when I arrived, just as lunch had finished. I'd been stuck in traffic. No doubt he was on his way to write some more drivel. We didn't speak and I was keen to get at what was left of the food.'

Suspecting that Gavin had little to contribute to the investigation, Carton dismissed him, requesting him to send in Conway Graves.

Graves fiddled nervously with his watch strap as he sat facing the DI.

'I understand you and Peter Merrison had a falling out. Can you tell me about it?'

'Well...er...yes. He stole a plot idea from me. We'd been talking at a crime festival and I told him what the twist in my next book would be. A new way of killing someone in a locked room. That's the sort of thing I write. I'd had a few drinks, so I suppose I said more than I should have. He used my idea in his book and it topped the best seller lists last year. I couldn't afford to sue, and, anyway, I had no proof that I'd told him. But I knew what the bastard had done.'

'So you had a motive for killing him.'

'No, no, not at all. My murders are strictly on the page.'

'Were you surprised to be invited to the party?'

'A bit. We used to be the best of friends. Perhaps he wanted to make up. I was curious, which is why I came.'

'When did you last see him?'

'A year or so ago. I arrived about four today so he was already in his study.'

'So you never spoke to him?'

'Actually, I did. There was a box from his publisher on the doorstep when I arrived. Gina asked me to carry it up to him. I knocked on his door, told him he had a parcel, and he grunted in reply. I then went downstairs for a cup of tea.'

'OK. Thank you, Mr Graves. That'll be all.'

The inspector turned to DS Muir.

'Let's get back to the station, Shona. I need you to trace that parcel's journey and check that the Scotch was in it. It may have been poisoned and we need to know when. I understand everyone's staying the night, so we'll talk to them again tomorrow.'

---

'I'm afraid you misled me, Inspector,' said the pathologist, when he telephoned the following morning. 'You told me Mr

Merrison died at seven o'clock but it was clear, when I arrived at seven forty-five, that he had been dead longer than that. Of course, I can't be precise, but he was cooler than I would have expected.'

'But two people heard him die.'

'They can't have. He was dead, at a rough guess, an hour or so earlier.'

'Thank you, doctor,' said the detective, his thoughts in a whirl. *How can someone have died an hour before two people heard him die?*

'Shona,' he called. 'Go back to the house. Check where everyone was that afternoon. I'll follow on shortly.'

---

'So what have you found out, Shona?' asked Carton, in the kitchen at the Merrison house.

'We know where everyone was during the afternoon, guv. Gina took Peter tea at three-thirty and had a cup herself with Alison, who had arrived shortly after lunch. She was then busy in the kitchen until Alison asked her for the key. Derek arrived for lunch and spent the afternoon dozing, drinking and reading. Gavin arrived late for lunch but there was some food left for him which he ate. He went for a walk and was back at about four thirty, then read in the lounge. Alison helped Gina for a while, then left her at about five to do some work, again in the lounge. Conway arrived at around four and sat in the lounge reading a forensic scientist's autobiography and making notes for his next book. Caroline had a business meeting with Peter in the morning and went for a drive after lunch, looking angry. She returned at about a quarter to five. Then she went to do some work in her bedroom.'

'So everyone was in view of someone else from about five onwards, apart from Caroline and Gina.'

'Looks like it, guv. Of course, anyone could have left the lounge, briefly, at some point, but they would have been noticed.'

'Would they? Derek was half-cut, Conway and Alison were working and Gavin was absorbed in a book. Would they really have seen anyone leaving if someone sneaked out, quietly?'

'I suppose not. But something's clearly worrying you, boss.'

'It's just that I can't get over what the pathologist said about time of death. He was adamant that it was earlier than seven.'

'You're not saying that a dead man stood up, and got himself poisoned all over again, surely?'

'No. But I think we're looking at a particularly ingenious murder. What did you find out about the box?'

'The publisher's office confirmed that they dispatched it for delivery yesterday and that the bottle of Scotch was inside it, along with a congratulations card. I contacted the courier firm who said that the driver left it on the doorstep at three-seventeen and emailed Peter to say it had arrived. Forensics found loads of smudged prints on the outside, one person's on the books, presumably from whoever packed them, and nothing on the bottle. No DNA yet.'

'So, it's possible someone intercepted it and either poisoned the whisky or substituted another, lethal, bottle. That means it must have been someone who was here at some point between three-seventeen and four o'clock, when Graves took it up to Peter.'

'That's just about everyone.'

'We'd better have another chat with them all and look closer at motivation. Let's start with Alison.'

Peter's PA sat nervously in front of the detectives.

'How long had you been with Peter?' asked Shona.

Alison's gaze flickered and she answered slowly.

'About twelve years. I met him when I was working at the BBC and they were televising one of his books.'

'What did you do at the BBC?'

'All sorts. Costumes, props, general dogsbody. Peter said my efficiency impressed him. He offered me a job and I've worked for him ever since.'

'Has your relationship has always been purely professional?'

Alison flushed and fidgeted.

'Yes, of course. He's been faithful to Gina all the time I've known him. If you're suggesting we were having an affair, forget it.'

'OK. OK. Did you leave the lounge after you finished helping Gina, until you went to fetch Peter?'

'Apart from a loo break, no.'

'All right. Thank you, Alison.'

'She's lying, guv. I'm sure she was screwing Peter. Her body language gave it away.' Shona said. 'We'd better ask Gina if she knew.'

'OK. We'll have her in next.'

'Before you start,' said Gina, resignedly, 'I knew he was sleeping with Alison. All those tours, celebration dinners out of town and London meetings. It was inevitable. I didn't really mind. I'd long since stopped fancying him and it took the pressure off me. It was the lying I hated. But not enough to kill him. I will miss him, you know.'

Gina looked wistful rather than bereaved.

'Oh. I see,' said Carton, taken aback. 'Then perhaps you can help us find out who did. I understand you were in the kitchen most of the afternoon, some of the time with Alison.'

'That's right. Strangely, I didn't mind her helping. She went to do some work at five-ish and I didn't see her again until she came down for the key.'

'Was anyone behaving oddly during the day?'

'Oddly? No. I don't think so. I suppose Derek was a bit grumpier than usual, and Caroline was upset about something. She could hardly speak to Peter at lunch. There was definitely an atmosphere.'

'What do you know about the parcel?'

'Only that Conway said he found it on the doorstep and was happy to carry it up to Peter's study.'

'Thank you, Mrs Merrison. You've been most helpful. Could you ask Caroline to step in, please?'

'Why did you fall out with Peter, Caroline,' asked Carton.

Caroline looked like a small rodent catching sight of a grass snake.

'Isn't it obvious? The bastard was moving on. After all the firm, and me in particular, had done for him! New publisher, new agent, new PA – a clean break from everyone who had given him a career. If it wasn't for us, he'd still have been working in the bloody Civil Service.'

'So, you hated him.'

'I was angry, yes. Who wouldn't have been? Are you suggesting I killed him?'

'Some might say you had a motive. You were away from the house for much of the afternoon and on your own after that. Can anyone confirm your movements?'

'No. I needed to be on my own.'

'Hmm. Can you tell us anything else that might help us?'

'I don't think so. Derek was pretty pissed off about losing Peter as a client but sought solace in Scotch, as usual. Alison looked glum and I heard Conway say to her that Peter still hadn't paid for his plagiarism. Gavin seemed completely indifferent to things. You do know that he once wrote an article in which he said that writers of popular fiction should be put to the sword?'

'No, I didn't. That's helpful, Ms Felton. We'll need to speak to you again, so please stay on the premises.'

'But I have a meeting in London later today. How long are you going to keep us here?'

'Not much longer I hope,' replied Carton.

Caroline glared and left the room.

A bleary-eyed Derek Ford offered nothing of use. He confirmed he'd been in the lounge all afternoon and that he didn't see anyone leave although, as he'd been drinking and sleeping, that was hardly surprising. He said he was disappointed about losing Peter as a client but not angry, pointing out that he would still get his commission from Peter's previous titles.

'In truth,' he said, 'I was getting a bit tired of Peter. He'd become a bit of a prima donna and I'd sensed a parting of the ways was coming. That's the publishing business for you, I'm afraid.'

Carton let Derek go and spoke to Peter's son next. Gavin Merrison was hostile and uncommunicative, stopping just short of going 'No comment'.

'What did you mean when you said popular writers should be put to the sword?' asked Carton.

'It's a metaphor, Mr Plod. You can Google it if you don't know what one is. I merely meant that they were an affront to literature and shouldn't be published.'

'I'm fully aware of what a metaphor is, thank you, sir. So you weren't advocating murder – or parricide for that matter.'

Gavin seemed surprised by Carton's vocabulary.

'No, certainly not.'

'Did you notice anyone enter or leave the lounge after you returned from your walk?'

'No. I was immersed in the sublime delights of Proust. I wouldn't have noticed a rhinoceros.'

'Thank you, Mr Merrison. That will do.'

———

'A charming fellow, guv. But where's this leading?'

'To an arrest, Shona. I realised how it was done when I got into my car this morning. There's one more thing I need to check, but, before I do, I need to make a phone call.'

Five minutes later he found Alison in the kitchen.

'Ms Fearne. I'm sorry to be so formal but I need to caution you before I ask you any more questions. It's just routine, and you're not under arrest.'

He recited the caution while Alison listened nervously.

'You said that Peter sent you a text at ten to six,' he began. 'May I see it?'

'Yes of course. Here's my phone. I've unlocked it.'

Carton looked at the message, nodded and continued to fiddle.

'That's fine, Ms Fearne. I can see the message, received from Peter's phone at the time you said. But I'm afraid you made a mistake.'

'What?'

'You forgot to delete Peter's Bluetooth speaker from the paired devices in your settings menu.'

Alison paled.

'You see,' continued Carton, 'I think you slipped out of the lounge with no-one noticing and went into Peter's study at about half past five. You served him whisky poisoned with cyanide, which I suspect you put straight into his glass, and chatted with him for fifteen minutes or so, then recorded him dying, on your phone. You locked the door behind you and slipped the key under the door – there is a big enough gap. I checked. Then you returned to the lounge, prepared to say you'd been to the toilet, if anyone asked. You played back the recording over the portable speaker on his desk when you and Derek went to fetch Peter, so it seemed as though he had only just died.'

Alison swore, pushed open the back door to the kitchen and dashed to her car. Revving the engine, she sprayed gravel over the rhododendrons as she accelerated down the drive.'

'Aren't we going after her?' asked Shona, astonished.

'No need. I phoned and asked for a patrol car to block the gates. The only place she's going is the nick.

'So what happened? How did you work it out?'

'I thought his body was rather cold when we arrived, especially as there was a heater in the room. When the pathologist said that death probably occurred before seven, I couldn't work out how two witnesses heard something which had happened an hour or so previously. I twigged when I started the car and my phone connected via Bluetooth.

'But why Alison?'

'Motive. She was losing her job and probably her lover as well. She had to be present when Peter was found and she asked Derek to accompany her so she had an alibi for the supposed time of death. She must have found out on the internet how to make cyanide – a dangerous thing to do, according to the pathologist.'

'All a bit circumstantial, though. But her behaviour proved you right.'

'I bluffed a bit there. I didn't have the authority to search her phone, so I didn't actually look at her settings, just the text. When she let me look at the message, which, of course, she sent from Peter's phone, I pretended to fiddle with it.'

'Not admissible in court, surely?'

'I didn't do anything to compromise what Digital Forensics will find, so there's no problem.'

'Very clever, guv. I suppose it's a case of 'The pen is mightier than the sword, but no match for cyanide.''

'Ouch, Shona. That's awful. You can get the coffees when we get back to the station.'

---

*It is possible to make cyanide from reasonably readily available chemicals, but I have no intention of explaining how.*

# The Tipping Point

THE KILLING WASN'T METICULOUSLY PLANNED but neither was it completely spontaneous. Years of psychological torment had slowly built up Nadine's resolve to end the situation, one way or another. But she'd never had the courage to act.

Mark knew how to make her feel worthless. Before they married, he professed his adoration, said he supported her career, and that he valued her independence. Once they were married, things changed and he started to criticise her constantly. He was never satisfied with the way she dressed, the food she cooked and her performance in bed. He derided her work, supporting victims of child abuse, as 'a pointless snowflake job' and undermined her confidence to the point where she had to resign. He stopped her going out and prevented her from seeing her friends. He also made her get rid of her cat.

He lashed her with his tongue rather than his fists, but the abject misery he caused was just as bad as if he had beaten her. Once she left work, she had no financial independence – he had made her transfer her bank balance to him and had cut up her credit cards.

The tipping point came when he destroyed her water-colours. Painting had been her solace, done in secret while he was at work. But he came home early one afternoon and found her painting at the kitchen table, her portfolio beside her.

'What's this?' he jeered. 'I didn't know I'd married bleedin' Rembrandt.'

Nadine said nothing.

Deliberately holding her current work upside down he sneered.

'This is rubbish. It doesn't look like anything. You tryin' to be the next Picarsehole?'

He ripped the half-finished painting in half and then seized her portfolio, scattering its contents over the table. His eyes gleamed maliciously as he held up each painting in turn, tearing it apart slowly in front of her, inflicting the maximum amount of misery on his wife.

'Clean this mess up. Get me a drink and cook my dinner. I'm being made redundant and got stopped for speeding on the way home. I'm not happy.'

Mark stomped off to his den and slammed the door.

---

Nadine's hatred crystallised into a diamond of icy fury. She poured a substantial measure of whisky into Mark's favourite cut glass tumbler. The ornate pattern would work in her favour, she thought, as she ground up five of the promethazine tablets she took for her hayfever and stirred the powder into the drink. He wouldn't see the cloudiness in the liquid or spot the sediment in the bottom. Neither would he notice any odd taste, as he tended to gulp, rather than sip, his Scotch. In a mood like he was in, she could probably serve him vinegar and he'd hardly notice. She took the drink into her husband's den knowing he would be watching porn on his laptop until dinner.

Half an hour later, Nadine returned, her heart thumping. She knew that alcohol increased the sleepiness caused by the tablets, but would they be enough? To her relief, Mark was snoring in his chair, completely unconscious. He was at her mercy.

For the first time in three years, she glimpsed a hint of freedom. She savoured this and wanted it to continue. Could she really take the next logical step and kill him? If she took that fatal course, how would she get away with it? She knew that if she let him wake up, the horror of her marriage would resume, and she would never escape. She had taken the first step, but did she have the courage to follow it through? When she glanced at his laptop and saw the vile, sadistic images there, the decision was made for her. She knew that the world, not just her own life, would be better off without him. But how to do it?

Being married to a tyrant had ingrained in Nadine the need to avoid mess. That rather ruled out knives and smashing his head in with a blunt object. She had no handy source of poisons and she didn't own a gun – this was England, after all. That really left strangulation or suffocation and she wasn't sure if she was strong enough, especially if he started to wake up. And if she were to stand any chance of getting away with it, she would have to use a method which wouldn't look like murder.

Eventually, she came up with an idea. She found a large plastic bag in the kitchen, crept up behind Mark's chair and slipped it over his head, holding it firmly against his shoulders with gloved hands. He started to wake up, and his panicked inhalation sucked the plastic into his mouth. Nadine tipped the chair back so he couldn't get up or hit her, and held on to the ends of the bag, her muscles screaming as she fought to keep him still. Eventually his struggling became weaker, and he lost consciousness. Nadine kept the bag in place for several minutes to ensure he was really dead.

———

Pouring herself a whisky, she sat trembling on the sofa, wondering what on earth to do next. Mark's body was heavy and she wasn't sure she could get him into the car by herself. That ruled out dumping his body in the countryside or a river. Anyway, he would certainly be found, and that would immediately show he'd been killed unlawfully. She couldn't face the thought of cutting him up. The mess would be ghastly. Mark had insisted on the garden being paved, with just a few plants in pots, so burial there was impossible, even if she had been strong enough to dig a grave.

Could she make it look like suicide? Mark's redundancy might provide a credible motive, she supposed. He had loved his job and similar opportunities in the local area for a middle manager in retail were rare, so losing it was a nightmare for him. His encounter with the police hadn't helped his mood, either. He already had nine points on his licence, and a driving ban would devastate him.

Then she remembered an item she had heard on the radio – *Woman's Hour*, wasn't it? – dealing with an odd sexual practice. It was about people who were strangled, or put plastic bags over their heads during sex, to intensify the experience. The important thing was to release whatever was stopping them from breathing just in time to avoid permanent damage, and not everyone managed this. Here was Mark, in front of his laptop, streaming porn. Could that work?

Nadine lifted Mark's limp hands and placed them around

the base of the plastic bag as if he was holding it himself. She put her tablets next to his computer, touched his fingers to the packet and undid his trousers and boxers. The dregs of the drugged whisky went down the toilet and she added fresh drink to the rinsed glass. She cleared away all evidence of her torn paintings and continued preparing the dinner as if nothing had happened.

Half an hour later, Nadine removed the bag from Mark's head, and dialled 999, her nerves screaming. Would she be convincing enough? Would a police officer see through her subterfuge?

'Emergency. Which service do you require?'

'Ambulance I suppose. My husband's dead. He had a bag over his head and isn't breathing. I don't know what to do.'

Nadine did her best to appear flustered and confused, realising that her call would be recorded. In reality she was calm and collected, measuring every word. She followed the call handler's advice to check Mark's breathing again and even attempted CPR, after pulling him onto the floor. She had to behave convincingly. While waiting for the ambulance, she put drops of lemon juice in her eyes and practised sobbing, every inch the suddenly bereaved widow.

'I'm very sorry, Mrs Wallace, but your husband is dead,' said a paramedic, her voice respectful and sympathetic.

'I'm afraid we'll have to wait for the police to arrive before we can move him. The circumstances are a little unusual.'

'I suppose so,' said Nadine, looking embarrassed. 'I didn't know he did this sort of thing. It came as a dreadful shock.'

'Can I make you a cup of tea or something?'

'No, no, it's alright. I've had some whisky.'

The paramedic looked away and busied herself collecting her equipment.

———

An hour later, two detectives knocked on Nadine's door. She showed them into the lounge and sat facing them, sniffing into a tissue.

'I'm sorry for your loss, Mrs Wallace,' said DC McKern, reciting the usual platitude. 'I'm afraid we have to ask you some questions.'

'Alright. I'm still coming to terms with it. I may not make much sense.'

'We understand. When did you last see your husband alive?'

'When he came in from work. About five.'

'How did he seem?'

'Desperately unhappy because he had just been made redundant and was stopped for speeding. He thought he'd be banned. I got him a drink and he went to his den.'

'What did you do then?'

'I started cooking the dinner. When I called him, around six, there was no answer, so I went to fetch him.'

'And you found him with a bag over his head in front of his computer. And his clothing in disarray.'

'That's right.' Nadine looked embarrassed.

'Did you touch anything?'

'Yes. I took the bag off his head as soon as I saw him. I put it on the desk. It's still there. The ambulance controller said to try CPR, but it didn't work.'

'Well, it was good you tried. We'll need to take the bag with us, and his computer. I don't suppose you know the password?'

'Yes. It's Joffrey007. We laughed about it. Combining a villain with a hero.' Nadine faked another sob.

'Had Mark seemed down at all recently?'

'Thinking back, I believe he could have been. He may have been expecting redundancy, I suppose. I did wonder if he'd been taking my tablets to help him sleep, but he denied it. I saw them next to his laptop, though – perhaps he thought they would calm him down, but they're not antidepressants.'

'We'll need those as well, I'm afraid. And any recent bank statements. I'm sorry to ask you, but was your marriage OK?'

'Yes. We were fine. The odd disagreement over where to eat or go on holiday. But nothing serious.'

'Were you aware he watched pornography on his computer and er... pleasured himself while doing so?'

'Certainly not. I never knew what he got up to in his den. I thought he watched sport. It came as a complete, horrible, surprise.'

'OK. We may need to talk to you again. We'd like to look round Mark's den, please.'

An hour later they left, apologising for the intrusion, and she was able, for the first time in years, to think about the future.

---

'And what, in your opinion doctor, was the cause of death?' inquired the Coroner.

'Asphyxiation caused by the placing of a plastic bag over the deceased's head,' replied the pathologist. 'Traces of promethazine, an antihistamine, were found in his body which, in combination with the alcohol he had consumed, would have made him extremely sleepy and, to some extent, unaware of what he was doing.'

'And is it likely that he put the bag over his own head?'

'It is. The situation is typical of autoerotic asphyxiation that went wrong. Some people like to enhance their sexual pleasure by temporarily depriving the brain of oxygen. Unfortunately, on occasions, they do not resume breathing in time and the results can be fatal.'

'Were there any injuries suggesting that someone else was involved?'

'No. He had some scratches round his neck, made by his own fingernails, consistent with him trying to remove the bag in a panic. There were no other injuries.'

'Thank you, doctor.'

The Coroner summed up.

'In considering my verdict, I have taken into account the likelihood of suicide since Mr Wallace had just been made redundant and was likely to lose his driving licence. While this is possible, I do not believe he wished to kill himself as he had no previous psychiatric history, was in a happy marriage and could rely on his wife's support to see him through his difficulties. He indulged in a potentially dangerous sexual practice which appears to have cost him his life. On balance I conclude that he met his death by misadventure. My condolences to Mrs Wallace.'

DC McKern called on Nadine to return her antihistamines and the items removed from Mark's study. She was sorting through a pile of documents on the kitchen table when he arrived.

'I'm afraid some of the material on his laptop was borderline illegal. Our IT people wiped it, so you won't need to see it if you use the machine.'

'Oh, I won't. I'm binning it. Too many unpleasant memories.'

'I understand. You must be relieved it's all over.'

'A bit. But I'm still coming to terms with the loss of Mark. We were so happy together and I didn't know about his other side. It was such a shock.'

'Well, again, I'm sorry. I'll leave you in peace now.'

As McKern drove away, something he had seen came into focus in his mind. A press cutting, partly covered by a birth certificate, on the kitchen table. It showed a young Nadine holding up a trophy with the heading 'Local schoolgirl wins prestigious acting prize.'

'I wonder,' he thought. 'I wonder....'

*The drowsiness caused by several antihistamine drugs is enhanced by alcohol consumption, although not to the lethal level of some other drug/alcohol combinations, such as barbiturates.*

## Getting Away With It

JASON KNEW they would never arrest him for murdering Gorman. Slipping ketamine into the coffee flask was easy. He knew Gorman would drink from it once he pulled off the M6 for the Lakes. Fifteen minutes later, on the winding mountain roads, Gorman would fall asleep and plummet to his death. Jason smirked as Gorman pulled out of the car park in the distance, confident that he would be a hundred miles away when his promotion rival died.

Gorman felt strangely tired despite the coffee he had gulped to make up for a restless night. Within a hundred yards, his steering became erratic and he slumped over the wheel, his foot still on the accelerator. He didn't see his observer's terror as his SUV slammed into Jason's body, crushing internal organs and stopping his heart.

Jason was right: they never did arrest him for murdering Gorman.

*This was a challenge to write a story with a twist, in just 150 words.*

# Death on the Doorstep

## Monday 18th May, 7.30am

WHEN JOHN TREGORRAN'S border collie, Bonnie, shot off along the footpath ahead of him he assumed she'd seen a rabbit. But, as soon as he caught up with the dog, he realised something was seriously wrong. Two people were lying on the ground in front of an old cottage, as if in some desperate embrace. A woman was on her back, her head resting on a bloody doorstep three metres from the path and her feet in a patch of mud. A man was on top of her, covering her smaller frame with his corpulent body. Were it not for the dog, barking in front of them, they wouldn't have been noticed from the path, as a partially open gate blocked the view.

'Hello,' John called. 'Are you OK?'

An idiotic question, as he soon realised.

Trembling, he approached the figures and checked for signs of life. Nothing. He backed away from the bodies and called the police, his fingers clumsy on the keypad. Obeying instructions to stay put and not touch the bodies, he put Bonnie on a lead and paced around for twenty minutes until a police car pulled into the parking space behind the cottage. Two police officers, dressed for the countryside, produced their warrant cards and introduced themselves.

'Mr Tregorran? I'm DS Simon Rose and this is DC Cara Lane. Thank you for calling us.'

Rose noted down John's details while Lane strung police tape around the scene.

'You found the bodies at about seven thirty. Is that right?' Rose asked.

'Yes. I always walk Bonnie along here around that time. She ran ahead, barking, and I followed. I've never seen anything like this before. Fair gave me a shock, it did.'

'It must have been very distressing for you. Did you touch anything, at all?'

'I felt for a pulse in their necks, as you're supposed to do, but there was nothing. The man was still warmish, but she was colder.'

'That's very observant of you,' said Rose, encouragingly. 'How about Bonnie? Did she approach them?'

'She didn't go through the gate and I called her away as soon as I saw them.'

'That's good. Did you see anyone else around?'

'No. I'm usually one of the first out this way in the morning. Sometimes there are cyclists or runners on the path, but I saw no-one today. I was here around ten o'clock last night, and they weren't there then. Bonnie would have found them.'

'OK. That's very helpful. Did you know the couple at the cottage?'

'I didn't – it's a holiday let. People come and go. I might have seen the woman out running once, but I can't be sure.'

'Right. Thanks. Now I'll need you to show me where you

stood and how you approached them. Don't worry, DC Lane has covered them up with a sheet. I'm sorry to ask you, but we need to eliminate your shoeprints from anyone else's.'

John showed the detective where he had walked, flinching slightly at the sight of the mound under the sheet.

'That's it for now, Mr Tregorran. Thank you very much for your help. Someone will call round and take a formal statement from you later today, when it's more convenient.'

John whistled to Bonnie, who had been dozing in the sun, totally oblivious to the drama, and walked slowly back down the path.

---

'What do you reckon, then, Sarge?' asked Lane, as they waited for the police forensic physician to arrive. 'He collapsed on her and knocked her head on the step? She slipped in the mud while going out for a run – she's in Lycra and her trainers are dirty – and he collapsed when he found her?'

'Could be either. He looks like heart attack material. Definitely not a runner and his clothes look as though they've been slept in. We'll know more after the PM. Here's the doctor now.'

Rose took photos of the bodies and their surroundings on his phone before the doctor began her examination.

With death pronounced and the bodies removed to the hospital, Rose and Lane inspected the stone-built cottage. It was cosy and characterful, although a flat-screen TV and a DVD player contrasted with the old-fashioned decoration and furnishings. A laptop lay open on a coffee table with several empty beer cans beside it. A couple of glasses with the dregs of a greenish liquid in the bottom sat on the kitchen worktop and a blender surrounded by a heap of vegetable peelings suggested the preparation of a healthy smoothie. A faint smell of bleach was discernible over the odour of stale beer and slightly decomposing kale.

'Looks like their name is Conway,' said Lane, rummaging through a pile of papers on the kitchen table. 'Jessica and Steven. And here's the letting agreement. They're from Birmingham and took the cottage for a fortnight, ending next Saturday.'

'OK. Get in touch with the West Midlands force. Ask them to send a uniform to their address and see if the neighbours know of any next of kin. We may find some relatives' numbers on their phones when the techies take a look at them but that might be quicker.'

'Is it me?' mused Rose, as the two detectives locked up the cottage and prepared to leave. 'But something doesn't feel quite right. If Steven fell on Jessica while she was alive, surely she would try to get out of the way? It looks like she just lay there.'

'So, you reckon she was dead or unconscious when he fell?'

'Maybe. Mr Tregorran said he was warmer than her, but larger people cool down more slowly than smaller folk. And there's something odd about that step, but I can't quite put my finger on it.'

Before becoming a police officer, Rose had completed a degree in forensic science and had also worked as a CSI for a year. He was keen to use his knowledge but didn't want to tread on the specialists' toes by appearing 'too clever'.

'You could be right, Sarge, but the DI would never sanction calling out a full CSI team just 'cos something doesn't feel quite right.'

'No, she wouldn't. But we'll leave the tape in place and I'll cover the step with a plastic sheet from the car.'

Rose received a call from the pathologist that afternoon.

'Those bodies you sent me. Both died less than four hours before I received them. She was quite straightforward. A skull fracture from an impact with a flat surface leading to a fatal haematoma. Her skull was unusually thin – it wouldn't have taken a massive amount of force. She was fit and healthy. He was a puzzle. It looks as though he had a heart attack but his arteries were not as furred up as I would have expected and there was no sign of chronic cardiac disease, despite his weight. I'm wondering if he was poisoned with something. I'll recommend to the coroner that a full Home Office post mortem is carried out and I think you would do well to treat his death as suspicious.'

Rose leapt to his feet.

'Looks like we'll get that forensic team after all,' he called to DC Lane. 'I'll brief the DI and she'll get it organised. In the meantime, I'll arrange for a PC to stand guard at the cottage. It's officially a crime scene now.'

Rose reported the pathologist's findings to DI Amy Ford and she called the two detectives and a couple of uniformed constables into her office.

'Mr Conway's death looks suspicious so we have to move fast,' she said. 'I want checks on any nearby properties. See if anyone saw or heard anything during the night. Judging by the map, there's only a couple of cottages and a small farm close to the scene. Check the campsite a few hundred yards further on as well. As soon as possible, please, before holidaymakers go home. I want dog walkers spoken to this evening and I need someone out there at dawn to talk to anyone normally about at that time. We'll have a formal briefing at 3 pm tomorrow, but please let me know of anything significant in the meantime. Simon – would you allocate tasks? I'll notify the DCI, but I'll probably be the SIO.'

## Tuesday 19th May

By ten o'clock the cottage and the path were bustling with Tyvek-suited technicians. Rose and Lane, similarly garbed, collected documents, the laptop and Steven's mobile. Jessica's phone had been found on her body and was already in the hands of Digital Forensics. Rose walked around the cottage, trying not to get in the way of the CSIs, looking for anything unusual. One or two things caught his attention and he sought out Derek Fellowes, the crime scene manager.

'Derek – can you ask someone to take a look at this patch on the wall? It doesn't seem quite as dusty as the rest and there's no obvious reason for that. And could you get someone to look closely at the blood on the step? We'll need those glasses and their contents for examination as well.'

'I have done this job before, you know,' replied Derek, sourly.

'Yeah. Sorry. I'm getting ahead of myself. I was a SOCO before I joined as a copper.'

He smiled, hoping to mollify his colleague.

While Rose and Lane were busy at the cottage, DI Ford notified the DCI, assembled a full team of detectives and support staff, set up an incident room, and started a policy book. She planned to visit the cottage later on but, for the moment, it was more important to set the wheels of the investigation in motion.

At the 3pm briefing Ford summarised what they knew so far.

'Jessica and Steven Conway. Found this morning by a dog walker on the step of the holiday cottage they rented. She died from a head injury consistent with striking, or falling onto, a flat, hard surface. He seems to have had a fatal heart attack without previous heart disease. A second PM tomorrow will look for signs of poisoning.

'We expect some initial forensic results by midday tomorrow, but toxicology reports on samples taken from the body won't come in for some days,' she continued. 'Their phones and Steven's laptop are being examined by IT and we expect something back tomorrow morning. Door-to-door found nothing, and we know from walkers and runners staying at the campsite that the bodies probably weren't there until the early morning, although they may not have seen them through the gate. This ties in with the estimated times of death.'

'What do we know about them, guv?' asked DC Lane.

'She was a retired PE teacher and he was a former office worker. They came up pretty clean on the PNC, apart from a couple of speeding offences, but Steven was cautioned for being drunk outside a sex club in Smethwick a year ago. He denied going in. West Mids are still trying to find next of kin and, when they do, someone will need to interview them. Anyone fancy a trip to Birmingham? You don't get to visit the sex club, though.' She smiled slightly.

One or two hands were raised, albeit slowly.

'Right. DS Rose will allocate tasks and we'll reconvene tomorrow at the same time.'

## Wednesday 20th May

Rose and Ford visited the cottage the following morning. Without the bodies and the CSIs present, Rose was able to take in the scene at his leisure. He spent several minutes looking at the bloody doorstep, frowning as he studied the cracks and fissures in the slate slab.

'Something bothering you, Simon?' asked Ford.

'Yes. I thought there was something odd when we first saw the place. I'll need to check with the CSIs, guv, but it looks as though the blood is just on the surface. It doesn't seem to have seeped into the cracks in the stone, which is what I would have expected if the wound had happened here. Also, the blood is mainly on the front edge of the step.'

'So?'

'The doc said the fracture was from an impact with a flat surface, not an edge. I don't think it happened here.'

'Well what do you reckon? An intruder killed her and moved the body then Steven had a heart attack when he found her? Or Steven killed her himself, moved her body and then died?'

'Could be either, though we found no sign of forced entry,' replied Rose. 'She could have been out for a run and fell on a rock, or someone hit her with something flat, I suppose. She wouldn't necessarily have died immediately – the doc said she may have been able to move around a bit before she died. She was wearing a fitness tracker so we can check that out. It's with the techies. Why was she on her back, though?'

'Perhaps she was on her way out for a run and slipped on this patch of mud? Steven then found her, tried to revive her and then collapsed?' Ford suggested.

'Not impossible, I suppose. And those scenarios don't explain Steven's death.'

'Well let's not jump to conclusions. Remember the Holmes dictum about not theorising without evidence. I think the toxicology results will be crucial.'

'Yes, guv,' replied Rose, still looking thoughtful.

## Thursday 21st May

There was little news at Thursday's briefing, apart from a report from the officers who had travelled to Birmingham. They had discovered that the couple had no children but both Jessica and Steven had brothers who agreed to come down to Cornwall to identify the bodies. Ford asked DC Lane to meet them from the train and arrange overnight accommodation.

## Friday 22nd May, 11am

The investigation had stalled for a few days as the team waited for results from the second post mortem, toxicology and IT. When these came through DI Ford called them together and summarised.

'I showed the lab's report on Jessica's fitness tracker to the pathologist. She had been for an early morning run, taking about half an hour. The record of her heart rate is interesting. Shortly before the run it hit a sudden peak – she must have exerted herself or something alarmed her. Then she went for the run and it remained somewhat elevated once she was back. It increased again to a sharp peak than fell back to a low level and finally petered out. That was when she died. The timing fits with the pathologist's estimate of her time of death.'

'Anything else from IT?'

'Yes. There was some very nasty porn on Steven's laptop. Extreme BDSM and torture. There was no internet at the cottage, but he'd brought downloaded files with him.'

'Nice bloke,' muttered Rose.

'I've saved the best bit till last. The tox results and the pathologist's report are back. We've got a cause of death for Steven. He was poisoned.'

An excited murmur ran through the team.

'He was killed by digitalis, from foxgloves. I'll spare you the chemistry but samples from the second PM contained traces of it. His stomach contents included particles of foxglove leaves and so did one of the smoothie glasses and the blender. So much for a detox diet. Foxgloves can stop your heart, and there are plenty of them growing along the path where we believe Jessica ran.

'One other thing: CSIs found a plastic bag with Jessica's blood in it, and a towel with traces of blood and bleach, caught in reeds at the edge of a lake beside the path. There were also traces of blood on one of the walls in the kitchen – it had been cleaned with bleach but not well enough.'

'So what do we think happened?' asked DC Lane.

'I've an idea,' said DS Rose. 'But I'd like to go back to the cottage to check.'

Ford, Rose and Lane returned to the cottage that afternoon. After half an hour wandering round the building and the outside, Rose was ready to offer an explanation.

## Monday 18th May, 6am. Five days earlier

Jessica came down for her pre-breakfast run to find beer cans scattered over the coffee table and Steven slumped in a chair, snoring. His laptop, on a coffee table, was plugged in and switched on. Out of curiosity, she refreshed the computer. When images of women being tied up and tortured came into view, she nearly threw up. It was clear that Steven, in his drunken state, had forgotten to hide the files and shut down the machine.

Jessica felt as though she'd been hit in the face with a brick, and her breathing almost stopped for a minute. This holiday was supposed to be a last chance to save their marriage. They would eat healthily, take exercise and try to enjoy themselves together. Steven had promised to lose weight to ward off obesity and protect his heart. But he was still drinking heavily and was clearly more interested in the filth on his laptop than in her.

Shutting the lid of the machine, she left the cottage and pounded along the footpath, hoping that the exercise would alleviate her despair. But it didn't and she realised it was never going to work between them. How it had got this bad she couldn't explain. Steven had been attractive, considerate and healthy when they first married. They would go for walks together, ramble over the Peak District and take active holidays. Their sex life was great and, she believed, he never looked at another woman. Now he was an overweight drunken slob with vile habits and looked as if he was heading for a heart attack any moment.

At the very second she thought of a heart attack, she passed a clump of foxgloves beside the path. Barely noticing them she continued with her run but, by the time she reached them on her return, an idea had insinuated itself into her mind. *Suppose Steven did have a heart attack. Her life would be her own again and the world would be better off without him. The idea was preposterous. I'm not the murdering kind. How would I get away with it?* But she knew that foxgloves could stop the heart and

Steven's weight and lifestyle would divert suspicion away from her.

Returning to the cottage, with a large handful of foxglove leaves in her pocket, she prepared two separate smoothies based on carrot, kale and wheatgerm. In Steven's she put the foxglove leaves, adding sugar to disguise any odd taste. She jabbed him in the ribs to wake him up and pressed the concoction on him.

'What the fuck are you doing?' He burped. 'I was fast sleep and my sodding head hurts.'

'Here. Drink this. It'll shift your hangover.' She managed to suppress her distaste for him.

'But I want bacon and eggs. You know I can't stand this vegan nonsense.'

He farted and looked at her aggressively.

'You promised you would eat healthily on this holiday. This is much better for you. You won't want bacon after you've had this.'

'OK. But I'm going to the bloody pub for a pasty and chips at lunchtime.'

He gulped down the smoothie with obvious distaste.

*In your dreams*, she thought, and, once Steven had swallowed the mixture, she could contain herself no more.

'You're at it again, aren't you?' she spat.

'What?'

He looked guilty, but with a hint of defiance.

'The porn. I found it. You were too drunk to switch off your laptop. You said you'd stop after they threw you out of that sex club. Stupidly, I trusted you. You've blown it. It's over. Shit, we used to have something really good and I thought this holiday would repair things. Get us back to how it used to be. But you've screwed up once too often. And you'll pay.'

Rage erupted through the fog of Steven's hangover and he stumbled to his feet.

'You nosy cow. I'll watch what I want. And I'll do it to you if I feel like it. I'll tell you when it's over.'

Jessica stepped back as Steven lurched towards her, his hands outstretched. The heel of her trainer caught on an uneven flagstone and she toppled backwards, her head hitting the rough stone wall behind her with a sickening crack. Her eyes went blank as she slid down the wall, leaving a trail of blood on the stone. She lost consciousness immediately, unaware that life would drain out of her in the next few minutes.

Steven stood rooted to the spot for what seemed like an age, his mind in turmoil. *Is she dead? It was an accident, wasn't it? Would they think he killed her deliberately?* he agonised. Eventually it dawned on him that he could make it look as though Jessica had fallen, either when going out for her run or when she returned to the cottage. He put a plastic bag over her head to contain the blood and half carried, half dragged her body into the garden, arranging it with her head lying on the doorstep and smearing the stone with her, now coagulating, blood. He rubbed some mud on her trainers to make it look like she had skidded.

His heart beginning to race, he rushed back into the cottage and used a towel soaked in bleach to clean the blood off the wall. Satisfied that he could see no visible traces, he went back into the garden and crossed the path to the lake. By now he was beginning to feel ill. His heart seemed to be bursting and everything had taken on a yellowish tinge. He managed to put the towel in the plastic bag and throw the package into the lake. *Shit. What's wrong with me. I'm really ill. The bitch must have bloody poisoned me.* He staggered back towards the cottage. As he reached the door his heart finally stopped and he collapsed on top of Jessica, stone dead.

# Friday 22nd May, 2pm

After his final look around the cottage, Rose shared his thoughts with his colleagues.

'It looks like a double murder, or at least murder and manslaughter.'

'How do you work that out?' asked a puzzled Lane. DI Ford smiled, realising that Rose was on to something.

'OK. I think Jessica must have found the muck on Steven's laptop – that's why her heart rate shot up first thing. I think she then went out for her run and, at some point, thought of poisoning him with foxglove leaves. She picked them from beside the path – I noticed some not far from the cottage – and I bet we'll find traces on her clothing. She put the leaves in his smoothie and persuaded him to drink it. She then confronted him – her heart rate went up again – and he killed her. Either he deliberately smashed her head on the wall or she tripped on a raised flagstone as she retreated from him – there's one close to where she fell. Her left-hand trainer had a small amount of damage, and there was a faint bruise on her heel consistent with this scenario.

'Steven realised Jessica was dead and covered her head with the plastic bag to carry her outside. We found some bloody hairs stuck to the inside of the bag. Then he removed it and arranged her on the doorstep. By now the blood on her head was too thick to soak into the cracks in the stone, but he smeared some along the edge, not realising that the wound wouldn't look like the result of an impact with the sharp surface. He tried to clean the blood off the wall, with bleach and a towel, but the SOCOs still managed to find traces. At this point he would have been starting to feel ill, as his gut began to absorb the poison. He threw the bag and towel into the lake and collapsed on top of

Jessica as he staggered back to the cottage. Bonnie found them soon after. No-one else seems to have been involved.'

'A proper little Poirot, aren't you?' said Ford approvingly. 'It certainly makes sense. It's a pity we can't prove it. It's a good enough explanation to put in the report to the coroner, though. Case closed, I think. Write it up, and then the drinks are on me.'

*The cottage in question is one we stayed at in Cornwall, with a lake alongside and a path with Foxgloves growing in profusion. We don't drink smoothies.*

# Death on the Tracks

GEORGE REYNOLDS SHUT off steam as his train approached Mexton station, reached unsuccessfully for the whistle and collapsed.

Fireman Desmond Barrow panicked, then composed himself. He'd watched George at the controls, and he knew how to operate them, but could he stop the train in time? Jumping over George's prostrate form, he hauled on the brake lever, at the same time pulling on the whistle that produced a banshee shriek. Wheels screeched as they bit into the rails and the train juddered to a halt some fifty metres beyond the platform.

Trembling, Desmond checked George's neck for a pulse. Nothing. He climbed down from the engine, ran along the trackside and hauled himself up into the first carriage, where Joe Dunster, the ticket collector, was waiting.

'What the hell's George playing at, young Desmond?' he demanded. 'He's scared us half to death. The passengers...'

'He's dead, Joe. Least I think so. Is there a doctor on the train? He just collapsed. I had to stop the train myself.'

Five minutes later Joe helped a silver-haired, keen-eyed

woman onto the footplate. She examined George's body and then turned to Desmond.

'How was he behaving before he collapsed?' she asked.

'He said he was hot and thirsty, but we always are when we're running, especially in summer. He also said one of the signals looked funny, but it seemed all right to me. Why's that?'

'Based on what you've told me, and from his dilated pupils and flushed appearance, I suspect he's been poisoned with atropine. I've seen it before, in A&E. You'd better phone for the police and an ambulance.'

---

While they waited for the emergency services, Joe, a retired British Transport Police sergeant, informed the passengers that there had been an incident, but there was no reason for them to worry. They were to remain on the train until it could be reversed into the station. In the meantime, the buffet car would provide free tea and coffee. Desmond waited anxiously in the cab for a qualified driver to take over.

---

Detective Sergeant Jack Vaughan and DC Trevor Blake showed their warrant cards as Norman Crowcombe, the Station Master, led them into his office.

'What can you tell us about this death?' asked Jack.

'It was an awful shock, officer,' Crowcombe replied. 'The driver of the five-thirty arrival, George Reynolds, died at the controls as he was pulling into the station. Doctor Bishop, here,' he indicated the woman standing beside him, 'believes he was

227

poisoned. The fireman managed to stop the train after it passed the platform.'

'What would have happened if he hadn't?'

'It could have crashed through the buffers and ended up across the main road. Very nasty.'

'Hmm. What about the people on board?'

'No-one was hurt. They're still there and can't get off until someone reverses the train back to the platform. I'm a qualified driver, so I can do it when you've finished with me.'

'Right. Thank you, Mr Crowcombe. Bear with me, please. I just need to make a phone call.'

Jack stepped out of the office and called DI Emma Thorpe, returning three minutes later.

'OK. We're treating this as a suspicious death, Mr Crowcombe, so we'll need to speak to everyone on the train and also all the employees on duty today. An ambulance is just arriving and the paramedics will examine Mr Reynolds. No-one else is to board the engine until the CSIs have finished, and I'll need contact details for everyone who entered the cab this afternoon.

'I understand, sergeant. I'll get you the names you need. Most of our staff are volunteers, but I'm sure they'll be happy to co-operate.'

Jack nodded and turned to his colleague.

'DI Thorpe has asked us to take statements. She's sending a couple of DCs to help. Can you have a quick word with all the passengers on that train? Get their contact details and ask them if they saw anything odd on the journey. Do people normally leave the railway at the other stations?' he asked Crowcombe.

'Almost never. They come for the return trip. There's a small museum and snack stall at Yarrowford where the up and down trains pass each other. Two trains run at any one time, and Yarrowford is the only section with double tracks. There's usually a wait of ten or fifteen minutes and some people get off to look at the memorabilia and buy sweets and so on. It's only staffed when trains are running. There's no one at the other stations apart from here and at Highchester, the end of the line.'

'I'll need the details of all the staff and volunteers, please, whether they're on duty or not.'

'Yes, of course. I'll phone and let Steve Webster, the General Manager, know what's happening and then I'll move the train.'

---

Just as Trevor and Jack, aided by DCs Kamal Chabra and Sally Erskine, finished speaking to the people on the five-thirty, the last train of the day arrived, its passengers bemused by the blue and white tape strung incongruously round the previous train's engine and the Tyvek-suited CSIs at work in the cab. Some tried to linger and take photos, but were ushered out of the station by the detectives. When the bustle of departing steam fans had ceased, Jack interviewed George's fireman.

'Desmond,' he began. 'I understand you were quite heroic today. Can you tell me exactly what happened?'

Desmond fidgeted in his seat and replied.

'George said he started to feel funny about half way between Yarrowford and here. He said he was hot and thirsty, so he drank his spare bottle of water. Then he couldn't see a signal properly. As we came into the station, he grabbed his chest and fell over. I stepped over him and managed to stop the train before it hit the buffers.'

'Well done, lad. What did George eat and drink on the journey?'

'He brought a sandwich from home and ate it at Yarrowford. He got a fruit drink there and also some water.'

'What happened to the bottles?'

'He put them in the firebox. He always did. Said it wasn't worth taking them home for recycling, and it was extra fuel.'

'How was he thought of by his colleagues?'

Desmond looked uncomfortable.

'To be honest, I don't think many people liked him. He thought he was better than the rest of us 'cos his dad was a driver and his grandad used to drive on steam. He insisted on driving whenever he felt like it, so the others didn't get much of a turn.'

'How about you?'

Desmond shrugged.

'I think he was trying to stop me training as a driver. He said I still had a lot to learn as a fireman, but that was crap.'

'Did anyone hate him enough to kill him?'

'Shouldn't have thought so. I mean, it's a bit extreme, isn't it?'

'OK, Desmond. You can go now. Thank you.'

---

'So, if it was poison, it was in either his sandwich or the drinks he bought at Yarrowford,' said Jack. 'We need to talk to George's wife and the person selling the snacks. Pity we haven't got the empty bottles.'

'Do you suspect Desmond, then? asked Trevor. 'We've only his word that George burned them himself.'

'Too early to say. Right, can you ask all the railway staff we haven't seen to present themselves here for interview tomorrow morning. Look at the passenger lists and see if we need to speak to anyone again urgently. The techies will need George's phone. We'll go and talk to his wife. Joe Dunster, the ticket collector, has already told her what's happened.

Mary Reynolds was a slim woman of about sixty. She wore a high-necked, long-sleeved blouse, despite the summer heat, and neatly pressed trousers. She had obviously been crying, but she was calm and composed with the detectives.

After the usual condolences, Jack asked her how things were between her and George.

'Pretty much like any long-married couple,' she replied. 'Ups and downs but nothing serious. He had his railway to keep him busy once he retired, and I have my garden and my book group.'

'Did he have any enemies?'

'He never mentioned any. He often said how much the others on the railway respected him.'

'I see. I think you know we believe he was poisoned. Did you make him his sandwich yesterday?'

Mary coloured slightly.

'No. He always did it himself. He said I never got the proportions of cheese and pickle right.'

'And his drinks?'

'He usually bought them at a station.'

'I see. One more thing. Where were you yesterday afternoon?'

'At book group and then the supermarket. When I got back there was a message on my phone to call Joe. I switch it off when I'm driving.'

Jack nodded approvingly.

'Thank you, Mrs Reynolds. Please get in touch if anything relevant occurs to you. I'll arrange for a family liaison officer to come and support you. Again, we're sorry about what happened to George.'

As the detectives drove away, Jack looked pensive.

'Something's a bit off there, Trev, but I can't put my finger on it. I'm sure it'll come to me. Oops.'

He braked sharply to avoid a herd of cows crossing the road, all thoughts of Mary Reynolds forgotten.

'OK, everyone,' called DI Emma Thorpe, as the Major Crimes Team assembled in the incident room on the following day. 'We have a suspicious death on the restored steam railway that runs from Mexton to Highchester. I've notified the coroner's officer. Jack and Trevor have been digging around and I'm now formally opening an inquiry. This is Operation Firebox. So, what have we got, Jack?'

'It looks like an engine driver, George Reynolds, was poisoned and died as his train was coming into Mexton station,' he replied. 'Had the fireman not managed to stop it, there could have been a serious accident, with possible loss of life. A retired doctor, who was on the train with her family, suggested it was atropine that killed him. We took a statement from the fireman and also spoke to his wife. Neither of them said he had any enemies. Trevor, Kamal and Sally spoke to the passengers, briefly. No-one saw anything odd, but we've got their details so we can re-interview if necessary. We're speaking to the staff – mostly volunteers – at the railway station this morning. One of the volunteers, Joe Dunster, is ex-British Transport Police, by the way. Seems a decent bloke.

After the morning's interviewing, the detectives returned to the office and briefed Emma.

'I've been through the passenger list again,' said Trevor, 'and nobody stood out as being of particular interest. They were all in family groups, apart from a couple of solo steam fans. No-one connected with the railway, apart from those working, was on the train. Nobody saw anything odd, either.'

'I've spoken to most of the staff here,' said Jack. 'People didn't really like George, but they appreciated his skills as a driver. How about the Highchester staff, Kamal? You went to speak to them.'

'Nothing of note,' DC Chabra replied, 'but Jackie Liddiard, who runs the stall at Yarrowford, said George only bought a bottle of water from her.

'Well, so far, we've got no motives and no suspects, although Desmond was peeved that George blocked his driving aspirations. I don't see him as a murderer, though.'

OK. Thanks, Jack,' said Emma. We need to run PNC checks on everyone involved and take a look at George's finances – and his wife's. Dr Durbridge is carrying out the PM this afternoon, so we should have confirmation of how George died tomorrow morning. Meet up at eight o'clock, please.

---

'It was atropine poisoning, probably from the Deadly Nightshade plant,' said Emma at the start of the next day's briefing. The berries have a slight taste, so they were probably in something sweet or strongly-flavoured.'

'In other words,' said Trevor, 'his cheese and pickle sandwich or the fruit drink. We'd better get that pickle analysed. That's the only thing we can test.'

'Yes, please,' replied Emma. 'And have another word with his wife when you collect it. Maybe she's hiding something.'

The detectives' musings were interrupted by an IT technician carrying a laptop.

'Look at this, boss,' she said. 'I downloaded it from the victim's phone.'

The detectives stared, astonished, at video footage which showed a man standing unsteadily on a snowy platform, in a light snowfall. A train pulled into the station and, from behind a porter's trolley loaded with trunks and milk churns, the end of a wooden pole suddenly appeared, hitting him in the back and propelling him into the path of the train. The phone jerked round and picked up a shadowy figure emerging from the other side of the trolley and slinking away. The video concluded with a close-up of the pole.

'Murder!' said Emma. 'No doubt about it. But we were never called in, were we?'

'I vaguely remember something about an accidental death on the railway last Christmas,' replied Trevor. 'I'll dig out the details. I assume that George was blackmailing the person in the video. A clearer motive for killing him would be hard to find. Looks like we're after a double murderer.'

'Indeed. Was there anything else on the phone?'

'A few things,' replied the technician. 'There's a video here of a couple embracing and another one of someone putting food into a rucksack. There's a photo of a press article reporting a Cyril Parfitt's conviction for interfering with children, and another video of someone slipping two ten-pound notes into her purse.'

'More blackmail material,' said Emma. 'And possible motives for murder. Take some stills back to Mexton station, please. Identify and reinterview the people featured. In the meantime, Trevor, dig out the details of that conviction. Find out why it's significant. I think a word with Joe Dunster would be useful, assuming he's not in any of the videos. As an ex-copper he could have some useful insights.'

'So, Joe, who are these people?' asked Jack, showing him the videos.

'Well that's Zoe Bridgewater, the ticket clerk, apparently pinching money. Clare Washford, the shop manager, is putting food into a bag. The bloke being pushed onto the tracks was Pete Watchitt, a guard. I can't make out whether the killer was male or female. The name on the press cutting is unfamiliar, but the picture resembles Steve Webster.'

'How about the couple?'

'The male's Norman Crowcombe and the female's Jackie Liddiard. He's married but she isn't.'

'Thank you. That's helpful. What can you tell me about Mr Watchitt's death? Were you there?'

'It was the last of the Christmas specials. I was the onboard Santa and we had a photographer take a publicity shot of me and the kids, on the train, for a poster. It's on the waiting room wall.

'I didn't see what happened to Pete. The platform was icy and he drank quite a bit at the Christmas lunch for non-driving staff. The coroner assumed he was drunk and had just slipped, so she recorded a verdict of accidental death. No-one doubted it.'

'Who else was on the train?'

'Mark Wedmore was the guard, Desmond was firing and Alan Wells was driving. He left because of the shock.'

'Do you have any idea who might have wanted to kill Mr Watchitt?'

'No-one specific. He was a bit of a ladies' man, apparently, so I suppose there might be an aggrieved husband somewhere. I'll ask around, if you like.'

'That could be really useful, but please don't let on that you're helping us.'

'Of course.'

'Good. Now we'll interview the potential suspects, starting with Norman Crowcombe.'

'Mr Crowcombe,' began Jack, using the station master's office as an interview room. 'Two people have died here in the past nine months – Peter Watchitt and, now, George Reynolds. We now have evidence suggesting Mr Watchitt's death wasn't accidental and we think the deaths could be linked. Can you think of anyone who might have had a grudge against him?'

Crowcombe licked his lips nervously before replying.

'He preyed on women. His charm made him irresistible. No-one's wife or daughter was safe.' He hesitated. 'You're bound to find out that he seduced my daughter. But I had nothing to do with his death. I promise you.'

'We'll come back to that. How much blackmail money was George demanding from you? We've seen the video of you and Ms Liddiard.'

All the colour drained from Crowcombe's face.

'A hundred a month or he would show the video to my wife. Yes, I suppose I've got a motive. But I was nowhere near George the day he died. I didn't even speak to him. You can ask anyone working'.

'We will, Mr Crowcombe. How about when Mr Watchitt died?'

'I was helping out at Highchester station. They were short of staff down there.'

'OK. Thank you. That will do for the moment. Please ask Ms Bridgewater to step in.'

Zoe Bridgewater met the detective's gaze without flinching.

'I knew George had that video. He tried to blackmail me with it but I told him where to go. The fact is, I was changing a twenty for two tens, not stealing them. The till balanced at the end of the day, and I also mentioned it to Norman, who said it was OK. George had nothing on me and, obviously, I had no motive.'

'How about Pete Watchitt?'

'A creep. He tried it on with me and I slapped him. He got the message.'

'Where were you when he died?'

'Waiting for a taxi, with a couple of others, on the forecourt. We'd all been drinking and were leaving our cars at the station.'

'I'll need their names. OK, thank you. Would you send in Ms Washford, please?'

'Is this about the food?' asked Clare Washford, nervously. 'Zoe said you've seen the videos on George's phone. There was a gap between running days, and the food would all have gone to waste, so I donated it to a homeless shelter. I cleared it with Norman at the time. George accused me of stealing it and said

237

he would go to the police if I didn't sleep with him. He looked so disappointed when I refused.'

'How about Pete Watchitt?'

'I admit I did succumb to his charms one night and we parted on good terms. Then I found out he'd been trying it on with just about any female on the staff, and some of the passengers, too. That changed my mind about him – but I didn't dislike him enough to kill him.'

'OK. Thank you. We'll talk to Jackie Liddiard now. Can you send her in?'

Jackie's interview was brief. She admitted having an affair with Norman but denied knowing about the blackmail. She said that the snack stall didn't stock fruit drinks.

'That'll do for now,' said Jack. 'Let's get some lunch, then we'll talk to Steve Webster. By the way, do we know why Joe retired from the transport police?'

'I looked into that,' replied Trevor. 'Apparently, he lost it with someone who was hitting a woman on a tube station platform. He assaulted the bloke, who turned out to be the woman's husband. No charges were brought against Joe, but he was invited to resign rather than face disciplinary action.'

'Hmm. Probably not relevant. Hardly grounds for blackmail.'

The two officers ate their sandwiches in the waiting room, looking round at the immaculately restored building and taking in the colourful posters on display. Webster arrived shortly afterwards and took them to Crowcombe's office.

'Mr Webster,' began Jack. 'Or should I call you Cyril Parfitt.'

Webster paled.

'It's all right. I'm not here to talk about your past offences. We're investigating more modern crimes. The deaths of Pete

Watchitt and George Reynolds. Is there anything you'd like to tell us?'

Webster took a deep breath before responding.

'George was blackmailing me. He said he would publicise my new name and convictions on social media. That would be the death of the railway. No family groups would come, even though I'm hardly ever on the trains or stations and am never alone with children. I didn't need a DBS check. He didn't want money, he just wanted me to arrange the rotas so he could drive whenever he felt like it. Of course, I complied.'

'So where were you when George and Pete Watchitt were killed?'

'At the time George died I was driving back from a three-day conference for managers of heritage railway lines, in Swindon. When Pete died, I was in hospital having a kidney stone removed.'

'All right. We'll verify those alibis.' Jack thought for a moment. 'Is Mark Wedmore on the station?'

'Yes, I saw him a moment ago.'

'Good. I need a quick word with him. You can go now.'

As Webster left, Jack turned to Trevor.

'Can you fetch Joe Dunster, in a few minutes? Ask him if we can pick his brains, cop-to-cop as it were. I think we're about to get a result.'

---

'So what are your thoughts on this sorry mess, Joe?' asked Jack. 'It looks like Zoe and Clare had no reason to be blackmailed and Webster was nowhere near the station on either occasion. Crowcombe was a victim but claims to have an alibi which, at the moment, doesn't seem awfully strong. I'm not sure whether

Jackie had a motive or not, but she certainly had the opportunity. Desmond had opportunity, but a weak motive, but we only have his word that George destroyed the bottles. What do you reckon?'

'I'm glad you asked me, because I've been thinking. There's one person you wouldn't have interviewed as a possible killer. Barry Witton, the porter. He didn't turn up for work the day after George died. I think he was due to go on holiday. Now, I found out that Watchitt got his daughter pregnant and dumped her. I didn't mention it before the inquest because we all thought his death was accidental.'

'But Barry wasn't on George's train,' Trevor interjected.

'No, but he could have given George the poisoned drink at Yarrowford, waited, and come back on the last train. Nobody checked the passengers on that service. I'm sure he was here for the Christmas specials, too. He could have killed Watchitt without anyone noticing. Apart from George, that is.'

'Well, that's really fascinating, Joe,' said Jack. 'But it's also total nonsense.'

Joe swallowed, nervously. Trevor moved unobtrusively to block the door.

'You see, there are one or two things we found out that made me think. You left BTP over an incident where you assaulted a wife-beater, so this is something that obviously upsets you. When we saw Mary Reynolds she was wearing clothing to conceal bruises, not entirely successfully, I must say. We suspect that George beat her and that you hated him for it. But is that a motive for murder? Unlikely, since you could have taken him round the back of the engine shed and given him a seeing-to. So you must have been on the video, killing Watchitt.'

'But I was the Santa on the train'

'No, you weren't. The Santa on the poster in the waiting

room has brown eyes. Yours are blue. I had a word with Mark Wedmore. You gave him a bottle of Scotch if he would take over your Santa duties on the run and keep quiet about it. You said you had a secret romantic tryst. But why kill Watchitt?'

Joe crumpled and put his head in his hands.

'It was my daughter he impregnated, not Barry's. I loathed Watchitt and his attitude to women. He deserved to die.

'George showed me the video and said he had other evidence as well. He wanted three hundred a month, which I couldn't manage for long, so I had to get rid of him. God, I wish I'd never volunteered on this bloody railway.

'I've been friends, platonically, with Mary ever since she came down here. I knew what George was doing, but I couldn't persuade her to leave him. I recognised Deadly Nightshade in one of her plant books. There's some growing in a siding at Highchester station. A handful of berries and some sugar went into the fruit smoothie I gave George at Yarrowford. Mary had nothing to do with it and didn't know about the blackmail. Please believe me.'

'I think we can accept that. So, Joseph Dunster, I'm arresting you on suspicion of murdering Peter Watchitt and George Reynolds. You do not have to say anything...'

---

'Any sympathy for him, Jack?' asked Trevor, as Joe was driven away.

'None. He could have caused a serious accident if Desmond hadn't stopped the train. Odious as his victims were, there's no excuse for murder and, as an ex-copper, he should damn well know it.'

*Readers based in the West Country, and heritage railway fans everywhere, might recognise some of the names in this story...*

*There is a delightful modern 'traditional' nursery rhyme involving Deadly Nightshade. I haven't been able to secure the rights to include it here, but you can find it at: https://medium. com/resistance-poetry/skipping-rhymes-for-the-new-age-3a9c5e0e90a5*

## The Lock on the Toilet Door

COLIN MOSELY WAS DETERMINED to kill his wife. He'd put up with her for far too long. The pursed-lipped glares of disapproval at almost everything he did; the constant criticism of his appearance; and the general atmosphere of disappointment she radiated all confirmed that any flame they once had between them had long been extinguished. And, with no evidence whatsoever, he was convinced that the village postmistress fancied him. So, Valerie had to go.

He wanted to make her death look like an accident, or natural causes. That ruled out actual physical violence. He knew nothing of motor mechanics, so he couldn't tamper with the brakes in her car and he didn't understand electricity enough to try to electrocute her. Poison seemed to be the answer, and he resolved to find out as much as he could about the sinister substances used by murderers over the centuries.

He had long been a devotee of TV crime dramas and had read dozens of thrillers in which poisons featured. He scoured the internet for true crime stories involving toxins, but steered away from the more erudite articles, as he didn't really understand much about chemistry or biology. All he knew was that poisons could kill people and that the ideal substance for his intentions was out there somewhere. He made copious notes in an old exercise book, kept hidden from his wife in his bedside cabinet under a pile of motoring magazines, and detailed various means of employing poisons as and when the ideas came to him.

Whatever he used, he had to find a way of getting Valerie to take it. It would need to be something that didn't taste too bad and could be concealed in food or drink. That ruled out most poisonous leaves and berries, unless he could put them in a curry or a chilli con carne. But Valerie didn't like really spicy foods and he feared that their taste would stand out in a cottage pie or tomato soup. But she did like chocolate. He came across a 'Golden Age' mystery involving chocolates poisoned with some obscure chemical, and a rerun of a *Taggart* story which also involved that *modus operandi*. An episode of the TV series *Professor T* was particularly promising. A killer was putting something called ethylene glycol in chocolates, and people were dropping like flies.

Within a week he had purchased, online, a bottle of ethylene glycol and a syringe with several needles. He bought a box of liqueur chocolates, extracted some of the liquid fillings and injected the sticky liquid. *That should do it,* he thought. *I'll give them to her tonight.*

Valerie Mosely was surprised when her husband presented her with the chocolates. Gifts from him were unusual, to say the least, and his claim that someone was selling them cheap at work seemed a little suspicious. But a chocolate was a chocolate, and she had little hesitation in tucking in while watching the television. Six chocolates later, her film had finished and she announced she was going to bed.

'Are you feeling alright dear?' asked Colin, regarding his wife's frown with hidden excitement.

'Yes of course. I've a slight headache, and the end of the film made me cross. It was so implausible. I need a decent night's sleep. I'll see you in the morning. Oh, thank you for the chocolates. They tasted a bit odd though.'

Once the bathroom was free, Colin prepared for bed and retired to his room. He could hardly sleep as his imagination went into overdrive, picturing the poison ravaging his wife's organs. These thoughts percolated into his dreams, when he finally dropped off, but metamorphosed into images of a judge donning a black cap and a noose swinging menacingly.

He jolted awake, just before his alarm went off, to the sound of Valerie singing merrily in the kitchen as she made the tea. Pushing the thoughts of long-abandoned executions from his mind, he sat, appalled, on his bed, wondering what had gone wrong.

He went back to the internet and looked further into ethylene glycol. He found out, after much confusion, that it would take about a hundred millilitres of the stuff to kill an adult and he had managed to get, at most, a millilitre into each chocolate. Furthermore, the treatment for ethylene glycol poisoning is alcohol, so even if he'd managed to give her a dangerous amount, the liqueur could have counteracted it. No wonder the wretched woman was still alive. Damn! He would have to find something else.

---

Colin's next port of call was cyanide. He was disappointed to find that you needed a licence, and a very good reason, to purchase it. *It wasn't like that in Agatha Christie's day*, he lamented to himself. But his mood lightened when he read that apricot kernels contain something very like cyanide, and somebody once died as a result of eating too many. Returning from the health food shop, he was dismayed to find that the kilo of dried apricots he'd bought contained no stones. Fresh apricots were less easy to track down in the village, but he found some in a larger store in the nearby town. He spent over an hour removing the kernels from the stones in a large bagful of fruit, and pounding them into a thick paste, in his shed. Now he had the poison; how was he going to administer it? He thought the best bet would be to put it in something that already tasted of apricots. He stirred a spoonful into a jar of the apricot jam that he knew Valerie always had on her toast on Sunday mornings, and also put some in her apricot yogurts. The latter was a complete failure, as she spotted the fibrous bits of apricot kernel and threw the yogurt away, threatening to complain to the supermarket whence it came.

With Christmas only a few months away, mince pies were appearing in the shops and Colin persuaded Valerie to buy some. Carefully raising the lids, he added some of his paste, plus a drop of brandy to hide the taste, and marked the poisoned pies by breaking off a fragment of crust to ensure he didn't accidentally eat one. Valerie enjoyed them immensely, possibly because of the brandy.

This onslaught of cyanide-bearing foodstuffs had no effect whatsoever on Valerie's health, though she did ask him why he was always smelling of fruit and what all those wasps were doing around his shed. He allayed her suspicions by claiming he was experimenting with making apricot and peach wines. *Back to the bloody drawing board,* he thought, and, once again, consulted the internet.

---

*Paraquat! That's the stuff!* He read with glee how many deaths worldwide had been attributed to this lethal weedkiller, only a teaspoon or two of which could prove fatal. At the first opportunity, he visited an out-of-town garden centre where he wasn't known. Asking for paraquat, he was disappointed to find that it was no longer available. The young man in the pesticides section was extremely helpful, however, recommending an alternative which was 'just as good'. Colin bought a bottle of the concentrated solution, paying cash so as not to leave a credit card trail.

The chemical had a bit of a smell so, once again, he had to find something which would disguise the taste. In their more civil moments, Colin and Valerie would watch a film together on the television, with Colin drinking lager and Valerie sipping whisky. She favoured the peaty malts and that, thought Colin, would be the answer. He added some of the weedkiller to the bottle and suggested a Sunday night movie session. He probably spent more time watching his wife for signs of poisoning than he did watching the film but, as they had both seen it before, he had no trouble discussing the plot and the actors' performances.

To his dismay, Valerie grimaced at the taste of her Scotch. She persevered with several mouthfuls but, eventually, tipped the remains into a Swiss cheese plant in a pot beside her armchair. She complained of slight nausea at bedtime, but otherwise remained perfectly healthy, despite having swallowed some of the weedkiller. A furious Colin looked up the chemical online and discovered that it was not particularly poisonous to humans – and that the days of the Swiss cheese plant were numbered. *Why didn't the idiot at the garden centre centre say so*, he raged, before realising that the lad's job was to recommend stuff to kill weeds, not wives.

Colin spent hours combing detective novels, websites and books in the library, looking for something else to kill Valerie with. Poisonous mushrooms had been used by several authors, but he couldn't tell one from another and he didn't even know where mushrooms grew locally. Every other substance or plant he came up with was either strictly controlled, easy to detect in a post mortem or simply unavailable in this country. *How the hell can I get hold of Heartbreak Grass, Jequirity Beans or the ordeal poison tree in an English village, for goodness sake? he bemoaned.* On the verge of abandoning his project, and miserably coming to the realisation that he would be stuck with Valerie for the rest of his life, Colin's attention was caught by an item in the online news describing how a worker at a local swimming pool was taken to hospital after mixing some chemicals together and inhaling the fumes. He looked into the case in more detail, ran a number of searches and came up with a cunning plan which, he told himself, could not fail. And he could make it look like an accident!

Rehearsals were important, Colin believed, and he was carrying out a trial run with the chemicals involved in the windowless downstairs lavatory, while Valerie was upstairs taking a nap. He had filled the toilet pan with strong bleach and was working out how to balance an open bottle of acidic toilet cleaner on top of the cistern so that it would fall over when Valerie entered the room and pour its contents into the bowl. He had just set up a suitable arrangement, with the bottle of cleaner perched precariously on a jar of face cream, when the fluffy pedestal mat on which he was standing slipped from under him. He tumbled forward, banging his head on the cistern and watched, in a daze, as the cleaner poured into the bowl.

Clouds of pungent, yellow-green chlorine gas billowed into the room and he started to choke. *Must get out.* Colin turned to the door and yanked on the handle. The lever came away in his hands and the door remained locked. *This was what I planned. Fixing the lock was crucial. But I don't remember doing it. What's the matter with me?* he thought, panicking. *I'll flush it away. That should do it.* He groped for the handle on the cistern. In a frenzy, he jerked it downwards several times but, unaccountably, it failed to flush and the gas continued to erupt from the toilet. *The fan! Oh, shit! The switch is outside.* His lungs burning and his eyes streaming, Colin banged on the door and called desperately for help, his feeble cries punctuated by agonising coughs. But no one came. *Wake up, you stupid bitch,* he tried to shout, to no avail as his lungs filled up with fluid and he lost consciousness.

---

Valerie Mosely snipped off the nylon line attached to the edge of the pedestal mat that she had pulled part-way into the hall.

She dropped it in the kitchen waste bin, washed her hands and put on her coat. She would reconnect the linkage in the toilet cistern later and replace the door handle, before calling for the local GP to confirm Colin's death. Stepping lightly out of the door, she dropped Colin's notebook into a handy skip and walked happily to meet the charming gentleman, from the village estate agents, who had invited her to go for a drink after work. Without scheming Colin, things were definitely looking up!

*Chlorine gas was deployed by the German army during the First World War and some of its effects are described in the Wilfred Owen poem 'Dulce et decorum est.' The wife of the chemist who devised this means of warfare, herself a chemist, committed suicide for the shame of what her husband had done.*

# Fatal Dose - taster

*Fatal Dose, my third novel features a serial poisoner stalking the streets of Mexton, my imaginary town. DC Mel Cotton and her colleagues have the challenging task of tracking the poisoner down. Here's a taster from the beginning of the book.*

Gordon Howell left the Greek deli with a look of anticipation on his face and a bag of sticky pastry in his hand. He was looking forward to eating his baklava in the park, as close to the children's playground as he could get. His thoughts were curtailed abruptly when someone collided with him, knocking his honeyed treat from his hands.

'Oh, I'm so sorry,' said the stranger, reaching down to pick up the bag, 'That was really clumsy of me. Are you hurt? Here's your cake.'

Gordon scowled but grudgingly admitted that he wasn't injured. He wasn't one to start a row and didn't want to draw attention to himself, so he just grabbed the bag and stalked off, with further apologies from the stranger floating in the air behind him. He reached the park and sat down on his usual bench, the afternoon sun warming his face. He knew he shouldn't be there but he couldn't help himself. He pulled out the baklava, which seemed none the worse for its impact with the pavement, and bit blissfully into it. Perhaps it was the incident outside the shop that affected his mood, but it didn't taste as sweet as usual. Nevertheless, a baklava was a baklava and he wasn't going to waste it.

Half an hour later Gordon had finished his snack, the playground was empty and he decided to head for home. He stood up and noticed that his muscles were tingling and twitching slightly. He felt odd and noises seemed to be more intrusive than usual. By the time he reached the park gates he was feeling distinctly uncomfortable. It must have shown, because a man in a paramedic's uniform, wearing a face mask, stopped him and asked if he was all right.

'Yes. Just feeling a bit odd, that's all.'

'Can I give you a lift anywhere?' the man asked. 'I've just come off duty and I'm in no particular hurry.'

'That's kind of you. But I think I'll be fine.'

Gordon debated with himself. Was this person to be trusted? He'd had plenty of experience of people turning on him, but no-one here knew his real name, so it should be safe. And, by now, he was feeling rather ill.

'OK then. Thank you. I live in the flats on Felton Street. It's not far.'

'No problem. I know where the flats are. We've been called out there a few times. This van's mine.'

He gestured to a dark blue Transit parked a few metres away.

'Sorry it's not a more comfortable ride, but I do some light

252

removals when I'm not working. I'll just put my rucksack in the back.'

The man opened the back doors, dropped in his bag and turned to Gordon. A lightning blow to Gordon's stomach doubled him over. He could hardly breathe and offered no resistance as the man pushed him into the van, sweeping up his legs from under him and slamming the doors.

Gordon's head banged against the side of the van as it accelerated away. He felt sick, disoriented and, above all, terrified.

'Why are you doing this? Who are you?'

'Who I am is irrelevant. You don't know me. But I know who you really are. And you can guess why I've taken you.'

The kidnapper put a CD into the van's player and pressed play.

'Here's a song for you to listen to while we drive. It's by an American singer, Tom Lehrer. It's called *Poisoning pigeons in the park*. He sings the praises of strychnine and you, my friend, are my pigeon. Enjoy.'

For the next two hours the van was constantly on the move with the song playing repeatedly. Gordon vomited. His muscle twitching turned into excruciating bouts of convulsions. Periods of calm, during which he sobbed and pleaded for his life, gave way to ferocious cramps when he felt his muscles were being torn from his bones. Every sound, bump, or flash of light through the van's window triggered more pain. Eventually, he could breathe no more and he expired in agony, his face scarlet and his body arched as the contracted muscles in his back pulled his spine out of shape.

The driver switched off the CD player and parked the van in a public car park, avoiding CCTV cameras. It would stay there until the middle of the night when he would dump Gordon's body in the location he had selected. A message sent.

The corpse lay on its back, just outside the school gates. Only the head and feet touched the ground and, judging by the terrible grin on the dead man's face, he had stared into the depths of hell and laughed.

'This wasn't an easy death,' commented Dr Durbridge, the pathologist. 'I'll take some samples, but I'm ninety percent certain this is strychnine poisoning.

If you enjoyed this taster of *Fatal Dose*, you can buy the book from Hobeck Books, your local bookshop or online at Amazon.

# Acknowledgments

Firstly, my constant gratitude goes to my wife, Jen, for helping to get my scribblings fit for public gaze. I would also like to thank my friends and fellow members of the Weston-super-Mare writing group Writers in Stone for their support and encouragement and, of course, Rebecca and Adrian at Hobeck Books for continuing to publish my books!

BRIAN PRICE

## About the Author

Brian Price is a writer living in the South West of England. A scientist by training, he worked for the Environment Agency for twelve years and has also worked as an environmental consultant, a pharmacy technician and, for twenty-six years, as an Open University tutor.

*Fatal Trade* was his first full-length novel and has quickly been followed by more novels featuring DC Mel Cotton. He has also contributed to a number of short stories to a local writing group's anthology, called *Cuckoo*. He is the author of *Crime Writing: How to Write the Science*, a guide for authors on the scientific aspects of crime. He has a website on the topic **www.crimewriterscience.co.uk** and advises crime writers on how to avoid scientific mistakes in their books. He was once credited with keeping author M.W. Craven out of jail, as a result of advice given.

Brian reads a wide range of crime fiction and also enjoys Terry Pratchett, Genevieve Cogman and Philip Pullman. He may sometimes be found listening to rock, folk and 1960s psychedelic music. He is married and has four grown-up children.

To find out more about Brian and his crime fiction writing please visit his website: **www.brianpriceauthor.co.uk**.

## The Mel Cotton Crime Series

*Fatal Trade*

*Fatal Hate*

*Fatal Dose*

*Fatal Blow*

*Fatal Image*

Available from book retailers.

*Fatal Beginnings* – a free prequel novella available if you subscribe to Hobeck Books www.hobeck.net.

# Hobeck Books - the home of great stories

We hope you've enjoyed reading this novel by Brian Price. To keep up to date on Brian's fiction writing please subscribe to his website: **www.brianpriceauthor.co.uk**.

Hobeck Books offers a number of short stories and novellas, including *Fatal Beginnings* by Brian Price, free for subscribers in the compilation *Crime Bites*.

Also please visit the Hobeck Books website for details of our other superb authors and their books, and if you would like to get in touch, we would love to hear from you.

Hobeck Books also presents a weekly podcast, the Hobcast, where founders Adrian Hobart and Rebecca Collins discuss all things book related, key issues from each week, including the ups and downs of running a creative business. Each episode includes an interview with one of the people who make Hobeck possible: the editors, the authors, the cover designers. These are the people who help Hobeck bring great stories to life. Without them, Hobeck wouldn't exist. The Hobcast can be listened to from all the usual platforms but it can also be found on the Hobeck website: **www.hobeck.net/hobcast**.

Hobeck Books – the home of great
stories

We hope you've enjoyed reading this novel by Brian Price. To keep up to date on Brian's latest writing please subscribe to his website www.brianpriceauthor.co.uk

Hobeck Books offers a number of short stories and novellas, including Fatal Beginnings by Brian Price. Look for subscribers to the compilation Crime Bites.

Also please visit the Hobeck Books website to see all of our other superb authors and their books, and listen to the occasional Hobeck podcast too.

Hobeck Books also presents a weekly podcast, the Hobeck Crime Vault, hosting Helen and Rebecca, talking about all things book related, tales from real life, recommending the best and newest authors in crime fiction. The Hobeck crime catalogue is heavenly.